MIST & DAWN

STARFIRE TRILOGY BOOK 1

PATTY JANSEN

THE ICEFIRE WORLD

CHAPTER 1

The Island of Skulls: a rocky knoll in the eastern ocean, far out of sight of the Chevakian mainland's coast.

The dark, algae-covered cliffs rose out of the sea, inhabited only by thousands and thousands of seabirds. Waves crashed at the foot of the cliffs. If anyone were to define inhospitable, this island would be it.

A small sailing boat drifted around the treacherous point of the island into the only bay along its shores. In the shelter of the foreboding cliffs, the wind dropped out of the sails.

Standing on the deck, Tylve tightened the mainsail, and loosened the front sail, which billowed out to catch the gentler breeze.

The fabric flapped, and with the flapping, fragments of lightstream oozed down the sail. Her father's spirit travelling with her.

They fell from the beam like rain made from light, onto the deck, where they disappeared. Lightstream could not survive in wood. It was attracted by metal and glass.

Now that the boat was in calmer water, the roar of the wind and the slapping of waves against the hull died, to be replaced with the screeching of the thousands of birds that lived on the cliffs of the island.

They flew overhead and circled in the sky. They squawked to each other on the cliffs, where the thousands of young sat on every flat space of the rocks, fluffy white and grey puff balls that were almost invisible until they moved. The young were not so small anymore. Most of them sported an untidy assortment of adult feathers and would be ready to leave the nest very soon.

Tylve's sailing boat drifted in between the rocky outcrops. Her experienced gaze went over the surface, taking in the flow of the waves as shaped by the treacherous currents underneath. Many ships had come to grief on the sharp rocky points.

This was not called the Island of Skulls for nothing.

A narrow beach of white sand sheltered right in the secluded part of the bay against the cliffs that rose like a foreboding wall out of the sand.

Tylve steered the boat in that direction. Every second week when she came here to read the barygraph and replace the paper in the machine, the wind was just strong enough to take the ship to the beach on wind power, but she held the oar ready, just in case.

There were no tusked lions on the beach today. Good. Although their recent presence had left tracks in the sand, rounded depressions of their bellies, sharp gouges of their flippers and deep holes of the long tusks of the males.

When the boat drifted close to the beach, she loosened the ropes on all the sails so that they flapped and discarded the last bit of lightstream. She ran to the bow with the oar and stuck it in the water to hold off the bottom from crashing into the sand. It looked safe, but the currents moved the sand around a lot and there were rocks underneath.

Tylve had been coming here for most of her life, first with her father, and then by herself to honour the family tradition. They'd always been weather reporters for Tiverius, the faraway capital.

She jumped into the water when the boat was almost at the beach and pulled the bow onto the sand. A rope hung off the end, which she ran up the beach to a rusty metal loop in the rock face where she tied it up.

Well, that was done.

She then went back into the boat and collected her barygraph kit. A sturdy leather satchel that contained new sheets of paper, spare parts for the machine, and any tools she would need to replace them.

She checked them and found that the pliers had attracted some lightstream glow.

Yes, it was often quite bad on this insignificant speck of an island. This island was as far East as people could travel, and judging by the old stories of sick and dying crew marooned on this island, not everyone could travel this far as this.

But her family had come here for generations, and rumours went that they could do so because they had southern blood, which made them somewhat resistant to the deadly effects of too much exposure to lightstream. As child, Tylve had loved playing with the sparks.

Tylve shouldered the bag and ploughed through the sand. The beach only looked inaccessible from the sea, but you had to be on the beach to see the small narrow stairway hewn into the rock. It was difficult to spot if you didn't know where it was, because the metal railing that used to run along the entire track had rusted off and fallen into the ocean many years ago.

The bottom steps were very rough, eaten away by the force of the ocean, encrusted with barnacles and slippery seaweed. You needed to know where to put your feet.

Tylve climbed with the birds circling overhead, squawking their alarm. Their nests were on the rocky shelves, little more than collections of driftwood, on which they laid speckled eggs and where the fluffy little chicks hatched. After a favourable spring with many successful broods, the cliffs were bursting with young, testing their fluffy wings and their neighbour's defenses of their territory. They were noisy and highly alarmed at the sight of this visitor.

She climbed and reached the rusty remains of the railing and the path that snaked its way up the cliff face.

For the next while, she was too puffed to think much about anything else except climbing. The path was steep, the steps uneven, and in the places where the sea water didn't reach, moss grew on the stone, making the steps slippery.

Every now and then, she checked instinctively over her shoulder, but from this position you couldn't see the beach, and you couldn't even see the bay, only the vast and empty ocean.

After a while, she reached her destination, a flat piece of land on a ridge from where you could see out to the east and well as the west.

It was not the highest point of the island, but a little plateau where some tufts of grass hung on for dear life and where it was flat enough to put up a tent.

Not that she had ever done that, but she could imagine that people would. They would have to eat sea birds, but they didn't seem to be afraid of people, and would be easy to catch.

She had been told that in distant history, people had collected these birds and made oil out of them.

In the middle of the flat space sat the only bit of modern technology on the island. Inside a glass cage on a pedestal of stone stood a machine with a round barrel, paper strung around it, a little pen that moved up and down and a bellows that generated the movement.

This particular barygraph was quite new. Tylve had installed it here herself, hauling it up the cliff in its awkward box so it wouldn't get damaged.

She had even picked the thing up all the way in Tiverius herself, travelling with it across the country on the train and on trucks.

She took a cloth from her bag and wiped the salt spray off the glass. This was not necessary, because the device would function well enough with dirty glass, but she liked her machine, for which she had done so much work, to be clean.

Then she opened the door, remembering how rusty and difficult it had been to open the door on the old machine that was literally falling apart with rust.

This machine was beautiful and clean, and she would make sure that it stayed that way. Every two weeks when she came here to change the paper, she wiped the outside with oil so that the corrosive salty water would not find purchase on the metal. She greased the seal to the door so it would stay watertight when rain came.

She took out the barrel and unclipped the strip of metal which held the paper in place. It fell into her hands. Judging by the readings, it had produced lots of spikes and valleys. It measured the strength of lightstream, and during her visit to Tiverius, and meeting up with the chief meteorologist, she had questioned whether she still needed to do this every two weeks. Sure Tiverius paid for her to do it, but she could probably make more money by simply catching more fish, because the price of fish had been high recently.

But the chief meteorologist had told her that hers was one of the most important measuring points in the country, and he'd shown her the maps he made of seasonal variations in lightstream. And he told her how they used these maps to calibrate the large machines along the coast that diverted lightstream from the continent. And he showed her that her data was even used on the other side of the continent in Arania, where she had never been and would probably never come, to calibrate their machines as well.

So, instead of letting her off the hook, he had provided her with a new machine.

And the machine continued to show her what it had shown for all her life, a track of regular spikes and valleys that had barely changed over the years, even if the rumours were that there had been changes in the strength of lightstream in the past twenty-five years since she had first come here.

She folded the paper up and tucked it away in the waterproof pocket in her bag.

Then she took out a clean sheet of paper, wrapped it around the barrel, slid the two ends under the strip, and tightened the strip with the wingnut bolt.

Then she put the cylinder back on the machine, making sure that the pencil sat against the paper, and that everything else was fine.

Great, that was that done.

She shut the door to the cabinet and picked up her stuff, ready to go back to her boat. It looked like the weather was on the verge of clearing up, and shafts of sunlight speared between the clouds. One such shaft hit a rock nearby, reflecting brightly off the white wings of a cluster of sea birds that seemed to be excited by something that lay on another patch of grass.

It was not far from where she was standing, and there was a kind of natural goat track along the cliff face. The track was purely coincidental, because there were no goats on this island.

Once, she had walked along this path, just to see where it ended up. It led to another point from where you had a far-reaching but empty view over the ocean.

The closer she came to the spot that the birds were interested in, the more uneasy she felt.

In her experience, bird flurries usually meant there was something to eat. And something to eat almost always meant something dead.

Sometimes dead legless lions would wash up on the beach, or dead fish would wash up after a particularly nasty storm. But that was on the beach.

The birds would carry dead fish up to their nests and squabble over the remains, but this was something much bigger, far too big to be carried by birds.

For something to have died up here, that meant something would have been able to climb up here. There were no goats on the island that she knew of and she had never seen a rabbit. There was not enough grass.

When she came closer, the birds flew off. She was left staring at what was clearly the skeleton of a human. A man, she thought.

The bones had been pecked clean by the birds, but bits of flesh still adhered. She had been here only two weeks ago, and she was sure that if this body had been here two weeks ago, it would have had more meat on it, so there would have been even more birds and she would have noticed them. In other words, this body was less than two weeks old.

In that time, he'd washed up on the beach, climbed up here and had died, and the birds had eaten most of him.

The man's clothes had mostly been torn away by the birds. They were quite flimsy, made of blue fabric that was stained by the weather, decaying flesh and bird shit. He wore black shoes made from some kind of fabric, with long laces.

Around the neck of the skeleton lay a metal band with a thicker, stone-studded amulet on it. Its front face had two glass or gemstone beads.

Tylve pulled at the amulet, but the band's fastening was firmly closed and the diameter of the band was smaller than the skull, which still had pieces of flesh stuck to the back.

She shuddered. No way she'd touch that.

Could she maybe turn the skeleton over?

She pulled at the fabric around the body and shoulders, but it upset a puddle of rancid fluid that had pooled within and—urgh, the stench.

Well, there was only one way to solve this.

She set down her satchel and dug out her hammer. It had a blunt end for hammering nails and a pointed end to use as a crowbar to remove nails. You could also use this end to prise open the door to the barygraph cabinet if it was stuck.

She hefted the hammer above her head and brought it down, pointy end first. She had to close her eyes before the hammer hit the neck.

It landed with a sickening crunch that didn't have the desired effect, and she had to hit it twice more, this time more precisely and with her eyes open. Ew, ew.

The last blow separated the skull from the neck. It went rolling down the slope, followed by the birds that were watching her from a distance.

It came to rest against a rock and birds fought over the slimy bits that had fallen out on the way through the grass.

Ew.

Somehow chopping the head off a fish was much easier than this.

How had this person ended up here?

She hadn't seen any sign of recent visitors on the beach.

But maybe this person had made the mistake of leaving their boat untied, which meant the current had probably carried it off. Then again, it rained a lot and there was a bit of food on the island in the form of birds and eggs, so why would this person have died so soon after arriving?

Lightstream?

She picked up the metal band which had fallen in the grass. It was heavy, and made of a non-corroding metal. It was well made, but gave no clues about its function. A piece of jewellery, no doubt, but it could help identify the person to those who had known him.

She put it in her bag. Underneath the ripped fabric of his shirt, she found another gadget, like a compass with a window and a needle set in a metal receptacle with one pointed end on one side and a handle on the other. She put that in her bag, too, and then scoured the dead person's clothing or whatever was left of it, but found nothing else.

It was very strange.

Since there was nothing else left to do, she picked up her bag and made her way back down to the boat.

Little about this affair made sense. If this person had travelled here alone, then there would have been a boat. The beach was the only place to access the shore. If the person had not been alone, then where were his companions?

On the way down, Tylve had an extra close look to see if she could find any signs of people having visited the island.

The path was mostly rock. People could climb up without leaving a trace, and she saw nothing out of the ordinary. She also felt that if he had left traces, she would have seen them on the way up.

Most of the beach was swallowed up by the sea at high tide twice a day. On the far end of the beach, she had noticed the impressions made by the tusked lions, which would often sleep on the sand.

The males were dangerous and could kill a person. Maybe he'd washed up, had been attacked by the tusked lions, and had climbed up to get out of their way, after which he'd died from his injuries. Yes, that could have happened.

But then, where was his boat?

The ocean would reclaim anything that washed up on the beach, but it was rare for an entire boat to disappear without a trace.

So she walked the length of the beach once again.

She found bits of wood, but they were old and all looked different, so she didn't think they had belonged to the same boat, or even any boat that had come to grief recently.

She also found a few fragments of long tubes of a see-through material like glass. Glass didn't float, but this material did. They were well and truly smashed against the rocks, so it was hard to see what they would have been for.

Some contained a dark, foul-smelling residue.

Tylve found no other signs of human activity.

Maybe he'd washed up around the point and had swum here?

That would be dangerous on most days, but it was a possibility.

This was truly the only beach where you could access the island, but maybe these people been stupid enough to try to climb up from the other side.

After pushing off her boat, she steered around the point. The island was only small, and she might just as well check on all sides.

The sea was a lot rougher on the exposed eastern side. A thin strip of treacherous rocks lay at the bottom of the cliff. The boulders were huge and waves crashed between them. Many of the crevices were big enough for a person—or wreckage—to disappear into, but Tylve couldn't check.

It was too rough to get close. Trying to access the island from here would be insane. But she studied the rocks and waves, and around the next point, she noticed a light coloured object strung between the rocks.

She was still a bit far away, so she went as close as she dared and loosened the sails.

Once the boat was stable, she pulled out her spyglass.

Items of debris lay between the rocks. There were several smashed up boxes, a large piece of material that looked like a sail, but was ripped and scattered over a number of rocks, probably by the waves. The material was dark in colour on one side and white on the other. It looked quite thick. Quite heavy for a sail.

Come to think of it, a sail would sink, so there was probably a mast or a boom attached, even if she couldn't see one.

There was also a large crate smashed against a rock lower on the shore. One side hung open, showing the inside with a metal plate with many tiny holes in rows. Most of them were empty, but some held broken transparent tubes like the ones she'd found on the beach. It was too far away to see if they also contained foul liquid.

So this was where those things had come from. They'd been taken around the corner by the current, but not the sail and the other debris—because those things lay too high on the shore.

Those rocks only got wet when the sea was extremely rough. But the weather hadn't been bad enough recently.

So did this mean the man had washed up on the rocks, dragged the remains of the boat out of the influence of the waves and had gone to look for help?

He'd managed to pull off the incredible feat of swimming around the point to the beach, he'd clambered up the steps and had died of cold when realising he was on a tiny island in the middle of the ocean.

They didn't call this the Island of Skulls for nothing.

She shuddered. What a horrible and lonely death. Had he been alone or were his companions still floating around, maybe on another island or on the bottom of the ocean?

She completed the loop around the island but saw nothing else unusual.

Tylve unfurled the large sail and set off home, tossing out the fishing net when she had put a good distance between herself and the island. Just in case any bodies floated in the water. She wanted to catch fish, not dead people.

Only when she was well on the open ocean did she stop feeling like someone was watching her, and did her nerves calm.

She took her bag to study the strange contraptions she had taken from the man's body. Seated at the tiny table in the ship's cabin, she wiped bits of dirt and adhering gunk off the metal and then wiped clean the glass. It looked like the ovals on the top were buttons and you could push them. They went down a little and then sprang back up. It was hard to figure out what they were for, though. Those buttons didn't operate the band's fastening, or didn't open the lid on the case, if indeed it could be opened.

When she pressed one of them, a tiny flicker of light went through the glassy material of the button. She guessed this was the lingering effect of lighstream. When a piece of metal or glass became infected with lightstream and you held it against another piece of metal or glass, sparks would often arc from one to the other.

Well, she still had no idea what this was and would have to ask a few people in town.

But when she picked the thing up to put it away in the satchel, she accidentally pressed both glass buttons at the same time.

A flash went off. She gasped and almost dropped the thing.

What was that?

CHAPTER 2

A vehicle had stopped in front of the house.

Ravi couldn't see it from the window of his room, which looked out into the yard of the house nextdoor, but he could hear the chugging and hissing of the engine echoing from the street in between the houses. The gate to the front yard creaked, and a door opened. Footsteps clacked on the paving from hard-heeled boots such as the doga guards wore. Men spoke to each other in the formal, military voices of the guards.

Ravi was sure this was the visitor his father said he was expecting. If so, he was late, and Ravi had been afraid he wouldn't turn up at all, throwing all his own plans into disarray.

He abandoned his desk where he had been staring uselessly at his study books, and went out into the hallway. It was late afternoon, and the light streamed in through the windows at the front of the house.

He peeked over the balustrade, taking care not to poke his head too far out, because he didn't want anyone to see him. There was only one thing his father wanted him to do more than study, and that was to mingle with the people in power to, as his father said, listen and learn.

If his father saw him—not studying—he would invite him down

to attend, and besides the fact that those meetings were always insanely boring, that would throw his plan into disarray even more.

This had to be an important visitor, because his father had opened the door himself, and he stood waiting for the person to enter the house.

A flood of golden light streamed into the hall.

The visitor stepped in through the door, a silhouette backlit by the afternoon light.

"Welcome, Proctor," his father said. "I'm glad that you found my note important enough to grace me with a personal visit."

Ravi couldn't believe his luck.

The proctor of the Chevakian doga, Calidius han Pasaki, visited often. His father was one of the proctor's trusted advisors and needed no "important note" to have the proctor's ear. It was all part of the formalities, but this visit meant that his father would stay in his study for quite some time.

"I hope you are well, Gerinius," the proctor said.

And the proctor always used full names. Yes, his father's name was Gerinius, but everyone knew him as Geri. Nobody ever called him Gerinius. The same as nobody ever called him Ravonius, which was his full name. It was Ravi.

Yet the proctor insisted on being called Calidius.

That just went to show how full of arrogance the proctor was, as were the rest of the senators in the doga, for that matter.

It encapsulated everything that Ravi's new friends at his self-defence training told him was wrong about the current government: out of touch, weak, obsessed with procedure and pomp, and not with solving problems, of which Chevakia had many.

The proctor had stepped into the hall. His father shut the door, and then they went into his father's study, under the overhang of the upstairs gallery where Ravi stood. They disappeared from sight. The door to his father's study closed with a snick.

This was his chance.

Ravi ran back into his room, slipped out of his comfortable shorts and put on long trousers. He ran his fingers through his hair, which was soft and curly. He'd probably cop a few comments about "baby hair" from his friends, but let's take things one step at a time, right? The meeting came first. The haircut and the appropriate clothes would follow later.

He left his room after shutting the door behind him. It was not that he kept any secrets in that room, but he just didn't like it when his mother came in there to get this or that thing or to change the pillows on his couch. The servants already changed the bed and cleaned the floors, and that should be enough poking into his private safe space.

Ravi went down the stairs, passed his father's study, where he could hear the voices of both men, and into the downstairs hallway to the living room. His mother sat at her usual spot in the corner, on a high stool surrounded by tables overflowing with paint jars, bowls of paint-stained water, jars of brushes and stained cloths. She held a brush and appeared to have just started the first strokes on a new artwork on the easel in front of her.

"What are you painting?" Ravi asked, because it was always a good idea to talk to his mother about her art first. It put her in a good mood.

"The district's chamber of commerce has commissioned a painting for their new reception," his mother said. "What do you think I should paint?"

Ravi gestured at the canvas, which had just a blob of orangey-brown paint on it. "You've already started. Surely you have already decided what is going to be in it."

He squinted at the indistinct shape on the canvas, but couldn't make out what it was. She usually worked like this. A blank canvas was not inspiring, she said, and she would put random strokes to inspire her imagination.

"I was thinking I might paint the building, or maybe the doga building. What do you think?"

"The chamber of commerce would be more interested in having a painting of their own building," Ravi said.

To be honest, he couldn't care less about what she painted. He didn't want to talk about this.

His mother often asked a lot of trivial questions that nobody else cared about. Do you think this jacket needs to be red or yellow? And then the figure wearing the jacket in the painting would be so tiny that you could hardly see the jacket.

"I was thinking they might draw inspiration from seeing the doga building."

She turned to her artwork, rummaging in the jar with brushes.

A kind of awkward silence fell in the room, a silence in which a confident person would have announced the thing Ravi was about to announce, but he allowed the awkward silence to happen, because he had practiced his words so many times in his mind, but now that he was here to say them, the words failed him, and he felt awkward and stupid. Surely his mother would see right through what he was trying to do.

"Yes? You wanted to say something?"

His mother had this annoying habit of over-emphasising the fact that she was listening, like she was making the space for a shy young child to speak. That was something you did to little children, Ravi had once explained, but she didn't seem to understand what he meant. He was shy, and he did want to say something, and the fact that he couldn't just say it, like a normal person would, annoyed him to no end.

There was no way that he could back down now.

He took a deep breath.

"I was going to tell you that I might not be there for the evening meal tonight." There. He said it.

She raised her painted eyebrows.

"Might not be?"

Of course, she also had a knack for picking out and emphasising the most poorly chosen word in every statement.

"I will not be," he corrected. He had to put his hand in his pocket to hide the fact that it was shaking.

And he then ploughed on, because it was getting late, the proctor had already turned up late, and his friends were sure to be wondering why he hadn't joined them already. They had arranged to meet in the city square after work, except Ravi didn't work, and he couldn't get out of the house that easily.

"I have agreed to meet some friends at the ulli hall."

His mother laughed, which was the worst thing of all the things she could do. "You play ulli?"

"Not much," he said. "But some of my friends were going, and they invited me, and I said yes, just to try it."

He was feeling more insecure about this by the moment. As if his mother could see through the big fat lie that it was. She had attended the art college, and would know that people who went to the colleges considered ulli beneath them, a game for the common people.

"What friends are these?"

"Just some people I've met at the self-defence training."

"Hmmm. It's nice that you made some friends there already."

"Yes." That was an awkward kind of yes, when you didn't know what else to say.

"And these friends absolutely have to hold this gathering—in the ulli hall—over dinner time?"

"It was the only slot of tables they could get. Playing ulli is quite popular with all the people at the training at the moment." The lies just piled up.

"But then, what about dinner?"

"I think there may be food, but if not, I was thinking that the cook could save me some, like she does with father when he spends a long day at the doga and comes back late."

His mother laughed again. "My, you have thought this through. You must really want to go then. Do you have money?"

"Yes."

From the small stash he'd saved whenever his parents gave him money to buy things like clothes, and he'd bought the cheapest thing possible, so he could keep the rest.

His mother had selected one of her paintbrushes, a sign that she was keen to get back to her work.

"So, is it all right to go, then?" Ravi asked.

"I guess so. You're twenty, so you need to start taking some responsibility."

How ever going out at dinner time translated to having more responsibility, Ravi wasn't quite sure, but he understood he had been given her implied permission to go, so he scurried out of the room, before she changed her mind, before his father had finished with his meeting, because his father would never let him go, not to play ulli, not to simply meet his friends, and definitely not for the reason he was really going.

Ravi looked at himself in the mirror in the hall, to make sure he hadn't accidentally put on something on inside out or back to front, so as not to give his friends even more opportunities to laugh at him.

The voices of his father and the proctor drifted through the door to his father's study.

Ravi had in the past attended quite a few of these meetings, while seated on the chair in the corner, while the men talked about "important things" and he tried desperately not to fall asleep. The men would be talking about budgets and political manoeuvres. They'd be talking about concessions they were prepared to make to get a majority of doga senators to vote for a plan. In his mind, he could picture the two men sitting on facing armchairs with a plate of tea and cakes between them and notes—of proposed laws or tables tallying likely voting numbers—spread over the table.

It was all very staid and boring.

At the bench in the hall, he swapped his house shoes for his outdoor shoes, trying to be as quiet as possible.

He was putting on his right sandal when his father's voice burst from the room.

"But this is a serious situation. You don't seem to comprehend that."

Whoa. That was not the type of language his father normally used to speak to the proctor.

Ravi half-rose, leaving the buckle of his sandal undone, while the proctor replied, his voice too soft for Ravi to hear.

His father's voice came again. "This situation is dangerous. It has the potential to unsettle the entire country."

What situation?

His shoe still undone, Ravi crossed the hall. The buckle made a little clinking noise while it dragged over the tiles, so he tucked it under the strap, and crept closer to the door.

The proctor said, "I simply do not agree with your assessment, Gerinius. When you've sat in the doga as long as I have, you've seen a lot of these movements come and go. They make demands and threaten unrest. We give them a few things they want. Not everything, because that's impossible. Then this takes the sting out of their arguments and they retreat. Meanwhile, we have so many issues right here in the city under our noses. This sordid affair of senator Suti and his cleaner. Really, if one was going to entertain a mistress, one should pick a better subject than a cleaning lady. And then senator Yori's rampant parties of debauchery—"

"Can the doga, just for one moment, stop talking about the affairs of senators?"

"People care about the affairs. It looks bad for all concerned. We have to instate a code of decency."

"While the northern provinces are getting ready to cut us off?"

"I've already told you not to worry. They're bluffing."

"They're not."

"They've been bluffing for many years. The northern provinces have always complained and made demands. I see nothing new."

"The army doesn't think it's like that. They're already setting up bases nearby. *Without* authorisation from the doga, should I add."

"Oh, they're just conducting annual training."

"Which they normally perform near the Aranian border."

"The army figured a change in setting might benefit the quality of the training."

"Sure, but it's highly suspicious that they're doing this now, of all years, when there are bands of northern youths stationing themselves along the river. Has that ever happened before—no, don't answer it. I know it hasn't. Wouldn't it be suspicious that this comes at a time when we have serious disagreement in the doga about the level of support for the north?"

"We know these people. Delegate Damio has explained that they're the youth division of the northern council and they want to organise their youth to increase their agricultural output."

"And you believe that?"

"What is there not to believe? Delegate Damio is supported by well-established families. They pay the district's taxes and they pay on time—which is more than can be said about some other groups, even some in Tiverius."

"What is that supposed to mean?"

"That the Third District has *still* not paid their dues."

"That's unrelated."

"No, it's not. Taxes mean we can help districts. If the city districts refuse to pay their taxes, then why should country districts do so? Our whole society will fall apart."

"The northern districts pay to curry our favour. They pay so that there are no questions raised in the doga about the fact that they're recruiting militias. And to be honest, if what the rumours say is true, and the soldiers the doga sends into that area for training behave as appallingly as they say, ransacking the villages for no good reason. Raping the young women, then this needs to be addressed."

"I refuse to believe those stories. They're rubbish."

"I don't think so, and clearly the northern council doesn't think so. I am deeply worried about where this will lead. We know there are discipline issues in the army. I have never seen this level of anger in the northern districts before. I implore you to listen to them, and I mean, really listen to them. They say that things have to change or they will cause a rebellion."

"Dear Gerinius, if being listened to is what they want, they can come to the doga in the regular ways. I'm not in the habit of stopping our business for any group on the street or a rebel army. If they have grievances, they know how to bring them to our attention."

"They can't, because—"

"Because their arguments and so-called proof are overblown or just plainly fabricated. If, as you say, you or anyone else, have clear proof of transgressions by the military, the doga is more than happy to investigate. You know that, and it has always been like that. We're a civilised country and will deal with disputes in a civilised way. We do not bow to thuggery."

Ravi backed away from the door.

It sounded like his father was losing the argument, and probably the proctor would leave soon, and his father would go into the living room and discuss the visit with his mother.

It would not be a pleasant discussion, probably yet again about some disagreement in the doga that, according to his father, no one in town understood about.

And according to his father, they didn't understand it because the vast majority of senators were old people who had sat in their cushy seats for far too many years, and even some of those representatives barely visited the districts they professed to represent.

Blah, blah. He didn't care.

His father said he was too young for this stuff and, in this case, that was probably a good thing.

A small noise drifted from the end of the hall, so, before a servant turned up with tea or something, Ravi quickly crossed the entrance foyer and slipped out the front door, doing up his sandal on the doorstep. He was free. For the first time in his life, he was going somewhere that had nothing to do with study, and nothing to do with his family.

If growing up and being responsible was anything like this, he liked it.

CHAPTER 3

Kotori stopped in the hallway in front of the elaborate wooden door that led into the King's private room. He checked his bag and straightened his astrologer's robe to mask the fact that he was quite out of breath after having walked up the stairs. One couldn't let appearances slip. People might think he was too old for his position.

The palace guards that stood on either end of the corridor watched his every movement. They were big beefy men, younger than him by about fifty years. Straight-backed compared to his bent posture, with big shoulders and muscular arms compared to his kindling sticks.

They watched him because it was their job, but probably also because they took a keen interest in who entered the king's rooms for purposes of gossip. Few people saw the king anymore.

Kotori knocked.

A voice responded inside the room.

Kotori couldn't make out the words, because the king's voice was not as strong and clear as it used to be, and Kotori's ears were also not as good as those of the young guards.

But he was sure the king would have told him to come in, since the king had asked for his attendance, so he pushed open the door and went into the room.

The first thing he noticed was the abundant warm light that flooded in to the king's private sitting room. He also noticed how warm it was in here compared to the coolness that the chill of autumn had brought to the stone and tiled halls of the Citadel.

A fire burned in the hearth, even if no other fires had been lit anywhere in the Citadel this early in the season.

The king sat in his chair by the window that overlooked the city of Kadrish.

From his position by the door, Kotori could see the domed roofs of the halls of the Citadel, the walls where the parading guards walked backwards and forwards carrying long spears, and beyond them, the roofs of the city across the hilly country that sloped towards the harbour, where he could see a boat come in on the glittering water of the western ocean. At the horizon billowed the clouds of the Mother's Veil, ever present, but never reaching the shore. Those clouds were blindingly white in the early afternoon sun.

Kotori walked across the room and stopped next to the couch that faced the king's chair.

The king's servants would put this couch here when a visitor came, but would take it away when the visitor left again, because the king did not like facing empty chairs. It made him feel lonely.

"Your highness," Kotori said, and he bowed.

From the top of his eyes, he could see the king's old knotted and wrinkled hands that lay on the spread that covered his legs.

"Don't be silly, Kotori. You are one of the few people I still want to see in this place. You're my family. Rise and make yourself comfortable."

Kotori did, taking his spot on the couch.

The last time he'd seen the king was not that long ago, although he struggled to remember when that had been. He didn't come up to the king's tower room so often anymore. The king looked old, his skin paper-thin and sallow, with deep wrinkles and spots of age.

The king met Kotori's eyes with his cloud-rimmed irises that had seen much good and evil in a long lifetime.

"You can say it out loud, brother of mine. I look terrible."

"I wasn't going to say that at all," Kotori said.

Making a comment like that would acknowledge his own age, and he was actually older than his brother the king, but for some mysterious reason, his health had remained much better. People joked behind his back that he was indestructible and would probably live until he was well over a hundred years old.

Kotori wasn't sure if he wanted to live that long.

"I am old," the king said. "And I am ill, and I probably won't last much longer."

"Don't say such terrible things," Kotori said.

"Don't perpetuate any lies," the king said. "We all know that it is true. No one lives forever, not even me. I've had a good life, but I sense in my bones that it won't last much longer."

This was all part of the ritual they went through whenever Kotori visited. The king had repeated different versions of those same words for over twenty years, but somehow the words had a real bite today.

"You called for me?" Kotori said. He pulled his bag onto his lap. "I've brought my star map and stones."

"You can put it away. I don't want a prediction. Heaven knows we've all put far too much stock in those in my lifetime."

Kotori's heart jumped. This was it. His brother had finally decided to appoint a new court astrologer, one who subscribed to the modern take on astrology: that it merely described the positions of objects in the sky, and not their meaning to daily life. This was the position held by the queen, who—

"I want you to help me keep the kingdom safe."

Total reset. Kotori jolted out of his thoughts.

Kingdom safe? "But I think we're pretty safe already," Kotori said.

"We are for now, but Chevakia is stirring. The great ruling body of the doga in Tiverius is a pale shade of what it used to be. They're old men, bickering over irrelevant matters. They don't control their own youth. The Chevakian youth is stirring, spoiling for fights. The army is out of control. Chevakia is facing difficult times. As their neighbour, we're facing difficult times. We've had no wars for over twenty years. Our soldiers are soft and no longer hungry for victory, or even to stand up in defense of the kingdom. What do you think will happen when I die?"

"Well, your daughter will become queen, as was enshrined in the new constitution."

Those words still felt unfamiliar on his tongue. Queen. Until recently, nobody in Arania had ever spoken that word. It used to be that the major princes, those who had risen through the ranks of the king's many, many sons, would battle for the position on the throne, but with one wave of his hand, King Orik had done away with those —admitted bloody and cruel—contests of power and now he wanted to put his daughter, yes, *his daughter*, on the throne.

"Yes, we changed the constitution, but I am not crazy," the king said. "I have heard all the rumours. I know that people in the Citadel and out are not happy, especially those who saw their influence greatly diminished when we stopped feeding our surplus of princes to the army and started giving money to the sciences and arts. They find the thought of having an artist in charge of this country galling."

"Well, it *is* galling, because a ruler needs to do so much more than playing pretty music."

"And do you think, dear astrologer, that is all my daughter does?"

Kotori desperately wanted to say *yes*, because that's what the princess did, but that would be rude, and he'd tried that avenue of discussion before, with little success. The king had made many efforts to educate the airhead. Private classes, visits to Chevakia and Peria to talk about statecraft had shown little effect.

The princess was only interested in playing music.

At least her mother had some useful skills, like calculus, that had some use. Even if he also very much disagreed with her conclusions, and her insistence that women be allowed to study.

The king continued. "My daughter has taken many classes on statecraft and is well-prepared for the task ahead. However, she is but a lone woman and I'd be a fool to suggest that she has the support of all the people she needs to support her. Like many in the armed forces, like—"

"Why don't you send your son to look after them?"

"Harek is only fifteen, and he needs to settle into sensibility before he can be trusted with a position of influence."

Ha. That was a diplomatic way of putting it. Harek was a spoilt brat who made it a point to always disagree with everything.

The king continued, "Anyway, Harek is too young. The men attached to the old ways are not happy about the impending ascension to the throne of my daughter. I worry that they will make use of the inevitable period of mourning and chaos after I die to further their interests."

"We have disposed of those ambitious princes," Kotori said.

He'd lived through that great purge, when people thought the king was about to announce he'd step down, and the three most powerful princes manoeuvred themselves into the most advantageous positions. Instead, he'd taken up with a new woman, married her properly, and it had been many generations since the king had married. In one fell swoop, he had sidelined and then murdered all the princes—his adult sons—in favour of the first child born from his new relationship.

Of *course* people had not been happy.

"Dear Kotori. Have you ever known men of power to give up so easily?"

Kotori shook his head. He had not.

"Right then. I want you to help me protect my daughter and my wife. When I die, which won't be too far away, I want you to make sure that my daughter can take up the throne and that those who wish to threaten her stay away."

Kotori met his brother's eyes. "How am I supposed to do that? I'm too old to carry arms and I was never any good with them, anyway."

Orik laughed. "Dear brother of mine, you never fail to impress me with your delicious combination of stupidity and cunning. It's quite an astonishing thing. If I wanted a man of arms, I would only need to call the guards in from the corridor. If I wanted a man of arms, why would I call for the court astrologer? In fact, why else would I call for the astrologer other than to make astrological predictions?"

"But you just said you didn't want—"

"Not for me, dear brother. You've known me long enough to be aware of what I think of the reliability of your astrological predictions."

Kotori's cheeks flushed. Yes, it was as bad as he suspected. The king didn't want him anymore. "I can make sure—"

"Be quiet. Listen, before you fill your head with nonsense. Which of the men of arms still consult you for castings of the stones?"

"Ehh."

"Colonel Betaro, right?"

"Yes. He's very traditional."

Kotori liked the colonel. He was another prince who had escaped the bloodbath following the king's changing of the constitution by virtue of having been only fifteen years of age at the time. But he'd grown up in the children's house, being led to believe that he would once have his own mother's house, only for mother's houses to become outlawed as soon as he was old enough to start his own.

"What about Leschek?"

"He moved to the country."

"And Pertak?"

"Yes."

Well, at least Orik's agents were still giving him the right information. Those two were Kotori's closest acquaintances, a brother and half-brother who had stuck by him for years.

"That's a decent start. Tell them that good fortune will come to those who support the queen and the princess."

"But's not how castings work—"

"Nobody knows how they work, least of all you. You cast a bunch of stones on a piece of fabric and make predictions based on where the stones land. How hard is that? Tell me how that has ever *not* been subject to a high level of imagination?"

Kotori's ears glowed. Just what was the king suggesting with these inflammatory remarks? That he, who had studied long and hard, simply made things up when people asked for predictions?

He stared at Orik, and Orik stared back.

They'd maintained this uneasy relationship for many years. Orik would needle him, and Kotori would always try to do the right thing.

"I'm not going to lie to men I trust," he finally said.

"I'm not asking you to lie."

Kotori breathed out. *He* thought the king was asking him to lie.

"I'm asking you to strengthen the position of the queen and princess in their minds. I know these men think little of women, and I want you to tell them that they should support the queen, because prosperity will come to them if they do."

"But you just told me not to lie—"

"Anyone can see that great prosperity will come to the ruler who recognises the value of knowledge over blunt force, of trade over war, of nurturing a few and nurturing them well over trying to raise many and failing them all. I don't need your star maps and pretty stones for that, but go ahead and use them if you think that gives your words greater authority."

Kotori opened his mouth, and shut it again. His brother was taunting him and making him into a fool.

"I only give predictions to those who ask for it." He knew that he sounded prim. So he added, "That is the tradition, handed down from the great Sizek."

"And yet you regularly give your opinions to everyone for free. Don't fool me with your statements of purity. You would not have made it this far if you were as pure as your words suggest."

Kotori found a seed of resilience. "I don't like your insinuations."

Orik laughed loudly. "No, I don't like them either, but that is the place we find ourselves in. I will die within the year. My wife will continue her quest for a fair country, but even with her support, my daughter faces a struggle against the men who won't give up their power and yearn for a return to the old ways. Men who would put my beautiful daughter in a mother's house to be violated nightly by those men and their friends, and instead of furthering knowledge, her time will be taken in pushing out a quick succession of brats that this country would need, under traditional rule, to wage wars to make sure that few enough powerful men survive so they can have mother's houses themselves. We have done away with that cruelty. We no longer need to train our young men to kill each other and let our young women believe that the best they can do is live in servitude to their master. I need you to plant the seed in the heads of these men that those who will continue the path I've set will lead prosperous lives."

"Ehh." Kotori could do no such thing. Why wouldn't his brother understand how castings and predictions worked? Why didn't his brother see that the princess had no interest in being queen, but only wanted to play music? That she had never uttered a word about what she would do with the country once she sat on the throne? That she would not inspire the people because she had no interest in doing so?

"Yes, I can see you want to protest, but dear astrologer, certainly you would have a foot to stand on if at least half of your predictions had turned out to be correct? So these are my words: you will tell these people what I said, because it's for your own benefit. Don't forget who pays for all your finery."

CHAPTER 4

The last strains of music faded away in the hall and through the tiers of seats in the audience.

For a few heartbeats, the musicians sat like statues and all those hundreds of people in the audience were quiet. Then the sound of applause broke out and reverberated through the hall. The musicians on the stage got up from their seats and bowed to the audience, including Loriane, in her sea-green dress, still holding her flute.

Lana's heart swelled with pride. That was her daughter down there. Neither she nor the girl's father, King Orik of Arania, professed to having one skerrick of musical talent, but Loriane had been different from birth. Graceful, talented, beautiful.

The members of the audience in the lower part of the hall were now getting up from their seats, some cheering with their hands raised. Lana recognised some of Loriane's friends from the music academy.

Even people on the balcony were getting to their feet, cheering, clapping, shouting.

As the first lights in the hall came on, Lana looked around, checking the faces of all those she hadn't been able to see during the performance.

Within a few moments, her pride turned to anger.

Where was Harek? He said he'd be there. He promised, this morning at breakfast.

"Wasn't that a beautiful performance, your majesty?"

She turned around.

The woman who had spoken was the citadel's seamstress, of all people, wearing the latest classy design. Not showy enough to upstage the queen or other high-ranked women, but just enough to exude class and style.

"It was, thank you."

"You must be so proud of your daughter that she can play such beautiful music."

"I am, thank you."

Lana took her overcoat from the back of her seat, her hands trembling with rage. Even the seamstress was here, but not Loriane's own brother.

On the stage, the musicians had gathered in a group. Most of them were in their final year in the music academy, like Loriane, and would go to a party to celebrate their graduation.

Loriane would come home later, and discussions about the performance could happily wait until then.

It was best to leave the young people to do what young people liked doing.

No need to bother Loriane with her brother's snub. Lana would deal with it, and oh, the dealing would be savage.

Lana bent to take the wheel brakes off Orik's wheelchair.

He had said little during the performance, but the full orchestra would have been loud enough for him to hear, and at least he hadn't fallen asleep.

"Let's take you home now."

He also hadn't asked to go home, a sign that he was having a rare good day when his mind wasn't muddled up. That was an improvement on his embarrassing performance at the merchants' meeting, where he had declared loudly in the middle of the proceedings that he wanted to go home.

Lana wheeled the chair up the ramp that led to the exit.

She smiled at the guards who waited there, ready for the two of them to return to the private quarters in the Citadel.

"Wasn't that a beautiful performance?" Orik said, as they were going through the quiet corridors of the private part of the citadel.

The hum of the crowd flowing from the hall into the courtyard drifted in through an open window together with the warm air of the autumn day.

She wheeled the wheelchair through the corridors, smiling to the servants they met and who told them how wonderful the performance had been.

Yes, it had been nice, but none of the pleasantries hid the ugly truth: Orik was old, Lana ran the king's affairs without the authority to do so, and the crown princess spent all her time playing music, which, no matter how wonderful it was, would not help her run the country. Loriane did all the work, but never spoke about her vision for the country.

And the princess' younger brother…

Lana didn't know what was up with him. With his recent fifteenth birthday had come a profound change in him: his withdrawal from family dinners, his terse replies to her questions about where he went for most of the day, and most worryingly, his appearance. He'd shaven most of his hair save for a ponytail at the very top and had tattooed his head. These days, he wore traditional leather gear treated with red oil. He wore a belt with a dagger inside the Citadel, no matter how often she told him to take it off. And when she said that she wouldn't have weapons at the table, his response had been to not come to the table at all.

They reached the king's private quarters and the trailing servants peeled off at the door.

Lana pushed the chair in front of the fire. It was hot and stuffy in the room, but that was the way he liked it.

"Something bothers you?" Even if he might look absent-minded, he was as sharp as ever. Many people made that mistake.

Lana could no longer hide her irritation.

"Harek wasn't there, and he promised me he would be."

"He probably had other things to do."

"He promised. Loriane is his sister. This is an important day for her. He couldn't even make that effort, yet, he's meant to be an observer to the royal council?" She hadn't agreed with that, not at all. He was too young, knew little about life outside the Citadel, and what was worse, people listened to every nonsensical word he uttered, especially the men of the army, because he was the king's son. That despicable Colonel Betaro was one of them.

"I don't know what gets into these young people." Orik briefly lifted his hands from his lap, blotchy-skinned, knobbly hands. The nails were much too long, but he wouldn't let anyone cut them, and since he was the king, no one could force him.

Even if Lana did almost everything else.

She said, "The young people don't know what the past was like and they're destroying all the gains we've made."

"No, they don't know. I am still king because of the softer rules. Back in the past, an old and decrepit man like me would have been deposed and killed long ago. But yes, parts of the army are still calling for a strong king. You can't vanquish that line of thinking with polite conversations and pretty music."

"So is that it, then? You don't want your daughter to take the throne as you promised?"

"Dear wife. You are really angry."

"Yes!"

"Dear wife of mine. You know I think you're an amazing, beautiful and ambitious woman. You and I know how much you mean to a lot of people, and how you've improved the lives of many in Arania, especially the women. But you and I both know that we have to step back and let our daughter govern the country as she sees fit."

He met Lana's eyes with his watery gaze.

"I know you want to protest, because you want to hold her hand, and I want it, too, but we know it's true. She is not you, and she is not me. She will do things as she wants."

"But she has no interest in governing! And her brother is not supporting her."

"Do not worry. They are but young. I've asked those in power to help support them. The country is in good hands."

"They don't even support each other."

These last few months, ever since it became clear that Orik's health was failing, were a string of frustrations for her.

She felt the abject failure of all the years she had fought to change the barbaric system in which princes had mothers' houses where women existed solely for producing the children that added to the prince's status. The world in which princes fought each other for the throne, guided by the nonsense sprouted by the court astrologer.

"I'll still talk to our son. He deserves to be made to feel ashamed of himself."

Orik shrugged. "Those who are shameless cannot be made to feel shame. All those who are young suffer from this infliction. You and I were no different. We adapt to the situation we find ourselves in as we age. Our children will be no different."

Lana left the room seething. She couldn't blame Orik. He was old and feeble and had forgotten many of the things he'd done in the last ten years. But he could at least… try.

Harek didn't normally listen to his father, although his father rarely spoke against him and instead doted on his son. Allowed him to become an observer at the council. Allowed him to go to military training. Because it was a thing men did.

Lana had different kinds of male activities in mind. Her son was never going to be a scholar, but he could be an engineer. Or an architect. Heaven knew the country could use those.

She didn't find Harek in his room, and nor was he at the Citadel's weapons training ground where he also liked to spend a lot time. He wasn't in the kitchen either, where he could usually be found after training.

Eventually, she was forced to ask the servants. Those in the kitchen didn't know where he was and hadn't seen him at all that day, but a guard told her that he had seen the prince leave the Citadel's gates earlier in the morning. Lana had last seen Harek at breakfast, and so it looked like the promise he gave at breakfast to come to the performance had been a complete lie from the start.

Anger grew. Supposing he was ever successful at supplanting his sister, as he had smartly never said aloud he wanted, but was so clearly the case, he didn't even have the courtesy to honour his subjects with his presence.

Someone like that could not possibly ever be a well-loved ruler.

Rulers who were not well-loved usually found out that there were knives that community members were happy to bring out at the first sign of weakness, no matter how much you scared your subjects into submission.

Lana had already told him this so many times. But talking to Harek was futile, anyway. He just did whatever he wanted.

Of course, there were far too many places in town where he could have gone for her to check every one.

Lana was about to go back to her private quarters when she spotted him coming in through the gates. She strode in his direction.

"Where were you?" she asked him.

He had the audacity to look surprised.

"What do you mean, where was I?"

"We were at your sister's performance this morning, and you promised at breakfast you'd be there."

To his credit, he didn't try to weasel his way out of it. He had promised in the morning, after all.

"Something else came up," he said.

"Something like what? What do you have to do in your life that requires immediate presence and absolves you from having to come to your sister's most important performance?"

"I had to help a friend."

He gave her a pointed look.

These days, he was taller than she was, and all his training made his shoulders broad.

He wore a traditional Aranian soldier's uniform, made of thick leather gleaming with red oil. It looked threatening and exuded a typical smell, which reminded her so much of the way men used to dress when she first came here. That was the time when the princes came into the mothers' houses to pick out the woman they wanted at night.

"Do I get to know who this friend is, who is so important that you can miss your sister's performance for their sake?"

"It's a delicate issue, and you will probably hear about it later, but I can't tell anyone about it, for my friend's protection."

Lana stared at him, astonished.

He was fifteen.

Where had he learned to speak like this all of a sudden?

And then another wave of suspicion washed over her.

"A delicate situation?" she asked, her voice low.

"That's what I said."

"Can I get a guarantee that this 'delicate situation' doesn't involve a girl and her or her family's reputation?"

"No, you can't, because it does."

"Harek!"

"What? I'm telling you the truth."

"That you've been with a girl and got her into trouble and now need to sort out the mess?"

He stared at her. His cheeks went red.

A million thoughts went through Lana's head, few of them kind.

We gave you all the education and taught you to respect women and the first opportunity you get, you get some poor girl pregnant?

Harek said nothing and stared back.

Lana was already sorry for having gone as far as she had.

It would be easy if he said, "Mother, if that is what you think about me, I'm finished with this conversation."

But he didn't.

His lips twitched. He continued to meet her eyes until that became too uncomfortable.

And the longer he said nothing, the more she feared that she was right, that all her education on the subject had driven him into the influence of the military men who still thought that women belonged in mother's houses and had started acting the part. He was the right age. Even now, there was never a shortage of girls throwing themselves at princes.

Families from the regions often still sent their girls to the city with the hope that some rich man would take them off their hands.

There were still mother's houses, because they had gone underground, even if the Citadel no longer encouraged them and no longer gave the men tax breaks for each woman they kept.

There were still men who did this.

"Have you finished?" Harek asked. "My archery training starts soon."

"No, but this will do for today. I'll be happy to hear more information once you feel inclined to share it."

"No, you won't be happy, and you won't hear it."

He turned on his heel.

"Harek! Don't be rude."

He kept walking.

She balled her fists against her sides as she watched him walk off, no doubt to meet some of those "friends" at some military style training. He was very tall and broad these days. Much more muscular than Orik had been, even when she first met him.

Back in the time when she had first come to Kadrish, the major princes like Nayek and Denori, or brutes like Sferuk, had terrorised the Citadel, including the women in the mother's house.

But of course, those men had all been Orik's sons. They'd been killed in the great battle for the throne that had resulted in her deal with Orik.

But you didn't just wipe out hundreds of years of brutal history with one agreement. Those men who hadn't been killed wanted to fight. They had elevated the past princes to near-divine status, ones like Colonel Betaro. It was no secret what they thought about the current prince. They trained for imaginary future conflicts. They dreamed of the past when any number of women would be clamouring for favourite mother status. They would use Harek to return the country to that world.

She would have to pull him back from that path before it was too late.

Even if there was a girl involved.

Even if Orik told her that everything would be fine.

And Loriane wasn't helping at all. She should be stepping up as crown princess, and Harek should be second in line. And neither of her children accepted that situation.

Loriane wanted to play music. Harek wanted the women.

And every day their father grew older, the time to a showdown came closer. And with every day, Loriane became less interested in running the country, and Harek became more obstinate. The future of Arania, and indeed that of the known world, lay in their hands.

CHAPTER 5

$\mathcal{M}$orning was Javes' favourite time of the day. When the sky was soft pink, the air held the crispness of the desert night and the hot wind had not yet picked up.

And this cliff face on the eastern side of the continent with its rugged terrain, sparse vegetation and wide views of the sea was one of his favourite spots to spend the morning, sitting by the fire making tea and porridge.

Javes was glad he'd never given up travelling. Not even when he took up the position of area administrator, not even when his household grew to four, or when they employed workers to look after the house, business, and animals. There was always someone in the kitchen wanting advice from him, about administrative matters, about the mail, about the telegraph lines or the roads, or the market stalls. And there was always work to be done in the camel shed.

He liked the peace and quiet.

Javes had already caught his two camels, and had fed them each some grain, which both were lazily munching while sitting on the top of the cliff. Over the last few days, during his trek through the desert, the pickings had been slim, even for camels, and his hope of finding some dead grass had been thwarted. Rain was unreliable and far in between in the desert, and seasons didn't hold much sway.

There were so many things to worry about: the crops, the grazing rights, the olive harvest and all the other administrative things that waited for him back in Ysherra.

There were questions about the building of schools and about the bus timetables and about who was going to go to the big meeting down in Watya next month.

All that would be waiting for him when he came back.

He looked out over the ocean, silver in the light of the sun that was still behind the bank of billowing clouds that always hung over the horizon.

He understood that in Arania these were called the Mother's Veil, and he now also understood that these were the same clouds, and because the world was a ball, the clouds covered the entire side of the world where the continent was not. What was on that other side?

Nobody knew. Many brave sailors from all parts of the continent had gone out on ships to discover and none had ever come back. Rumours were rife about the things that could be found there, from rich lands that housed a fabulous modern civilisation, or an ocean infested with monsters to waterfalls that plunged into bottomless depths. And most likely, the reason that those sailors died was that they suffered poisoning from sonorics.

Normal, rational people did not think too much about matters like this. The continent was kept safe by the machines that diverted the rays from the land. It was big enough for all. There was no need to go elsewhere. There was nowhere to go.

A few islands lay off the coast of eastern Chevakia, but they were mostly rocky atolls, populated by huge colonies of noisy pooping birds. If there were any beaches to access the islands at all, explorers had found them hostile. The rocky outcrops offered no food, no water, nothing at all that people valued.

The camels had their noses deeply buried in their grain bags, when Javes rose from the spot where he had been eating to pack up his modest camp.

He'd collected a lot of material on this trip, and the packs were heavy.

The water he'd collected from the muddy well yesterday evening had filtered through the cloth bag and was now clean. He topped up his water jars and gave the rest to the camels. He checked their feet for sharp rocks and thorns.

One of them, the younger male, was restless and wouldn't keep his feet up for Javes to check. He pulled his head upwards, making the rope slip from Javes' hands. He made funny faces with his lips as if there was another camel nearby.

Javes straightened and studied the land behind him and the ocean in front of him and the cliffs on either side of him and all the gullies and the coloured outcrops, and the smooth glistening areas where water came to the surface. He couldn't see anything out of place. The weather was normal, the sky was clear, there was no sign of impending dust storms. Dust devils were quite common, but they usually came with bad weather and the weather was beautiful and calm and silent.

Yet the camel was agitated, which meant something bothered it. Camels were always right. Even if you thought there was nothing, you always found out that there was a reason for the strange behaviour.

But Javes could not see it.

The smaller female camel didn't behave in the same way. She was going to be carrying most of the packs today, and he tied them to the saddle while she finished off the grain.

He tapped the male camel on the leg. It sat down with a groan to let him get on.

From the top of the saddle, he had a better view of the surrounding land, but still saw nothing out of place.

He tapped the animal on the neck. It started walking down the narrow path that led up the cliff, with the female following behind, tied to the male's saddle with a rope. They went down the gully with desiccated bushes and tiny patches of grey-green grass where moisture came to the surface.

They went up the path that zigzagged up the other side of the gully to the ridge behind the cliff.

At the top, he looked around over his shoulder, still not seeing anything.

The camel was still disturbed, looking over its shoulder and tossing its head.

But there was nothing that justified this behaviour. Meanwhile, Javes noticed that a rope on the female's pack hung loose and had gotten tangled, so Javes let himself slide off the saddle. He made the female camel sit and fixed up the ropes. They would only annoy the animal for the rest of the day.

At the moment he rose from the packs, he sensed someone or an animal behind him. Javes never travelled without his knife. He slid it out of his boot and swung around, facing—well, was that a man or a woman? He wasn't sure. The person was dreadfully thin, with white baggy scuffed and ripped clothes hanging from bony shoulders.

The face looked like a skull, and dirty hair hung in strings from the person's head. The fingers were like the legs of an insect, the skin scabbed and engrained with dirt.

Javes looked at this man, because he settled on that the person was male, despite the lack of facial hair, and the man looked back at him. He tried to speak, but his voice was so soft and rough that Javes couldn't hear the words.

He held out his hands as if to beg for help.

"What are you doing here? Where did you come from? Where are your animals?"

The man rasped a few words, but Javes had no idea what he said.

In the gully that he had just traversed, he could see no sign of animals, not even a dead ones, and there was no other sign of human habitation.

"Where did you come from?" Javes asked again.

The man again held out his hands and said strange words. He took a few steps forward. He was very unsteady on his feet and looked like he might collapse at any moment.

Still holding onto his knife, Javes grabbed his water bottle and handed it to the stranger with an outstretched arm.

Certainly, if this man was fleeing the law, he wouldn't ask for help?

The man grabbed the bottle with both hands and drank in big gulps. He was very careful with not spilling any. His hands were those of an office worker, with well-maintained nails and soft skin, which sported bleeding cuts.

His clothes were made from a thick type of material that Javes had never seen before. They were dirty and ripped, but must once have been quite beautiful.

His shoes were made from a shiny material, now also scratched and damaged.

Javes had never seen this type of outfit before.

What was he going to do? He couldn't leave this poor man alone, no matter how he had arrived here.

Javes put the hobbles back on the camels. The beasts were unimpressed, because they had only just gotten started, and both beasts liked walking.

He untied two heavy packs from the female camel and attached them to the male's saddle. This freed up the saddle on the female for the stranger to ride.

The man retreated a small distance and watched with wide eyes.

"You can come closer," Javes said. "This one's a bit grumpy, but he doesn't bite. At least not until you really annoy him."

The stranger said nothing, but glanced at the rocks at his back as if looking for a way to escape.

"No, he really doesn't bite. You do want to get out of here?"

He expected no reply and got none.

The man would be hungry. He'd be tired.

Javes dug in his packs and found a bag of dried salt meat. He held the packet out to the stranger, who stared at it, an uncertain look on his face.

"It's food," Javes said. "You eat it, like this."

He took a strip and tore a piece off with his teeth and chewed. The salty taste exploded in his mouth.

The stranger looked around, looked aside, and took a piece, quickly, as if he was afraid that someone was going to take it off him.

Javes asked, "Were you alone? Were there any others in your group that we need to rescue?"

Of course, the man didn't understand this, so Javes found a sandy spot and drew himself and the camels as stick figures.

"That's me and the camels." He pointed at himself and the two beasts. "What about you?" He pointed at the stranger.

The stranger pointed to himself and then held his hands up.

What did that mean?

Javes pointed to the drawing of himself in the sand, and then drew another separate person. And then added a couple of stick figures in a group. "Where are your companions?"

The man came closer and wiped them all out.

"Just you. You alone?"

The stranger repeated the word *alone*, but there was no comprehension in his voice.

"How did you get here? Where is your boat? Do we need to take things from there?"

But that was too difficult for the stranger to understand.

Damn, he'd have to check. This guy might be a murderer and his victim might be lying dead on the beach.

Javes wanted to be on the road. It was a good day's walk to the next waystation.

But he knew he'd be sorry later. When he got to Ysherra, the guards would ask if he'd checked for other people. He would ask that question himself to anyone who came to his office in a similar situation.

Javes walked up and down the cliff face, looking at the tiny beach below. Part of the sand was visible, but the narrow path that went down to the beach was very steep and hard to discern from here.

He hardly ever went down there, because he'd been there a few times and there was nothing to see on the beach. Sometimes, too, the tusked lions that often sunbathed on the beach were aggressive.

But he could see no signs of a boat. Or a camp. Or any other people.

"Is there any stuff down there that we have to take?" he asked, but asking the stranger anything was a waste of time, because the man clearly understood very little.

After chewing through his dried meat, which Javes didn't think he enjoyed, he had sat on a rock, with his arms linked around his knees. His eyes darted from one side to the other, but there was only empty ocean and empty sky, with the clouds on the horizon. There were no islands offshore, so surely there would have to be a boat or something that had brought the stranger here.

So Javes installed the man with some water and a few different types of dried meat and dried fruit to try.

He tied the camels together, took their hobbles off, grabbed the headrope of the male camel, and guided the animals down the steep path.

The stranger followed at a distance.

The path was even steeper than he remembered, and he had to use all his wits to remember where it was. This stranger must have done a pretty good job or have been pretty stressed to find his way up the cliff.

Eventually, he came down to the beach. Waves already rolled over much of the sand, and it wouldn't be long before the beach would disappear under the water.

Javes could see nothing on the sand that indicated where the stranger had come ashore.

He walked along the remaining strip of beach and found a few pieces of debris that he couldn't place. There were fragments of a box, bits of cloth that looked quite old, and some fragments of a transparent material that he had not seen before. Some pieces looked like they were fragments of little tubes as thin as his little finger. The material was lighter than glass and felt warm to the touch. He put some fragments in his pocket, and checked in between the rocks at the back of the beach for additional clues.

In every crevice, he expected to see a dead body or something equally disturbing, but apart from a few other and larger fragments of this strange material, he found nothing. Would it be possible that the stranger had arrived here overland? Maybe he was a fugitive, and had realised only after coming here that surviving on the desert coast was hard.

From where he stood on the beach, Javes could see the man sitting on a rock, looking out over the ocean.

His presence was an utter mystery, but yet, he should probably get going.

He climbed back up, and he was about halfway up the cliff, when he discovered a kind of provisional shelter made from a material that looked like sail cloth. A narrow path between large rocks led to it, and at one point he could even see footsteps in the dust. He hadn't seen it on the way down because an overhanging rock sheltered it from that side.

Inside the shelter, he found a bunch of strange objects on top of a bed of dried seaweed. A little box with a window, with salt crystals encrusting the inside, and sea water sloshing around behind the glass.

A nice-looking suit. Javes didn't understand why the stranger was not wearing that. It got very cold at night.

But when he picked it up, it turned out that the back was all ripped and stained with dark fluid. Was that blood?

The garment was next to useless, but he packed it up, anyway. He also took the thing with the water behind the glass and the flat box that he found under the seaweed. It was a bit bigger than his hand, made of metal and quite heavy. He couldn't figure out how or even if it opened.

One of the camels was making snorting noises outside.

When he came back up to the camels, he expected trouble, but the stranger sat in exactly the same position where Javes had left him.

"I got your stuff." Javes showed the items he had collected.

The man said a few words, accompanied by a dismissive hand signal.

It would be handy to know that he said, *Leave it, it's broken,* or *It's not worth anything.* Something like that.

This situation was so very, very strange.

But they needed to get going.

The camels were skittish and impatient.

The stranger at first didn't want to come close to the animals, and Javes had to demonstrate getting into the saddle, making the camel having to get up twice.

Camels didn't like being prodded into doing something, so the beast protested loudly, which made the stranger shrink back even further.

Had he even seen a camel before?

It took Javes a lot of convincing to get him to climb into the saddle, and then when the camel got to its feet, stretching its back legs first, the man let out a squeal of fear.

The female camel was very placid, but one thing she didn't like was a lot of noise, so she shied and jumped, and this made the man squeal more.

"Stop, stop!" Javes called.

He grabbed the camel tightly by the headgear so that it couldn't make any more sudden movements. But now he had to get onto his own camel, and for that, this camel had to calm down first.

"Sit still. Don't move."

He mimicked setting still, and eventually, the stranger understood.

He could then go to his own camel, and climb on.

Normally, he would lead, but he let the female camel go first for a bit, to make sure that the stranger didn't get into trouble.

It was slow going, because the path was narrow, and the camel kept stopping because she expected her mate to go first.

They needed to cover a reasonable distance to get to the next waypoint, and so Javes took the lead when he was convinced that the stranger had gotten the hang of it.

Every time he looked around, the man still sat like a statue in the saddle, and if Javes asked a question, he only moved his eyes in response.

This was going to be a long trip home.

CHAPTER 6

$\mathcal{I}$t was close to darkness when Tylve finally came back to the shore. After three days at sea, she was tired and hungry, looking forward to putting her feet up for a day or two before getting ready to sail again.

She had hauled in the nets a good while ago, and the baskets on the deck of the ship were full of silvery fresh fish, some of which still occasionally flapped their tails.

The catch had been quite good recently and if this continued, she would be able to save up some money to fix the roof at the back of the house, which overlooked the ocean and where the salt spray had eaten into the gutters and eaves.

The harbour in the village of Samira was small and ancient. Today, it was occupied by the familiar boats, the fishing vessels of families in town, and Councilmember Lon Dorkas's two carrier vessels that took fish up the river and brought the mail back down. The Dorkas family owned another two of these flat, rather unsightly boats, but they would be at work, somewhere between the wide river mouth where Samira lay, and the capital Tiverius.

Tylve steered the boat past the lighthouse into the harbour. Both the waves and the wind vanished here. She threw the grappling hook over the side and dragged it along with the remaining movement of the boat until the hook snagged in one of the underwater cables. She hauled up the cable, encrusted with marine growth and barnacles, fed it into the pulley on the bow and cranked the lever attached to the mechanism back and forth, so that the movement of the wheels in the pulley box pulled the boat closer.

The mechanism rattled the last few shards of lightstream out of the metal box that held the gears. Tylve gathered it up in her hand and flicked it into the water. She would do that all the time back when she would go fishing with her father. Stunning fish, she used to call it, until her father told her not to do this too openly because it would be seen by many in the village as a sign of something evil.

"I've worked hard at getting accepted by the villagers," he had told her when he'd sat her down at the table to warn her. She'd been about ten. "For many years, we of the Gathering were always on the outside. We got the worst deals, the dregs of everything. I worked my way up to the council. Don't you go and prove that everything they feared about us was right after all."

Cranking the lever was hard and hot work, but preferable to taking the oars, especially when it was as dark as this.

The glow of street lights in the main streets of the town spread a yellowing glow, in which she could see people moving along the quay.

Quite a lot of people, actually.

Samira was a small town that was quiet and sleepy most of the time, except a few times in the year when the domed building that poked over the houses took on significance. That was when people from up and down the coast roamed the streets, dressed in grey robes for the seasonal Big Gathering.

But the Autumn Gathering had been held last month.

So, was anything else going on?

The people were mostly walking in the same direction, but in small groups, or alone, and they walked at different speeds.

Where were they all going, and who were they?

The people who normally walked around on the quay were dock crew for unloading ships, but there were not that many ships at the quay, none that were being unloaded, which was a rare occurrence at this time of the day, anyway. These looked like ordinary townsfolk. They definitely weren't carrying anything.

At the quay, she tossed the ropes over the mooring bollards on the shore and tightened the boat's position.

The harbourmaster had seen her coming and had sent the young kids who would come to collect the fish.

Tylve let down the ladder and the two kids, a brother and sister, came on board.

"Four baskets! It's a good catch today," the boy said.

"Take a little something from it for your mother," Tylve said, winking at the boy.

"I will, thank you." He picked up a basket and carried it off the deck.

His sister, a beefy, short-haired girl who almost looked like a boy, picked up another basket. She was shy, but Tylve knew her as an intelligent girl.

"Do you know if anything was going on at the quay just before I arrived?" Tylve asked.

"What was going on?" The girl looked at her.

"I saw a lot of people walking along the water. They were all going in that direction." She pointed.

"Oh. Some guards from Tiverius came to town," she said. "They're looking for something, but no one knows what. Some people say an escaped criminal, but others say they're looking for stolen goods. I don't know about it either. That's just what I've heard. I prefer to stay as far away as possible from people from the city. They arrived yesterday afternoon and went around all the inns last night, and lined up everyone inside, and it looked like they were going to do it again this afternoon. So that's what you must have seen, because as soon as the news came that they were doing another round of the harbour, people started to leave."

"Did anything happen?"

"No, they just went for a drink in Pabito's place and stayed there."

Tylve snorted. "Pabito can't be too happy about it."

"No. He has no patrons left in the dining room. Not until these guards leave."

"Have they actually found anything?"

Guards came into town on occasion, more so this year than previous years. Half the time Tylve suspected there was a reason back in Tiverius that they did this, because they hardly ever seemed to find anything.

"Not that I know, but they've been talking to more people than they did last time."

"Who?"

"People in the street going about their business. They took Pandor out of his house in front of his kids, and yelled at him and threatened him."

"Pandor? Really? What did he do wrong? He wouldn't harm a fly." Pandor was the temple guardian and took his duty to his community seriously. As temple guardian, he might once have been a target of insults by people in town, those who did not belong to the Gathering, but she hadn't heard of any of that kind of behaviour since she was a little girl and her father had sat her down at the kitchen table.

People from Tiverius wouldn't even *know* about the Gathering, or get upset about it.

The girl shrugged. "That's what happened. All he did was ask questions they didn't like. Everyone in town should get out of the way of these guards. They'll be like the typical city people. They won't find what they want, and then they'll leave again to harass other towns."

The girl's brother walked past, carrying a basket of fish. "Hey, sis, are you again letting me do all the work?"

"Oh, eh. I'll help you. Will I see you later at the evening Gathering?" she then asked Tylve.

"Yes, I'll be there."

Tylve watched the two youngsters walk down the gangplank, each carrying a basket of fish.

Oh, to be that innocent age again. To trust everyone so blindly. To have adults you could look up to. Not that she thought she deserved to be that person that youngsters looked up to.

Tylve collected her pack from the cabin. The strange collar she had found still lay on the table that held her maps. She debated leaving it here. Having to dismember the fresh skeleton had been a more disturbing experience than she wanted to admit, but curiosity won. The town administrator had spent time in Tiverius and might be familiar with the latest gadgets. She wanted to know what the thing was, so the man hadn't died abandoned and lonely on the island for nothing.

So she opened the drawer underneath the map table, took a cloth from the neatly folded pile, and wrapped the thing before putting it in her bag.

The thought of putting an object that had touched rotting flesh with her clothes made her uneasy.

Then she climbed onto the deck, pulled the cover over the deck so that her boat was well protected from any rain that might fall overnight, and she walked down the gangplank to the quay.

The citizens who had been there earlier had long gone. The only sign of movement was a group of seagulls fighting over something dropped on the cobbles.

Tylve walked with her hands in her pockets and her bag over her shoulder.

The harbourmaster's office was already closed.

The sound of talk and laughter still came from the market warehouse, where the brother and sister had taken her fish.

It would be sold here tomorrow.

She turned around the corner into the main street, hoping to catch a glimpse of these guards in their fancy uniforms with shiny buttons, but they had long gone or were still inside Pabito's drinking room. Many of the shops were closed or about to close.

She stopped at the bakery for some bread, getting today's bread for half price just before the shop closed.

Away from the harbour, the main street wound through the town. Ages of history had left their legacy. The street was narrow and paved with uneven cobblestones. There were those in town who wanted to make the main street wider, but most of the locals objected to it.

Sure enough, you could get carts to come through, but carts and trucks didn't belong in towns where people walked. She'd seen in Tiverius where that led: wide streets that were too dangerous to cross. In Samira, the carts and trucks would just have to go around the centre to get to the harbour.

Tylve's house lay on the outskirts of the old part of town, on the road that went up the ridge immediately behind the old town centre.

Building space was tight here. The front of the house lay directly on the street, and there wasn't much of a backyard because the ground sloped steeply down.

From the back of her house you could see the entire bay and the river mouth and if the weather was clear, you could even see some of the smaller offshore islands. Not the Island of Skulls where she had collected this strange thing, that was much further out.

The view was why she'd traded her family's old house in town for this one after her father's death. Big houses were for families. No man in town had ever been interested in having a sailor for a wife.

The house was dark and quiet and smelled a bit musty. That was because of the leaking roof in the back room.

One day, everything would be fixed, and she'd sell her boat and she would sit here and look over the ocean all day. She would get a bird in a cage, one of those ones that could learn to speak so that she could teach it to sing rude sailor's songs.

She went to the kitchen, and she cut a piece off the bread she'd just bought and collected some cheese and salted fish.

She ate it while rummaging around in her bedroom in semidarkness and changed out of her sturdy fishing clothes into her town clothes.

It was already so dark, she was sure going to be late for the dusk Gathering.

Better ask for forgiveness first.

She stopped at the shrine in the hall, noticed how the little oil lamp was almost out of oil, and refilled the reservoir from the squeeze bottle in the tiny cupboard underneath.

The flame must be kept going, her father always told her.

Stuffing the last bit of bread into her mouth, Tylve left the house again and in the increasing darkness, walked down the street into town.

The temple with its marble pillars and domed roof was the first thing you saw of Samira if you came into the shore by sea. The dome was painted brilliant blue and was adorned with leaf patterns in glittering gold paint. When the sun hit it at a certain angle, the gold reflected the light and shone as bright as a beacon.

At the street level, the building was rather more modest, with plain walls and marble pillars at the entrance. Unlike with other community or government halls, there were no statues, because the Gathering disliked putting certain people above others. The Gathering did not teach the philosophy of a single visionary. It recognised the power of all people working together, like an ant's nest, or a beehive.

After she had taken off her shoes at the entrance and walked through the dark foyer into the main hall with its many flapping torches, she found the Gathering already in full swing. Many villagers sat on the plain wooden benches that surrounded the central mosaic floor and the low platform where one of the town's shopkeepers was talking about the subject of petty thievery.

There was barely any space to sit, but she found a spot at the very end of the top bench. Not where she, as a long-standing member and belonging to one of the original Samiran families, was used to sitting. But that was her own fault.

Many of the people in the benches at the front, whose backs she could see, were those she'd grown up with. The owners of the shops, the workers and butchers and weavers and their families, the owners of the warehouses and the market halls.

Did these people realise that their kids were playing spying games in the bench behind the adults? She repressed a snigger.

The shop owner was a long-standing member, and petty thievery was a favourite topic of his. He blamed, as usual, visitors from out of town.

And this had become a difficult discussion topic.

Seated here at the back of the congregation, it disturbed her how many faces on the benches opposite her she didn't know. Oh, some of them had become familiar to her ever since new people first started turning up at the Gatherings about two years ago. She even knew many of their names. They'd come from the inland towns, some even as far away as Tiverius or places like Twin Bridges.

For many years, Samirans had been persecuted, ridiculed and made to give up their beliefs, even within the town. For years, the old families—of which only a few remained—had been told to keep quiet, not to be overt, and especially not to talk about lightstream.

For years, Tylve's family, especially her father and uncle, had fought the town administrators who wanted to tear down the temple "because no one uses it" even if there had never been a single day that no one had come through its doors. But it had been rather empty on most days.

And now Samiran Gatherings were suddenly popular, and none of the townsfolk understood why.

Tylve liked how younger people from other towns had brought so much life to the daily Gatherings. These people would actually discuss new issues, rather than go over the same ones over and over.

Some townsfolk weren't happy, like this particular shop owner who had just been told his time was almost up by Pandor with the bell.

He'd still maintain that theft in his shop had increased and therefore these new people were thieves.

But since the Gathering's kids from Tylve's generation had fled the village years ago—and few had come back, the village had been bleeding life. They should welcome these new, much younger, families.

The shop owner had vacated the stage and one of the new people came forward. This was an older woman Tylve had seen a few times at Gatherings, even if she didn't remember the woman's name.

"I want to talk about the dangers that come with the visiting guards," she said. "They've been to our doors and have asked questions they have no right to ask. Their questions are about the Gathering and who comes to it. They ask for lists of names. They want to know where we live. Some women were so scared that they didn't dare go home."

"Yes, this happened on our side of town as well," another woman called from within the audience.

"They asked us about my son," another said. "I don't know how they know that we have a son, since he doesn't live with us at the moment."

"They asked about my daughter," a man said. "I told them she's gone for a year to serve her community, but they wouldn't believe me."

"The Tiverian guards have been mystified by our practices for as long as I remember," Pandor said, a calming, trusted voice in the panic. "They never liked us, and they sent scholars to study us and write up long reports about what we do and who we are. The guards will know about these scripts."

The woman protested. "This is more than that. They're seeking us out. They're asking about things that we've been doing for years. What is their obsession with us?"

"Welcome to being with the Gathering," yelled the original shopkeeper.

Yes, it had always been like this. If you had any interactions with people from out of town, you never mentioned that you were with the Samiran Gathering, because that would be an excuse for them to mistreat you and be rude.

The new practice of sending their children away for a year of study or whatever they did to "serve the community", was a new development that even Pandor had professed privately not to know where it came from.

The Samiran scripts said that young people, lacking responsibility for feeding a family, should volunteer time to help those in need. It said nothing about leaving home, or about staying away for a whole year.

Tylve had never done that when she was young. She had to help her father with the boat. They never had time for luxuries.

The discussion went on about the visiting guards. Several of the older villagers got involved. The guards were interested not because they were Samiran, the older villagers said, but because the guards didn't understand why so many people suddenly declared themselves Samiran.

It sounded like the villager wanted to know this, too.

A man, one of the new people, said, "That is none of the guards' business, because we have done nothing wrong."

However, Tylve knew those same questions were asked in bars. Why did all these new people suddenly have an interest in Samiran culture?

Pandor closed the discussion with a statement of unity, after which they all sang the song of Peace and Everlasting.

It was heartening to hear all those voices echo in the temple's vast space.

Disagreement is human, her father used to say. The Gathering encouraged people to disagree and talk so that they could agree on the important points.

People grabbed each other's hands and closed their eyes while they stood in the benches.

If she opened her eyes a sliver, Tylve could see glowing motes of dust and strands of light drift down from the skies. Lightstream. The spirits of those who had departed the mortal life.

The motes pricked her skin when they landed on her bare arms. They brought energy that coursed through her veins. She used this energy to make decisions that benefited future generations.

But then suddenly, a voice yelled discordant panicked words. People stopped singing. A few gasped and turned around.

A young boy said, "They're coming in."

Tylve stepped aside so that she could look out the temple door into the forecourt, where flapping torches lit the pavement.

A couple of guards had entered the yard.

Pandor strode across the hall to the temple's entrance. "Halt. Don't progress any further."

Five guards faced him, standing on the steps.

Pandor said, "You are entering the domain of our Gathering space. No one can come here who has not taken the oath of allegiance to our community. You need to have proven your purity of mind and swear your allegiance to the power of the sea and the sky."

The leader of the guards said, "We come in the name of Tiverius. You are officially part of the country and we have the authority to search this property for people and material that we feel may be of importance for the security of the country."

"You can't do this," Pandor said.

"Yes, we can. Unless you can produce a document from the Tiverian court that you are exempt from these powers."

"But you have to—"

The commander of the guards waved his hand and the group of guards crossed to the temple steps. They did not pledge their allegiance. They did not take off their shoes, and they simply pushed Pandor aside.

Several citizens ran to help him, and a few others formed a chain of linked hands to stop the guards from entering the building, but one of the guards grew nervous and pulled out his sword.

The villagers stumbled back.

"What is this?" Pandor yelled behind their backs. "We are peaceful citizens. You have no right to come in here. This is a property of cultural significance and if you want to search it, then at least abide by the rules of the country. Rules made in our capital."

The patrol leader jerked his head, and the group barged into the building, all of them still wearing their shoes.

People inside shouted. Many of those had not seen what happened in the forecourt.

Panic broke out. Citizens stumbled down the tiered seating.

The temple room had a second entrance on the opposite side of where Tylve stood. Someone flung open those doors, letting a stream of villagers into the night. Tylve followed the stream of citizens into the rear courtyard, which looked out over the roofs of town, the harbour and the ocean.

The last thing she saw was Pandor standing at the entrance, his hands at his sides. His voice carried into the night.

"We are a peaceful organisation and we will not allow anything that is capable of killing a person into the building. The Gathering is a place where we cultivate peace and community, not destroy it. Leave your weapons outside. And take off your shoes to respect our culture."

This was followed by the sound of a crash, and then the splintering of wood. A rough male voice laughed.

Tylve felt sick.

What sort of guards were these?

Unprofessional idiots.

What had Pandor done to attract their ire?

All the people who had been inside the room now stood in the back yard, which was not big enough for everyone.

They listened to the crashes and things being dragged over the floor. The men spoke in such strong dialect that she had no idea what they said.

What did they want inside the temple? All the people stood outside. There was nothing they would want inside the building.

Tylve waited, jammed into the courtyard with everyone else.

A few young townsmen came in the alley below with a ladder, which they set against the wall.

A few people had climbed down before someone at the back yelled that the guards were no longer in the temple.

Tylve followed the stream of people back into the meeting room.

But that stream soon stopped as those at the front halted inside the door.

Everything in the room, that holy, simple and beautiful room, had been smashed. Benches lay on their sides. Some were broken.

An oil lamp lay smashed on the floor, with the glass cover shattered over a wide area. The oil had run out over the tiled floor and was burning. Someone ran to stamp it out.

Then a woman said, "Where is Pandor?"

CHAPTER 7

*R*avi ran through the streets like a young boy who had been told he can play.

It was not until recently that he'd become aware that his parents were stricter than the parents of other young men. That not everyone his age had so little freedom and had to ask for permission for everything they did.

But he could partially understand it. Because his parents didn't have any other children, they were naturally more cautious. Because his father was a senator with direct access to the proctor, they didn't want him in situations where people could take advantage of him.

At any rate, they probably couldn't imagine that people wanted to go out at this time of the day, because all the houses where he walked past glowed with warm light and families could be seen moving within. You came home after work. You had dinner with your family, when you discussed grave and important things. Then you went to bed early.

Going to parties and bars was... for other people. Lesser people. Common people. Who didn't know how to do *wise things* with their money.

That's why he'd mentioned the ulli hall, because playing a game, to their way of thinking, was far more acceptable than going to a bar.

Especially *at your age*, which was also a thing his parents said a lot, even if he was twenty.

Gradually, the houses became smaller, and the streets became busier. The last shoppers were carrying purchases home from the market. There were those servants who waited until the last moment to get the best deals.

Then he reached the city centre, where the eating houses were getting their dining rooms ready for customers and some had already arrived, mostly people with families seated in corners where the children's chatter would not disturb anyone.

He felt a thrill of excitement. He never came here at this time. Maybe the last time had been when his parents took him to a play or something equally proper.

Oh look, there was the ulli hall. There were not that many people inside yet, although he was sure that would change, if the stories were to be believed. A waiter was cleaning the tables, and another was getting all the play sets ready.

But he walked past without going into the open door. Then he crossed the market square, where the stallholders were still packing up for the day.

On the other side of the market was a narrow street that ran down the hill into what was considered one of the lesser suburbs of Tiverius. The houses here stood close together and were so old that the stone was dark with grime. They were the original houses of the city centre, built without planning, before the doga had instated rules about neat, broad and straight streets that would continue to serve future generations, because they left plenty of rooms for carts and trucks.

It was in one of these old buildings that he was going to meet up with his new friends. The front of the complex was a dreary-looking warehouse, but a small alley ran along the side and provided access to a courtyard from which the sound of talk and laughter and music drifted.

Ravi had quickly ducked in here the other day when he was on the way to the library, just to make sure that he had the right place. He didn't want to look like an idiot for having to ask for it later.

The courtyard was full of people, and the back doors of the warehouse were open to make one big half-covered drinking room.

Ravi took a deep breath and went in. He tried to hold himself like he knew exactly where he was going. Like he came here all the time.

The place was busy, with many people sitting at the tables or standing at the bar. It was quite dark and hard to recognise people.

A dancer moved between the patrons, wriggling her hips to the beat of a drum played by a young man tagging along with her.

He found his group of new friends in the corner. He'd been afraid that he wouldn't recognise them without the pads and shields they wore at self-defence training, but there they were, seated around the table, already with drinks.

They had all come. Fali and Neba were self defence tutors he had befriended, and Keran was a fellow student.

"Hey, there you are," Keran said. "We thought you weren't going to come."

"I said I would, but I said I'd come later because I was busy."

"Oh, keep your hat on. I was only joking."

It didn't feel like joking to him.

Ravi shuffled around the table and sat next to Neba. He realised that he should perhaps have bought something to drink first, because there were already some empty glasses on the table, but then, maybe he shouldn't, because he wasn't used to drinking and he had better be careful or his parents would discover where he had been. Neba wasn't drinking either.

"Have you been here long?" he asked, because he felt awkward and didn't know what else to say that didn't involve talking about him being late and not meeting them at the square after work. He couldn't tell them that he didn't work, and he didn't have the freedom to do as he wanted.

"No, not very long," Fali said.

He was leaning back in his seat with his legs crossed and held a glass half full of a cloudy yellowish liquid. It didn't look like beer either. He was looking not at Ravi, but at a distant point across the room. Ravi couldn't make out what had caught his attention. The dancer was working the tables there, still followed by her drummer.

"I guess you heard the news," Neba said.

"Eh… news?"

"Ah. You haven't heard the news. What do they talk about in that… library where you work?"

"We just—eh—talk about books. Where to return them, and where people can find them."

Of course, he didn't actually *work* in the library. But in the self-defence training course, offered for free to all Tiverians over eighteen, there was a space in their discussions during breaks called "what do you do for a living?" and a clear answer was supposed to go into that space, and Ravi had used "librarian" to fill that void.

Because "study" and "listening to my father" would mark him as a rich boy and Ravi had quickly figured out that the general people didn't like rich boys, and especially those who had anything to do with the doga.

He was disturbed by how much the general people hated the doga.

Neba said, "Well, Fali is leaving because his unit got called up. He's going on the train tomorrow to patrol the Aramys River bridge at Watya. So tonight is kind of a farewell to him."

"Just like that?" Ravi asked. "He can't teach us anymore?"

"They'll get someone else. That's the army for you." Fali emptied his drink and clunked the glass on the table. He glanced sideways at Ravi. "Have you ever been to Watya?"

"No. I've never travelled north very much." He'd not travelled *at all*. His father used to travel a bit, apparently, but he had asked to be stationed permanently in Tiverius because *dealing with the hostility a senator in the regions faces is best left to someone younger*. His father's words.

"You could come to Watya if you sign up."

Ravi shrugged. Fali had told him yesterday that he was doing so well in his class that he should consider signing up. Signing up also meant he'd have an income, although apparently a soldier's pay was not that great, but Fali had also said he'd probably earn a promotion soon and the pay for officers was much better.

Ravi shrugged. He didn't want to talk about this again. He didn't know what to feel about the army, especially in light of the bad behaviour stories coming out, about soldiers ruffling up villagers and raping women. His father would never allow him to go, for one.

But part of him also wanted to see what the mighty Aramys River at Watya looked like, just to say that he'd seen it. He'd heard that the bridge was very long.

He deflected the subject. "What are you going to do up there?"

Fali shrugged. "Whatever the officers in charge tell me to do. It's likely to be fairly boring. We'll get lots of time for exploring."

"You're being stationed there to stop the northern rebels forming a militia?" He remembered what his father and the proctor had been talking about.

Fali met his eyes with an uncomfortably intense look. "They're not just rebels. People in the north *hate* the proctor and the doga. They're spoiling for a fight. Bastards need to be stopped once and for all. If the north wanted to be a proper civilised area, they should know Tiverius doesn't listen to thuggery."

"Yes. They have finally gone too far," Neba said, her face looking very serious. "I hope my unit also gets placed there. I'm just itching to teach those idiots a lesson."

"What have they done now?" Keran asked.

Neba said, "The northern council has set up what are clearly military training camps on the southern bank of the Aramys River in Watya."

"But they don't have their own army?" Ravi asked. Although his father had also mentioned something like this to the proctor.

"Northern districts have always had local troops. The argument was that they had trouble with Arania up there, and that was true, but Arania has ceased to be a problem years ago. The doga used to allow the northern militias to exist as long as they weren't openly active and they only dealt with Aranian border crossings, but they've become as brash as an Aranian prince looking for something to fuck. They've closed the river crossing for days on end for ridiculous reasons, like unpaid grants promised to the north. I guess they don't care anymore if we get upset."

"What are they training their troops for?" Ravi asked. The discussion between the proctor and his father was still in his mind. The proctor had used the word *rebellion*.

"To defend their new borders," Fali said, his voice dark. "They cordon off villages, letting no one in or out, effectively stopping Tiverius' rule in those areas. They expand their own rule."

Ravi considered, but only very briefly, mentioning that there had been reports of misbehaviour by Chevakian army troops and this might be what the villagers were protecting themselves against, but didn't.

They would ask where he got that information, and the reply *eavesdropping on the proctor* would get him into all kinds of trouble besides marking him as a hated rich boy. And on top of that, he might have mis-heard and misunderstood.

Keran snorted. "Nobody can trust the northern provinces."

He picked up his glass, realised it was empty, and put it back down.

Ravi really thought he should have gotten a drink, because he felt clumsy without one.

"In this time, no one can trust a politician," Fali said. "Certainly not the current lot. They just stoke the conflict by encouraging, no even challenging, the north to act. Did you hear what the proctor said the other day? *If they want railways, they can come and get them.* The stupidest thing I've ever heard. What if the north acts on it and Chevakians start fighting each other? Who gets to pick up the pieces? Not them, for sure. Not the proctor or senator Gerinius han Chevonian, who's only there because of his name. In fact, the lot of them are just there because of who their fathers were. They're all just feathering their own nests. No wonder everyone is fighting each other. That's what we're going up there to stop, but you wonder what the point is. The whole system is rotten."

Ravi's ears burned. Just as well he had never told anyone in the class who his father was.

"I have to start getting my guys ready," Neba said. "I want to be prepared when the call comes for our unit to join you guys."

"Do you think they'll send more people up there?" Keran asked.

"Yeah, I think so. You should sign up."

"Huh. My father needs me to help run the shop."

As far as Ravi knew, Keran's father sold metalware from a warehouse on the outskirts of the city.

"Then why did you want to learn self-defence?" Fali asked.

"Huh. To defend myself? We get louts coming in wanting stuff for free. Last time, my father had to chase them off with a length of pipe."

"What about you?" Fali asked, turning to Ravi.

"I've got my studies. I won't be finished until next year at the earliest."

"Why did you join the class?"

"Something new to do. It seems useful."

"You're good at fighting. You should sign up."

Yeah, he kept saying that.

Neba said, "I guess it's good that someone in the doga has finally picked up the courage to send someone up there to rein in this northern council."

"They're meeting soon, I hear," Fali said.

"Yeah, the whole rabble-rousing lot of them," Neba said, her voice dark.

"What will you do? Like, will you patrol the streets of Watya during that meeting?" Keran asked, looking at Fali.

"I doubt it," Fali said. "The northern districts are spoiling for a fight. If the army is smart, and I think they are, they're not going to pour oil on the fire. They know that if they walk the streets of Watya, they'll be lightning rods for characters who want to stir things up. They'll watch from a safe distance. We'll only go in when things get out of hand."

"Then they must be expecting trouble if they're increasing troop numbers up there?" Ravi said.

"We'll just be there to keep things quiet," Fali said. "The official word the command wants to be known is that the Aranians are stirring up something."

Neba rolled her eyes. "Yes, no one in Tiverius going to have the guts to say what's actually happening, that the doga has lost control of the regions. We have to be a complete country, they will say. We have to be lenient, they say, or Arania will take advantage of the situation. I am sick of this weak talk."

"But the rebels haven't actually done anything yet?" Ravi said.

"Ha, I can see you haven't been up there. There's been raiding and unlawful acquisition of property, like farm sheds and machinery. There's been recruiting of young people, boys and girls. They go to these camps for a year and goodness knows what training they get there. Many of the best soldiers in the past have come from the northern districts. They're going to be training those northern rebels in decent warfare. There's been thievery and obfuscation of the administration processes. If you would only read the reports, you'd see it."

"Peacetime governments don't send their own soldiers to control their own people," Ravi said.

That was one of the tenets of a free government he had heard many times from the tutors his father paid to teach him, learned academics and military men.

The doga could use the guards, but not the army.

"That's their issue. I do what the doga tells me to do," Fali said. "That's my job. Questioning things isn't. That's for the wise men to decide."

Fali got up to buy a round of drinks for everyone. He came back with a tray that contained the same cloudy drink for himself, beer for Keran and Ravi, and something that looked like juice for Neba.

The dancer followed him to the table in the company of the drummer. She started up a dance routine.

The girl was about Ravi's age. She was wearing a very short skirt made of scraps of fabric and a singlet that only reached to midway down her stomach. Both those items of clothing showed parts of the female body that were normally well-hidden. She wore a belt with dangling strings of coins that tinkled when she shook her hips. Bands around her wrists held many bells.

Her singlet was so short that it showed a good amount of bronzed, well-oiled skin. She leaned forward over the table, shaking her chest so that Ravi could see through the top of her singlet out the bottom.

He could see the silhouettes of the soft rounded shapes of her breasts, with the little nipple on top.

"Hey, pretty boy." Her voice was soft. She met Ravi's eyes through thick, purple-painted lashes.

Blood rose to his cheeks.

Neba snorted. She was a typical female soldier, tough, with her hair in a tight ponytail and clothing that covered all the indecent parts of her body.

She glared at the girl, who studiously avoided looking at her, but turned her attention to Fali. He whistled while looking into her singlet.

"Hey, soldier," she said.

He flicked his eyebrows.

She turned her back to him. The drummer whipped up the rhythm. The girl raised her arms and shook her hips so much that her very short skirt lifted up to show glimpses of her naked buttocks.

Fali whooped.

The girl then turned her attention to Keran, who got up and danced with her for a bit. He'd been drinking for most of the evening and kept wanting to put his hands on the girl's hips. She danced out of his way, but he backed her into a corner.

She stopped dancing. "No, no, no, no touching. If you want a private session, that's extra. Go and see the bartender for your booking. I'm rather busy."

Neba rolled her eyes and mumbled in a low voice, "Disgusting."

"If you don't like it here, we can go and sit outside," Fali said.

"I said you're disgusting. All of you. While you're ogling some chick's tits, never forget that the moment she's got you by the dick, she will steal your money or stick a knife in your back. You're so damn predictable and so damn stupid."

Fali snorted in a kind of awkward way.

Keran came back to the table. He bumped so hard into the table when he sat down that the empty glasses almost fell over.

Right. So he had emptied most of them.

Neba looked him over. "You better watch out. If you don't want to be pulled up at training tomorrow, don't make a scene."

"I'm not making a scene. I'm just having fun." But his speech was slurred.

"Yeah, right."

Ravi sipped from his beer. The training was the only thing that allowed him to leave the house for anything that wasn't study. The Scriptorium and the library. Those were the only places he was allowed to go.

The recruiters had come into the library and impressed upon the students that skills to defend oneself were important. He'd had to beg his father to be allowed to go to training.

He didn't want to risk being thrown out of the class. It was the only reason he knew anyone who was not an academic, people like Fali, Neba and Keran. People whom his mother would never even allow him to look at.

That dancing girl and her suggestions that made him feel hot was definitely not someone his parents would appreciate him to meet. But all of a sudden he wanted to pull out money he didn't have so that he could do… whatever it was that men of arms did to these girls and wherever they did it. Be a real man.

And for the rest of the evening, he thought about how he was going to approach her, each time to be reminded that his father controlled his money.

Keran got increasingly drunk, and Fali and Neba talked about military things, since they were both trainers.

Then Neba got up and told them that they should leave because soldiers didn't misbehave and didn't drink so much that they couldn't get up the next morning. She was looking pointedly at Keran.

Ravi was not a soldier, and Keran was not a soldier, but Fali said that she was right, because he'd leave on the train early the next morning.

So they left the bar and walked through the quiet streets.

Ravi left the group at the market square. He had told them his family lived in the merchant quarter, while the others all lived in southside.

"Will I see you later this week?" he asked Neba. Keran had kept a little behind, because he had trouble walking in a straight line. He now leaned against the wall that surrounded a house's yard.

"Sure. Unless I get sent out, too. Then you'll get a different tutor."

"You're really sure you don't want to sign up?" Fali asked again.

"I don't think my parents would let me," Ravi said.

"Your parents?"

"I'm an only child. I need to help at home."

"Ah."

An uncomfortable silence hung between them. Clearly not the reply Fali had expected. Why was he so keen for people to sign up? He might have a talent for fighting, but it would take a lot of training to become a soldier.

Ravi wasn't sure he wanted to be a soldier either.

"Well then, all the best until you come back," Ravi said to Fali.

Fali clasped Ravi's hand in a strong grip. "Practice those swings, and soon enough, you'll be recruited to join me."

"Bye, Keran," Ravi called out.

But Keran leaned over the wall, and looked like he was about to vomit.

Neba snorted. "Idiot."

Ravi walked across the square alone in the direction of his home.

Alone. Deflated.

If this was going out with friends, he felt kind of… stupid. Clearly, they had all been doing this for a long time, so that they didn't need to feel embarrassed when a dancing girl flashed her tits in their faces. Fali had given the girl a tip so that she would come over and he was experienced enough to not feel flustered and want nothing more than give her all his money so that she could teach him all the things. Fali probably already knew all those things.

Ravi was just… stupid. Not allowed to do anything. Clueless.

He hated his life.

CHAPTER 8

The weather in Kadrish was lovely at this time of the year. The days would be bright and still warm, the sun not too hot nor too cold, and the storms that marred the afternoons in late autumn had not yet started. The nights were a little bit cold, but that's why people used fires, and families would sit in the kitchen at night talking to each other, after having done the jobs that the hot weather in summer made them put off until later in the year.

But Kotori didn't find as much joy in autumn as he used to. He found the cold nights increasingly hard to take. His ears were not as good as they used to be, so he didn't find much pleasure in joining the others in the Citadel's kitchen to listen to the jokes and the banter. He found that too often, he thought the banter was about him, and he couldn't hear well enough to establish if this was so, and so instead, he grew anxious while he was around other people.

And he had increasing trouble with the students who had returned excited from their summer breaks. It seemed like every year those kids grew younger. They made increasingly immature comments behind his back, and because of the aforementioned problems with his hearing, he couldn't hear what they said.

When he walked through the library, like today, he could hear their voices mention his name over and over, *Kotori, Kotori, Kotori,* but when he stopped to listen, he could never catch them in the act of gossiping, and that led to his other major fear: that no one talked about him. That he was irrelevant, a relic from the past. Someone kept in his position only because people felt sorry for him.

He'd gone up to the tower to get the books he had left behind on his desk, another sign of his increasing forgetfulness, and when he walked back into the library, a man approached him in the entrance portal to the astrology tower.

"Astrologer, Pertak wanted me to tell you that he has returned."

Kotori stopped and faced the man in the semidarkness of the room. He was a regular guard employed at the Citadel.

"I'm teaching," Kotori said.

"Pertak insisted on seeing you. Colonel Betaro is here as well."

A cold feeling crept up Kotori's back. Those were the two men the King had suggested he convince to help protect the queen and the princess, and Kotori hadn't as yet decided what to do about the king's suggestion. Or rather, he hadn't decided how to do what the king wanted without compromising the ancient written rules about predictions and castings.

He asked, "Did they say what it's about?"

"Only that they don't have much time."

Right, he got the message. "Thank you. I'll see them. Where are they?"

"In the back of the library."

Kotori went into the grassy, tree-lined courtyard that lay between the astrology tower and the library. A group of students were sitting on benches in the shade. While Kotori didn't approve of lounging around by students, he did admit, even if only to himself, that the queen's drive to pretty up the bare look of the Citadel had pleasant results. He'd railed at the extravagance of having water tanks installed just for growing plants, and not even ones you could eat, but the result was not displeasing. As an added benefit, the courtyards were not as hot in summer.

But before Kotori reached the library's entrance, the sound of talk and laughter drifted into the courtyard.

Drat, the musical performance had just finished. He'd been invited to the music students' final event, but fortunately it had been during his tutoring time, so he had a good excuse not to go.

Not that he disliked music, not at all, but the queen would be there and any distance he could put between himself and the queen was a good distance.

But now a group of people—all the music students by the look of things—were streaming into the courtyard, laughing and talking, still in their performance finery.

And the crown princess was in that group and she was another woman he didn't want to get too close to.

Unfortunately, they had already seen him.

"Oh, look, it's the astrologer," a girl said.

The group opened out and all the students—most of them girls—surrounded Kotori.

"We just finished our performance," one of them said. "Did you watch?"

"I got an invitation, thank you, but I was teaching." He held up the book he'd gone to retrieve.

"Oh, I'm sorry you missed it."

"Well, someone has to work."

"Sorry. We won't disturb you."

Kotori wriggled his way from between them.

Then another one asked, "Astrologer, is the stargazing session still on?"

"Yes, it definitely is." Kotori turned around. "And I expect all of you to be there. Attendance has not been satisfactory." He pointed his finger around the group. "And it might just influence your end-of-year results."

His eyes met and held those of the crown princess Loriane. She was also in his astrology class, and she hadn't attended a single stargazing session.

She said nothing, but lifted her chin and regarded him for a moment through half-closed eyes. Her tall and willowy form invited assessments of aloofness. While there was a certain toughness about the way she walked, he had never seen her do any work, nor study. Infuriatingly, she still passed all her exams.

He couldn't look at that face for long without being reminded of the girl's mother and how the queen loved to humiliate him with statements about how wrong his astrology predictions had been over the years.

Then one of the princess' friends said they should go to the study hall, where they could buy something to eat while they studied.

Kotori watched them go. The "study hall" was the two-storey building that used to hold the mothers' house. Back then, it used to be the domain of the seductive, scantily-clad and beautiful women whom he, as astrologer, would pick out for the king to birth him lots of sons. They would dance and perform plays, and invite the men in. As astrologer, he would go in to make castings before a woman gave birth. Those women adored him.

Until he picked the woman who had changed everything. He could not get over that fatal mistake he had made. The king wanted a southern woman, and one had turned up, having been taken prisoner across the border. The king had been delighted, but the woman was devious and much smarter than all the men in the Citadel combined.

Kotori lived with the consequences of his choice every day.

Damn that woman. Lana, half-Chevakian, half-Perian. A foreigner who was in charge of the country.

Inside the library, the students were all working very hard, or pretending to work very hard, as he scurried through the reading room. They looked at him with bemused glances, and said things to each other that his ears couldn't make out.

Kotori hated being old. He hated being referred to as irrelevant, even though he knew that he was just that. He hated how the king reminded him that he should respect the girls in the course, but any questions they asked reminded him of just how stupid girls were.

He did not know what to say to them, because anything he said was always taken the wrong way. Once the queen even came to berate him about things he had said.

He walked across the stately reading room in the library, that venerable hall with its wood panelling, velvet-covered seats and study tables that were older than anyone still alive in the Citadel, including him.

The group of first-year students who sat there were mostly girls in the first year and he wondered what had happened to the boys to make them want to give up study as so many of them seemed to have.

Where were these boys? And why were there so many girls everywhere?

Back in the glorious days, the students respected him and bowed to him and didn't ask silly questions.

In the very corner of the library, in amongst the shelves, he found a small table where a couple of men gathered who were very different from all the students in the main part of the room.

One of them was a man who had just retired from the military, and he still looked very much the part, even without his uniform. Everyone still referred to him by his military title, Colonel Betaro.

The other looked travel worn, with deeply bronzed skin and dusty clothing. He had also stepped out of the military but much longer ago, and worked as a private informant. A spy. One of the best.

His name was Pertak and his experience was second to none, even if in the heydays of power, he also used to keep shady allegiances and would work for two rival princes at the same time. Since most of the princes had either moved away from the capital or had been killed, he'd been out of work. He was now trying to weasel himself back into the good graces of the king by spying on the regions.

The two men sat close to each other, speaking in low voices. They only looked up when Kotori joined them.

Both nodded. Kotori had been friends with both of them for most of his life. They had grown up in the same children's house. Betaro was a straight brother of his, and Pertak had a different mother.

"Had a good trip?" Kotori asked Pertak.

When they last met, a few weeks ago, Pertak was about to leave on a trip. The nature of Pertak's work meant he rarely told anyone where he was going beforehand.

"It was effective enough."

"Where did you go?"

"The border region, where else?"

As if the whole world was as obsessed with activities by Chevakia as the military people and spies were. And the border with Chevakia was very long and spanned most of the continent, from the mountainous region where Chevakia and Arania joined Peria and the precise location of the border was not settled, to the far north where the border petered out in the desert and no one cared much about where it lay.

"You mean Wellak and places like that?"

That was a town high in the central mountain range that formed the border between Arania and Chevakia. The train line started here.

"Yes. And other places."

"How are things up there?"

"Getting worse," Pertak's voice sounded ominous.

"How?" What was getting worse? The Chevakians had been quiet. The joke went that they were far too preoccupied by their internal struggles. And everyone knew that Pertak loved to make situations sound far worse than they were.

"I was just telling him." Pertak jerked his head at the Colonel. "Do you remember how much hostility we met when we last travelled together?"

"Yes, I do." Kotori nodded. It had been his last trip out of the city a few years ago. That was when he realised that he was getting too old for this kind of thing, facing the anger of the citizens when they realised he came from the Citadel and in their eyes this meant they could vent all their frustrations to him.

At first he'd been puzzled about why people did this, since the regions seemed prosperous and content.

His companions joked that this was the perennial fate of people from the Citadel travelling in the country.

Then a local had explained that the changes at the Citadel meant that farmers could now no longer send their daughters to the mothers' houses of the princes or the king, and could no longer count on that as a source of income. Sure enough, according to the king, the girls now had the freedom to study, but what was the point if those families had no money to do so, as people in the country frequently did, since they grew their own food and didn't need as much money.

"Well, the situation has only gotten worse," Pertak said. "The king and the princes liked the new rules because they no longer have to spend money to maintain a mothers' house. But each and every mother in those houses used to support her entire community. They'd send money and goods. The lack of funds sent back to the country over the past twenty years has started to bite. There is a lot of maintenance on the town's communal buildings and at people's houses that they haven't been able to complete, because many of the citizens have been unable to pay their usual council dues, and as a result the authorities have little money. They're angry with the capital for not giving them replacement funding. They say the king has only banned mothers' houses so that he and the princes could become increasingly rich. They demand action from the council and from the capital. And the anger is getting worse."

"What sort of things were they doing?"

"As soon as they knew we came from the city, they displayed extreme hostility towards us. The inn owner must have told the townsfolk that we were there, because the villagers were waiting for us outside and we faced a lot of angry questions. Everywhere we travelled, there were people outside in the street wanting to talk to us, they were mothers demanding that their daughters be admitted to the city academies for study if they could no longer go to the mothers' houses, but as we all know they have little hope of getting admitted, because most of these girls have never learnt to read or write, and there is no program inside the Citadel to bring girls from the country up to that level. Even the boys from the regions who want to study are often required to work in the fields, so they see their city-based cousins get ahead of them, and they're all very angry at the gap in wealth that this creates. Their city cousins are wealthy and they wear nice clothes, while the kids in the country work hard and the meagre money they earn pays for less and less of the things they want."

"Are these people getting organised in any way?" the colonel asked.

"I didn't see much evidence of that, but I can imagine they would be. It wouldn't surprise me at all, and if they haven't organised, it won't be long before they do. People might call these peasants stupid, but that couldn't be further from the truth. You only need to put a single spark into a powder keg like this, one charismatic young leader, and the entire situation can blow up in everyone's faces and then you have a Civil War and all of our armed forces are completely unprepared to fight it."

"This is the danger I fear," the colonel said. "The land is without leadership, military or otherwise. The princes of the past, like Denori or Nayek, might have been harsh, but the constant conflict between them they kept the army well trained, even if only for the single reason that as soon as a man started to become irrelevant, he was in danger of having his head chopped off, so people were very keen to keep on their toes, and if they knew they weren't going to make the requirements, they disappeared of their own accord."

Pertak said in a dark voice, "They disappeared across the border, yes, and they gave the Chevakians the benefit of all the years of investment we put into them."

This had been going on for many years, and was at least one of the good outcomes of the current situation. Arania was no longer bleeding its young and well educated people to other countries. But they had become soft.

The colonel snorted. "We must start to rebuild the army in a way that can ward off significant threats."

Kotori could not help but agree with that. "Just as well Chevakia is in a state of disarray and their doga is unable to string together a decent response to anything."

Pertak added, "But we have our own issues. The king seems uninterested in potential turmoil. I've been to report to him just now, but he just sat there humming music and didn't appear to listen to me at all."

"He's just attended his daughter's music concert," Kotori said. "He gets a little self-absorbed when you talk about his wife and daughter. Don't discount his intelligence on any other subject, though. He's as sharp as he was when he first came to the throne."

Pertak snorted. "Then why does he have so little interest in seeing what is happening around the country?"

"He is far too much influenced by the queen. He's besotted with this woman."

And there Kotori stopped, because he realised an opportunity opened up where he could talk about how the queen needed to be protected, as the king had asked him to do.

The colonel looked at both of them. "I agree. What do you see as the solution?"

Pertak said, "We need to get back to getting our young men in a state where they're angry enough to want to defend the country. We need to collect groups of courageous young men who are ready to lay down their lives for the good of the country. We need to revisit some of the institutions of our past, or we will become irrelevant and when and if Chevakia can be organised enough to want our territory, they will be able to just march across the borders and take our land. We need to stop that."

The colonel protested. "But the king won't support an expansion of the army, and I can't see the princess or the queen support it either. They were very much burned with the violence that was sometimes unnecessary, of the princes fighting for the throne and casting aside those less violent, and terrorising the women. I have tried for ten years, but cannot convince either of them that to have a strong army is a necessity."

"They are women and that is the problem," Pertak said, his voice dark. "The citadel is full of women and mealy-mouthed officials who agree with everything they say. You might have said that the princes were cruel rulers, and I might agree, but at least we had direction. This…" He spread his hands, sighed and shook his head.

"I agree. I wish the king would be more worried about this," Colonel Betaro said. "I have raised this with him several times already, but he doesn't seem to understand that this is serious. And that we're in trouble, and that we're weak."

Pertak added, "And that the waif who will inherit the throne won't have a real interest in it. She won't be as hungry as the old princes, who were forced to climb over the bodies of their brothers to sit on the throne, or even of the Chevakian proctors, who have to politically slay their opponents to get enough votes. She just gets... handed the prize and has had to do little for it, and she is unsuited, and not interested."

"The king wants her and her mother protected," Kotori said in a low voice.

"Of course he does," Pertak burst out. "He's besotted with both of them."

"So what would happen if he were to die, and they *weren't* protected?" Kotori was treading into very dangerous territory now.

"Not much good," Colonel Betaro said, looking at his hands.

"The fighting would begin again," Pertak said. "For the throne, I mean."

"Who would fight?"

"Everyone with half an eye on the throne would come out of the woodworks. Any of the princes still alive. Other contenders. Rich men from the regions, maybe even some of the people who fled the country, would come back."

"What about you?"

Colonel Betaro shrugged, clearly uneasy with the question. "I'd do what was required."

"Would you fight for yourself?"

"A soldier always fights for himself. Sometimes, he fights for the country, too, but not without fighting for himself as well."

"For the throne?"

"If necessary." Colonel Betaro did not meet Kotori's eyes.

Kotori said, "So, that would be a bad situation."

"That's understating it," Pertak said.

Kotori took in a deep breath and plunged ahead. "So, if we put up a strong man who supports the women and gave him enough power to keep him happy, then we could stop all the other contenders?"

"What are you saying? Someone to replace the princess?"

"No, to protect her and her mother and give them the feeling that they rule the land, but really, it's only an illusion. This happened in Peria for many years. They had a queen, but it was the council of Eagle Knights who ruled. The queen just did all the pretty things for the people. Shaking hands and accepting flowers."

"Having babies," Colonel Betaro added.

Kotori grinned. "You get the idea."

"Hmm," Pertak said. "Orik has left too much to the women, and as a result we are now in this mess. The men in the military don't want to listen to a woman."

Colonel Betaro said, "But where would we find a strong man who would be happy to be in that position without wanting the throne for himself? That is a big risk."

Kotori said, "I might have an idea. Give me a bit of time. I'll investigate. It might not be pretty, but it can solve a few problems."

Colonel Betaro met his eyes. "Anything better than this mess we have now."

CHAPTER 9

When Javes was confident that neither the stranger nor the camel was going to make sudden movements, he set the column in motion. They had a long distance to cover today and needed to get going.

The path from the coast up to the highest point of the platform was steep, so he walked and held his camel by the reins while leading the beast up. The female camel followed, and after a while she started nosing for bushes to pull out along the path, and Javes knew that she had settled.

Then he climbed on his own camel.

There was no opportunity to talk. The path was narrow and the beasts couldn't walk side by side. He had to keep his wits, in case one of the animals slipped or something fell off their packs.

They reached the top of the plateau when it was far closer to midday than Javes was comfortable with.

Here, the landscape was barren, with very little vegetation. If he came during the summer, he would put leather shoes on the camels to stop the soft pads at the bottom of their feet getting burnt.

But summer had turned its back, and at this time of year, the breeze became bearable, if also bone dry.

Once they were up here, Javes could finally pull the two camels next to one another and ask the man questions.

"I'm Javes," he said while pointing at his chest. "What is your name?"

He pointed at the stranger, who just looked at Javes' wrinkled and brown hand.

Javes again pointed to himself. "Javes."

Then he pointed at the stranger again.

Eventually, the man said something that sounded like Mindo.

"Mindo? Is that your name?"

He pointed at himself again, "Javes." Then he pointed at the stranger. "Mindo."

That seemed to satisfy the stranger. Whether it was indeed his name or not, it sounded like a name, so that would do.

"I am from Ysherra." Javes said, and he pointed across the desert. "Where are you from?"

But that was too much for this strange man to understand. He looked at the sky.

"Did you come from the sea or over the desert?" Javes pointed in the direction of the desert and in the direction of the ocean. The stranger pointed back at the ocean.

He'd come by sea. That was something, at least.

Javes wanted to know whether he had been alone, or whether there was a shipwreck elsewhere on the shore where they would find people who had perished.

But this was too hard to be expressed in sign language.

Now Javes wished he'd spent more time looking for signs of a wrecked boat.

But he *had* looked on the beach, and most of the coastline was inaccessible. The cliffs were sheer and too treacherous to climb. The rock crumbled easily. Sometimes you couldn't even get close enough to the edge to see the shoreline below.

The stranger kept being fixated by the desert plain ahead, as if he was afraid to fall off the camel's back, and barely looked sideways to meet Javes' eyes.

Had he come by boat?

Javes mimicked waves and formed his hands into the shape of a boat, but that was just met with blank looks from the stranger.

They rode in silence for another while.

Mindo kept looking at the sky. Javes tried to figure what he was looking at, but couldn't see anything unusual.

It was a typical day, cloudless, although it was very hazy, a sign of hot weather to come.

Javes tried asking, "What are you looking at?"

But that met with the usual blank look.

Then Javes thought it might also mean that he had come via a balloon. That sort of made sense, because the Chevakian army had balloons, and maybe one had been blown off course and landed in the ocean. But in that case, he would be able to understand the man.

Maybe he had even come by balloon from Peria. The ocean currents were mysterious, and big storms out at sea played havoc with navigation and could carry items for long distances. And Javes did not speak Perian. Mindo didn't look like the typical Perian, but then again, Peria was a long way from here. Could he even be Aranian, not a farmer, but from Kadrish or along the southern coast?

Quite often, Javes would come to the beach, and there would be debris washed up on the shore from places far away. Once he had even found a piece of a crate with writing in Aranian, although he suspected that it had a washed overboard from a ship on the Chevakian side of the continent.

The man was a mystery. He seemed civilised. His hands were scratched and one of his nails was bleeding, but they were not the callused hands of a worker. They were the hands of someone who was educated. Javes just couldn't understand why he spoke such an unfamiliar language and did not understand any Chevakian. Even the most ardent Aranians at least understood some of it. The man didn't look Perian either.

And his continued inability to communicate with the man made Javes turn to less comfortable possibilities.

What if he was a criminal escaped from jail? Of course, in that case, he was going to pretend not to understand anything Javes said.

But Javes liked to think that the man was honest. He'd given no indication that he was putting on an act. Also, if he was in hiding, he wouldn't have shown himself to Javes, right? He would have hidden in his tent and Javes would have walked straight past him without ever knowing he was there. Or he wouldn't have been calm and quiet while Javes took him back to the civilised world.

There had to be another explanation.

Years ago, when he was a student, he and a few other keen students had worked out the place of the world in the universe. This world was a ball that orbited a large world known in Arania as the Mother. According to those who had described it—and died soon afterwards—its huge striped circular body filled up most of the sky. The sonorics that came from it rendered the far end of the world, away from the continent that held the three countries, uninhabitable.

The Aranians used to send people out there on a ship when they wanted to condemn them to death. The sailors would wear a suit, but even they were not guaranteed protection against the harmful sonorics. Perians called it icefire. On the coast of Chevakia, they would call it lightstream.

But, meanwhile, people only lived on the continent and no one knew what was on the other side of the world where it faced the Mother. Whether there was only an ocean or an unknown land. Whether monsters lived on that land, or maybe people who could survive sonorics.

At one time, people had lived all over the land. Those people had built the ancient installations that still dotted the coastline that protected the continent from the deadly rays.

Javes and his silent companion made good progress during the rest of the day. When it was about to go dark and the sun cast long shadows over the orange landscape, they arrived at a low ridge.

Javes was glad to see it because he knew what was on the other side, and he was keen to rest and eat something.

When the camels crested the low ridge, Mindo shouted out. He pointed.

His face was more lively than Javes had seen it during the entire trek.

Yes, this was an ancient human settlement that spanned the width of the shallow and broad valley.

The centrepiece of the site were five metal bowls on pedestals in various stages of decay. The best preserved one tilted sideways so that any rainwater drained out before it caused corrosion. But even that bowl had missing panels. The most damaged one resembled a rusty stump on a sturdy pillar of stone. The metal lay as millions of rusty flakes on the surrounding ground.

The other ruins in the valley surrounded these five installations. Most of the buildings consisted only of crumbling walls. Most of the roofs had long gone, together with the doors and the glass in the windows.

These types of ruined settlements lay dotted throughout the desert. Javes knew of at least six sites. Each held a few old buildings and at least one, but usually two or three, pedestals that held a metal construction that looked like a giant bowl.

The windwalkers that lived in the desert used the more intact bowls to collect water, and insisted that this was their purpose, but Javes had seen too many that stood at angles and doubted it. Although the explanation definitely made sense and they were very useful for collecting water.

The windwalkers would carry damp soil into the bowl, which they had covered with a giant sheet of the transparent material that you could also find at these old sites. If you held a rod of hot metal to it, the material melted, and you could stick two sheets together. The windwalkers fashioned these into giant transparent tents, where the water rose from the damp soil and collected against the material and ran down the sides into the trays that hung there for that purpose.

This settlement was well past any chance of being useful to the inhabitants of the area, of which there were none, anyway.

Javes led the camels into the valley, noting the footsteps his camels had made a few days ago while going in the other direction on the way to the coast.

No one came here, and no one had been here in those days.

Mindo watched with wide eyes, his mouth open. His face held an expression that Javes found hard to place. Not fear, not wonder, but almost horror.

"I don't know what happened here and why these people disappeared," he said, not expecting a response.

He didn't get one. Mindo still stared from one half-collapsed installation to the other.

Javes added, "We're staying here tonight. I have to do some work at this site. We can look around in the morning."

To the edge of the valley, on a low hillside, lay a blocky building half-buried in the sand. It remained complete enough to still offer some shelter. For one, it had a stone roof.

Javes usually stayed here. He'd been here last only a few days ago on the way to the coast. The fire bricks still lay in the fire pit under the grate so that any rogue goats wouldn't eat them. Some goats had visited recently, judging by the hoof prints in the dust.

He took the packs and saddles off the camels and tied both of them up near the water trough that he had to uncover by dragging the lid off.

Then he lit the fire and told Mindo to fan the flames with a piece of cloth. Mindo did as Javes suggested.

Javes had set up one of his travel supply depots in a room at the back of the blocky structure.

The supplies contained extra water and extra food, packaged in boxes that kept any insects out, and also extra bedding and a tent.

He rummaged in the fast-falling darkness, hoping against hope that there would also be a connection box that he could hook into the telegraph line when they passed it, but knowing he preferred his travel time to be undisturbed by messages. And indeed, he didn't find anything of the sort.

He didn't feel comfortable travelling with this stranger without knowing his history.

When he had collected the extra material, he returned to the fire that was going well. Mindo had even filled a pot with water—from the animal drinking trough. Urgh.

Javes had to empty it again.

"This water is for the camels." He pointed. "Our water is in here."

Mindo said, "Ah." It seemed he understood.

Javes turned around to get the water bag—and noticed the writing in the sand.

It was… some small circles and lines and a circle so large that only part fitted in the sandy patch in front of the shelter.

"Did you just draw this?" Javes asked.

But it was a futile question. The lines intersected the recent goat hoof prints and there would be no one else who could have done this. Javes studied the diagrams in the dust.

What did this mean?

The curve of the large circle met one of the lines. Something was written in the space between those two lines. It looked like… a formula.

He remembered how, as a student, he learned how sailors on the ocean navigate. They used the position of the stars and the apparent distances between stars and the horizon.

He stared from Mindo to the scribbles in the sand. They were calculations of some description. Calculations of where he was?

That was… disturbing.

If he could do this, then he didn't come from a primitive place. And if he'd had any education on the mainland, he'd know at least a few words of Chevakian. Even if he was Aranian. And he didn't look Aranian.

Javes walked around until the drawing lined up with the brightest star in the evening sky.

It was almost completely dark now, with most of the light coming from the fire and Javes' light.

Across the valley, past other ruins and one bowl that lay in pieces around its pedestal, stood the most intact bowl. It pointed in the direction Javes was looking.

A chill crept over him.

Almost as if… these things had been built not to collect water and act as greenhouses for windwalker crops—which Javes had always doubted—but to look at the sky.

But how?

Mindo came to stand next to Javes. Wisps of steam rose from the pot that Javes had set on the fire. The air already acquired a cold bite.

"If you look over there, this little circle here is that star," Javes said, pointing at the respective items first on the drawing and then in the sky. "Then, by measuring how far the star is above the horizon at sunset, you can calculate where we are, providing you also know at what time the sun sets."

He was pretty sure that both Mindo had no idea what he said, and that these were precisely the things he had calculated. The man had to be a sailor. A captain or something, or a navigator who set the vessel's course.

Mindo pointed at the dots he had drawn and then at the corresponding stars in the sky. He pointed at the large curve had had drawn. He knew the earth was a ball. Even after all those years, that was also not widely accepted knowledge.

Mindo held up his hand and mimicked writing.

He wanted a note pad.

Javes usually travelled with a small book where he made notes about things he should do when he came home, but it so happened there were no blank pages left in the book. But he also collected paper out of the barygraphs along the way. The back of those recordings was empty.

He gave Mindo a sheet and a pencil.

Mindo took the paper on his knees. He drew a few things and then showed the paper to Javes. It displayed a balloon with two people in it.

"There were two of you?" Javes said, holding up two fingers.

"Two," Mindo replied.

"What happened?" Javes spread his hands.

Mindo balled his fists and mimicked fighting.

"Where is the other person?"

Mindo held up his hands. Did that mean he didn't understand or he didn't know?

Either way, Javes felt cold. What should he make of all this?

Things weren't well in the rest of Chevakia. The current proctor was weak and the senators of the doga deeply divided over many things. As regional administrator of the Ysherra district, Javes had always seen a weaker doga as a good thing, because it meant the north was stronger.

But he hadn't liked the stories coming out of Tiverius recently.

He took the piece of paper and drew arrows being shot from the ground.

Mindo shook his head and again mimicked fighting. The men had fought each other?

"But then, where did you come from?"

Javes pointed at the balloon with the two figures. He drew a land mass that was the Chevakian coast, with Peria to the south and Arania along the western coast. He presumed, since he looked and acted educated, Mindo would understand what it represented.

Mindo took the pencil and drew a circle away from the coast and pointed at it.

"There?"

Did this mean there were islands out there in the Mother's Veil and people lived on them? And that somehow, sonorics didn't kill those people?

It didn't kill people from Peria either. They were resistant to sonorics.

And now… those people out there had some kind of disagreement with each other that was bad enough for them to flee in a balloon… to a place where they hadn't visited for many hundreds or even thousands of years?

Also, there was another person out there who was angry with Mindo.

Someone who might be calling for help or who would come after Mindo with… who knew what kind of strange weapons.

This was deeply disturbing.

CHAPTER 10

*L*ana looked from the man who sat across the room to the papers spread out on her desk, a feeling of dread rising in her.

Foroli had come to her quarters and insisted that he wanted to see her immediately. He was still in his travel clothes and the scent of smoke from the train still hung around him.

He had brought a scrappy collection of documents, most of them hastily copied and poorly translated from Chevakian by the spy who had procured the information a few days ago.

Having grown up in Chevakia, Lana would have been better off without the translation, because the Chevakian verb forms clearly confused the poor spy.

The information, however, did not lie.

One copy appeared to have been taken from an official document of the Chevakian doga, authorising the establishment of an army camp near Watya, south of the bridge across the Aramys River. In the poor wording of the translator, a senator had told a military officer that *defensive action, if necessary* was authorised.

Lana held up the paper. "It says the doga authorises the Chevakian army to take defensive action—against what? Arania has no interest in that area. It's close to the border, but it's unforgiving country and only useful because of the river, and our soldiers can't carry that across the border, and there is no reason for Arania to cross the border to occupy the region, no running conflict, none of the usual claims of looting or robbery. What do they fear?"

Foroli met her eyes. "To be honest, we're not sure it is about Arania."

Lana frowned at him. As informant paid by and part of the military, he was usually full of talk about how good and dangerous the Aranian military was and that Chevakians would quake in their boots if only they knew. In the minds of these military people, information sourced from spies was *always* about Arania. Why the change?

"Then what do they fear? Can you make a guess?"

"It seems… some sort of internal thing." He hesitated and gave her a sideways look. Oh, he knew very well that she knew much more about Chevakia than he did. "They say it's between the capital and the north."

"An armed conflict? I don't believe the doga would use the army within the borders of the country. As long as I remember, there have always been tensions between Tiverius and the northern provinces. They're mostly about expenditure, or lack thereof, by the doga in the northern provinces. Those are sparsely-populated areas and past proctors often made the mistake of making promises that would never be sensible to honour. There are not enough people in the area to justify building the railway lines that senators promised in moments of madness. The northern districts know that, but sparring over this issue has become a national sport."

The man shrugged. "I'm repeating what the spies have told me. But I'm aware that your knowledge on the subject of Chevakia is greater than mine."

"Yes."

Because she had not simply grown up in Chevakia. Her father was Sadorius han Chevonian who had held the position of proctor longer than anyone in living memory. She had grown up hearing about what went on in the doga every day.

But that was more than twenty years ago, and back then, she'd been just a student.

She had lost contact with the senators of the doga since her father died. The new ones were of a different mould. No longer desperate for solutions to wars and other dangers that threatened to kill the population, they'd become political players tangled up in bureaucracy and protocol. The proctor Calidius han Pasaki was someone who only ever interacted with the Aranians via formal channels.

Lana didn't like him. She hadn't liked him when he was an arrogant fellow student in an older year at the Scriptorium with his gaggle of friends that all came from rich merchant backgrounds, mostly young men who derided Lana's passion for astronomy *because stars will never pay your bills.*

She liked him even less now. He was a brusque, uncompromising man who made it his mission to ridicule and dig dirt on his political opponents, and whose mission it seemed to be to do as little as possible. He had a reputation that he spoke before he thought, much less consulted with other members of his government about it. Careless and sloppy language led to arguments over his words, arguments over his commitment to Chevakia, and arguments between factions in the doga. Arguments that were more often about bribes, scandal and mistresses than about actual matters of government.

Even at the time her father died, the country had been sliding into chaos, but it was just as well that he didn't have to see what was happening to it now. He'd be turning in his grave.

She gathered the papers into a small stack. "Well, Foroli... Thank you for bringing this to me. Thank your informants on my behalf. I shall look at it all in detail. Continue gathering information as you were before. If I want you to make changes, I will let you know."

He bowed and made his way out of the room.

As soon as the door had shut behind him, Lana took the papers and went into the apartment's sitting room.

Orik sat in his chair, staring out the window.

Lana dragged the chair that the cleaning lady always put near the hearth over to join him.

"Something bothers you?" he said, without looking at her.

If ever she thought he was too old to care, he was always quick to remind her that his age had crippled his body, but there was nothing wrong with his mind.

She sighed. "Many things. I just got word from the informants in Chevakia. I don't understand what's going on there."

He snorted. "It's impossible to understand what's going on in Chevakia."

"They're mobilising forces in camps along the Aramys River."

"Huh. What's there?" Now he looked at her, a frown on his old and wrinkled face. "That's not even close to the border."

"No, but the troops have the authority from the doga to defend themselves in any way possible."

"Against what? We have no activity in that area."

"That was my first thought, too."

He met her eyes, frowning.

"Then what are they up to?"

"The spy suggested that the threat could come from internal issues."

"A strong statesman would never use his army against his own people."

"That's what I told him, too. There have been divisions between the north and south of the country for as long as I can remember. It's a national pass-time to make fun of the other camp. I've seen no evidence that this conflict has grown beyond the realm of sparring in the doga and making fun of each other."

Of course, the current Chevakian leadership could be described in many ways, but *strong* wasn't one of them.

"No." Orik shook his head.

"Unless..." He stared out the window. "Unless the doga has become so weak that the northern districts see an opportunity to grab what they can get away with and they put themselves in a position of power. The Aramys River provides water for the entire central farming district, where most of the food for Tiverius comes from."

Lana felt cold. "The northern provinces have become more prosperous through several good grain seasons. They've always wanted a dam in the river so they can irrigate their crops."

"See, there you go."

Lana delved deep into her memories of the country where she had grown up. Geography lessons at school. Meteorology classes at the Scriptorium. They had informed so much of her understanding of the world.

She said, "There was always a water reservoir at Lekata, of sorts, and waterholes all the way to Watya. They're natural holding ponds, but as the population has grown, the ponds are not big enough to provide a reliable source of water. The Aramys River is large, but it's also highly seasonal, and much of its headlands are in the desert where you get huge floods for a day or two per year and the rest of the time it barely rains, so the flow relies on water sinking into and seeping out of the rocks."

Her thoughts flooded with memories of a place she hadn't thought about for a long time.

It was in this country that she had been travelling when she had been captured, on the bus from Watya to Ysherra with her tutor. She was a student and had begged her father to be allowed to go on this trip, because the other students in her class got study placings in interesting places in the country, but her father was so worried about her that he gave her a placing in the library. And she got so angry about it that she forced him to let her travel to Ysherra.

She often wondered how different her life would have been had the bus not gotten bogged in the mud and had she not been captured and taken to Kadrish to live in the King's Mothers' House.

Even after she had regained her freedom many years ago, and had travelled to many places, she had never once made it to Ysherra. She heard that these days it was a larger town. Their main exports were olive oil and camels and camel products.

They had been on their way to see a fellow student. The Aranian soldiers had killed her tutor and the other people on the bus. She had only survived because the soldiers wanted women and she was the only woman on the bus.

Lana had also never seen her fellow student again. She understood Javes still lived in Ysherra and was a local administrator. She couldn't even remember what he looked like.

They used to correspond with each other about stargazing, and about history. And later, when the three countries had built the network of sonorics machines along the coastlines of the continent, and when they had calibrated them. That had been a wonderful time of collaboration. What had happened to that spirit?

She'd lost contact with Javes many years ago.

In fact, she'd lost contact with her country of birth and was no longer in touch with what was happening.

The Chevakia the spy had told her about was not the same country where she'd lived, where her father had led the doga.

She should swallow her pride and listen to the spy. He probably knew more about the place than she did.

She got up from the couch. "I'm going to ask Foroli for more information."

"You can never have enough information."

He sounded cheerful, but Lana didn't fail to notice how his hands trembled worse than usual. He was holding his tea cup with both hands.

Orik had warned of his impending death for years, but maybe life was finally catching up with him. Lana was running out of time to get the country and her children ready.

While on that subject, she could hear Loriane's voice in the hallway.

She went out.

Loriane had just come past the guards that stood at the entrance to the royal family's private quarters. She had a habit of greeting the guards loudly and flamboyantly. If anything, Loriane knew how to entertain people. She was loud and confident, all things Lana was not.

She was all smiles. "Good afternoon, Mother."

"Anything put you in such a good mood?"

"Anything make you grumpy? I'm looking forward to the end of my studies. I'm done with the music exams."

"Good. Now you can put more effort into other things."

Loriane stopped.

With her enormous mop of bushy hair and light eyes, she even looked like Lana's mother Loriane, who had fled, dirt poor and desperate, from the City of Glass in Peria.

"You clearly want me to study other things."

"Now you've finished with your music exams, yes, I think you should. In fact some of your tutors have complained to me that you haven't been to their classes."

"*Some* tutors?" Her eyes held this gaze that could look right through you. It was impossible to hide something from her. "I'm only aware of the astrologer's complaints. But he hasn't stopped complaining since I set foot in his class. He doesn't want me there and I don't want to be there. I think peering at star signs is dumb. The stars are all so far from each other, and the idea that the way we observe them means anything is ludicrous. Every word he utters is nonsense."

"I know, I know." Lana had frequently said most of her daughter's words in exactly the same order. "But stars signs are important to a large group of people in the kingdom you'll be leading. It pays to at least understand what motivates those people and how they make their decisions."

"Hmph. It's still a colossal waste of time."

"Loriane, make an effort. These men are dangerous. The astrologer is a powerful enemy to have when you're alone and a young woman on a throne many men think should be theirs."

"What about you? What about Harek?"

Lana couldn't hide her frustration. "I'm not always going to be around either, and Harek didn't even come to your performance."

"Mother, I don't understand why you keep insisting that Harek comes. If he doesn't want to be there, I don't want him there, honest. Give the seat to someone who is not going to hate it, and going to remind me that he does."

"You shouldn't be talking like that about your brother."

"Why not? He agrees with it. He doesn't like concerts and dressing up in finery. Let him be. That's my task, talking to all the civilised people."

"You're treating it like a game."

"It is a game. Everyone is taking part. You have to play the moves that you're good at. He's no good at discussions about culture and ideas. So I'm doing that. He can talk to the generals."

"Do you even understand how dangerous the situation is? Do you realise how very little stands between your right to the throne and your imprisonment in a Mothers' House where all you're allowed to do is spread your legs as often as your master decrees, and push out his children? Do you realise that Harek is already running with this crowd and that I suspect he's already got some poor girl in trouble?"

Loriane frowned. "Harek?" And then she gave a little snorting laugh.

"Yes. And it's *not* funny."

"It is. He would never do that."

"He did. He admitted it to me."

"No. I don't know where you heard that, but it's not true."

"It is."

"It isn't."

Lana glared at her daughter and Loriane glared back.

"All right," she said. "Give me a few days. I'll prove it to you."

Loriane snorted. "Good. That will be an excellent use of some poor spy's time. Meanwhile, I'm going to study."

She strode down the corridor to her room.

Lana went into her office and had to restrain herself not to slam the door.

Where in all the seven hells had she gone wrong to have landed with two such stubborn children?

CHAPTER 11

The market square in Kadrish was always a busy, bustling, noisy place, especially for those who didn't come there often.

Kotori didn't like it. He was familiar with just a few stalls that sold items he liked, which were not many. As court astrologer, he had no need for clothing because it came with the job. He didn't need to buy food because he lived in the Citadel where meals were provided, and he had no personal use for trinkets. His room was only small and the sense of useless opulence that came with owning one of those little clipped indoor trees grown in the greenhouses of Peria, or pottery from Chevakia, just gave him the shudders.

Dried prunes, he liked those, so he sometimes ventured into the streets to buy a packet, especially if his digestion gave him trouble. The prunes came wrapped in a triangular paper holder that allowed one to eat the prunes from the top.

He had bought a packet when he got to the market and, rather than take it home for measured use, he ate the prunes while walking through the marketplace.

Even if he knew he shouldn't.

But he was early for the meeting.

And he was nervous.

And the prunes were very good this year.

He glanced up at the forecourt of the weigh house where they had agreed to meet. No one was there yet. Half of him wondered if the boy was going to show up at all. He wouldn't be surprised if he didn't. With more than two generations between them, the boy might not be interested in meeting an old man, even if he was the court astrologer.

And another prune. He really shouldn't. Kotori dropped the pip of the previous one in a bin that stood next to a stall for depositing rubbish.

He turned a corner and walked back to the weigh house.

Ah, the boy had turned up.

He was alone, even if Kotori had said nothing about the presence of guards. He must have understood.

Kotori climbed the steps of the weigh house.

Harek noticed him and bowed. The boy gracefully combined features from both his mother and his father. His glossy dark and curly hair and his light eyes were definitely his mother's. His strong physique was like his father's, even if Orik these days was bent and thin.

"Well met, astrologer."

The set of his mouth was also his father's. Kotori was disturbed to see the beginnings of chin hair.

His voice had grown disturbingly deep recently and each time Kotori saw the boy, he'd grown another hand width. He might be only fifteen, but he held a commanding presence.

Kotori bowed as much as his back would allow him. "I'm glad that you could come, your highness."

Harek gave a small snort. It sounded like he would protest at being addressed by that term.

"Why did you want to meet me?" Harek said.

Straight into the matter.

"I prefer not to discuss that here. Too many ears might catch our conversation. There would be gossip. Let's get some tea in a private room."

"I don't like tea."

"Something else then." Something alcoholic? The boy was too young for that.

"I'd like to stay outside. If you must speak with me, you shouldn't need a secret place to do that, where I have no witnesses."

Kotori swallowed.

"But certainly you don't suggest that I would... I'm a very old man."

"I don't suggest anything at all. I'd like to be safe."

"Well..."

Seriously? Where had the young man learned this kind of behaviour? This level of distrust? As if he, the court astrologer of all people, would threaten a prince.

"From gossip," the prince added. "My sister's friends."

"Well..." Kotori repeated. "I don't know where else we can—"

"We can walk to the harbour," Harek said.

"I suppose we could." It wasn't far, but oh dear, now he wished he hadn't eaten so many prunes.

"If you can walk that far, astrologer. Otherwise, I can ask for a wheelchair."

"Absolutely not. I'm old but not decrepit."

Yet. Although he bet the boy was waiting for that moment. They all were. Like vultures around a dying cow. Him and Orik. The old vestiges of power.

They set off through the market square and into the street that led to the harbourfront. People in the market aisles gave them a wide berth as soon as they recognised them. Kotori looked over his shoulder a few times, but still couldn't see any guards.

It was not far, but Kotori was too out of breath to speak.

Yes, he definitely shouldn't have eaten so many prunes.

Harek's legs were very long and Kotori was keen to show him that he was still capable, even if he would have preferred to walk much slower. Kotori got hot and his insides gurgled uncomfortably.

He was sure he'd feel very sorry for himself tomorrow.

They reached the waterfront in silence.

Being the middle of the day, the harbour was quiet. The fishermen had gone out in the morning and they wouldn't start to return with their catch until the end of the afternoon, when the place would spring into life. A cargo ship lay alongside the main quay. A pile of boxes stood on the quay, but right now, nobody was there to load them.

A row of seagulls sat on the edge of the quay, their heads tucked in their wings. A pelican roosted on top of a pylon. It eyed Kotori and Harek as they walked past.

The birds were waiting for the fishermen to return to port.

Harek turned to the right. They crossed the bridge across the river mouth and onto the much quieter part of the quay.

"Now, what is it that you wanted to talk to me about?" Harek asked.

Kotori glanced over his shoulder. He would very much have preferred to talk in a private room. Who knew whether the prince had stationed spies along the route?

Kotori was no longer convinced that this was such a good idea, even if he had promised Colonel Betaro that he might have a solution. He'd considered the prince to be a blank slate that one could come and write one's own views onto, but even at fifteen, Harek appeared much more mature than Kotori had suspected.

But now he was here, and Harek had actually turned up, he couldn't walk back his decision. He had to push ahead with it.

"There has been talk," he began, and then said nothing for a while because he wasn't sure how to make his next point.

"Talk?" Harek said.

"Yes, about your father."

"What's with my father?" Those intense eyes made Kotori even more nervous than he already was.

He'd imagined feeding the boy sweet cakes and having a chat over cups of tea about his father's health, but Harek was not only not a boy, he was deeply suspicious, and reminded Kotori painfully of Prince Denori, who had more than once threatened to dislodge Kotori's head from his shoulders. And somehow having made it to eighty years of age without that happening made it all the more important that it didn't happen now either. Certainly not by someone who was only fifteen.

He should know what was good for him and should stay *away* from any princes.

"Your father is old," Kotori blurted out.

"So are you, dear astrologer. In fact, you are older than my father. Do you prefer that when we replace my father, we find a replacement for you as well?"

Kotori opened his mouth and shut it again. And then he opened it again.

"That's what you were going to ask me, right? Go up to my father and tell him that the wise men have decreed that he is too old to be the king and he should step down."

"Well… I… uhm…"

"You *were* going to tell me that."

Kotori let out a breath.

"You're not very good at this conspiracy thing, astrologer. Come on, I know my father is old, but if that is the only argument you've got…"

He was not only not a boy, he was a very arrogant young man.

Kotori found a seed of resistance. He was not here, at his age and in his position, to have this young lout make fun of him.

"Well, if you're going to be like that, I shall keep the information that a spy friend of mine has passed onto me to myself. Or I shall give it to your sister."

"Huh. My sister couldn't care less about anything you have to tell her."

He was undoubtedly right about that.

"Your mother, then."

"My mother hates you as much as my sister does."

Fair call.

He glared at Kotori and Kotori glared back. So they stood for a long time. The breeze ruffled Harek's ponytail. He had to squint against the sunlight.

Kotori sought for an angle to penetrate the boy's defenses.

Behind the prince's back was the wall of honour, for those condemned prisoners who would go out on boats from this very quay to meet the Mother.

They didn't do that anymore, because the new code of honour said it was cruel. The last ships had left many years ago. Instead, prisoners rotted in jail, and the country had to pay for their upkeep, besides the fact that no one saved their souls.

One of the many things that were wrong with the country.

"You can tell my father or you can tell me. What things is this spy talking about?" Harek asked after a long silence.

Ha.

"About the unrest in the country."

"What unrest?"

Double ha. "Have you not heard of it? Because the villagers can no longer send their daughters for the mothers' houses, the families don't have enough money to pay for the upkeep of works in the village."

"Then they should start a business or sell something. We did away with Mothers' Houses."

"The villagers *were* selling something, but now they can't and the extra women just become mouths to feed."

Harek gave Kotori a hard look. He didn't say anything, and it was impossible to gauge what went on in his mind. But now that Kotori had started along this path, he was forced to continue. And he wanted to continue, because those damned prunes he'd eaten were making an impending visit to the outhouse increasingly likely.

So he ploughed on. "When I was younger, a young prince like yourself would have a mothers' house and several successors already."

Harek stared at him for longer than was comfortable. Kotori looked out over the horizon, where the cloud bank that was the Mother's Veil reflected the sunlight.

Harek sneered. "And the villagers are upset that no one wants their pretty girls anymore?"

"Those girls are waiting for you."

"For me?" He chuckled.

Kotori's heart was hammering. He hadn't liked that chuckle. But there was no way of backing down.

"Sure, your highness, you know how to…"

"I don't know that's any of your business."

Kotori attempted a grin, but the thing was, Harek might know a lot more about this subject than he did, since his position of astrologer had required him to be celibate, and he had no interest in women's flesh, anyway.

"Mothers' houses are for princes like yourself. The girls choose to be there. They don't have to and never did have to go. But my brother has given girls access to the library and we see now where that has led us."

Harek looked at him in a *did we?* way.

"The people in the country are very unhappy that they can't send their girls, and might well increase their rebellious thoughts about it."

Harek squinted at Kotori again. "So, why are you telling me this and what do you want me to do with this information? Tell my father to open mothers' houses again? I'm sure he will be really happy with that suggestion—it gives him a reason to put you away or send you to meet the mother."

"I don't suggest that at all."

"Then what?"

"You can still have a mothers' house. You don't need to be as blatant about it. The girls will be guaranteed to be there voluntarily."

"Huh."

The prince didn't tell him to shut up, so Kotori plunged ahead. "There is an empty house just down from the main entrance to the Citadel. I know who owns it and I could entice the owner to sell it to you. If you want, I could arrange for you to meet some well-connected girls from around the country who would be more than happy to live there to serve you."

"And I'm supposed to pay their families?"

"That's how it works."

"Huh."

But he said nothing more, so Kotori took that as an encouraging sign.

Harek continued, "And then? I'd have all these women and children, and then what? Why do you want me to do that?"

"The army generals would be really happy to take the older kids off your hands. They would be really happy to open their mothers' houses again, too. They would be so happy, in fact, that they would not dispute your sister's claim on the throne when your father dies."

"Huh. If you're going to be like that, what makes you think *I* won't want to claim the throne?"

"Your mother and sister would never allow that."

"They would never allow the mothers' houses to reopen, either."

"No, that's why you can't be open about it. Only take girls from the country who put themselves forward."

"Huh." Then he again said nothing for a while.

Kotori was now trembling. Both from nerves, and the pressure on his bowels that the combination of nerves and too many prunes unleashed. "When will I organise this meeting?" he asked.

Harek snorted again, his eyes unfocused. "I'll think about it."

They walked back to the marketplace. Harek said he was going to attend a training session, but he slowed his pace because he said he realised Kotori couldn't walk as fast as he could, and he asked for an apology about that. But the reason Kotori didn't walk fast had to do with those prunes and much less with his age.

As soon as the prince left him in the marketplace, he scurried to the latrine. He only just made it in time.

CHAPTER 12

Ravi got home late in the night. At least it was late for him, because he had never been out for that long. The streets were already quiet, the shops had closed and shopkeepers had gone home.

He suspected that it wasn't actually that late for people who went to bars, because the sound of talk and laughter and music still drifted from the open doors of such establishments he passed.

Such as the ulli hall, where many people stood around the tables, cheering and deliberating team moves.

At home, his mother sat at the kitchen table.

The first thing she said was, "You're late."

"You didn't need to wait for me."

"I wanted to make sure you're safe."

"Of course I'm safe."

"Did you drink?"

"Why is that important?"

"Well…"

"I had one drink. I'm twenty. I never said what time I'd be back. I'm not drunk and didn't do anything stupid."

She gave him a disturbed look.

"You have lessons again tomorrow morning."

"It's not that late. I usually stay up way after this. I met up with some friends and we were talking. Am I allowed to do that?"

"Ravinius…"

"I mean it. These are just people I know. I'm allowed to know people, right?"

Meaning people his parents hadn't picked out as being appropriate for him to know. And after having heard Fali talk about the doga, he could understand why his father wanted that.

She sighed. "Your father wanted to speak with you. He's now gone to bed."

"He can talk to me in the morning."

He wasn't sure why she said this, because his father always went to bed early and got up very early too.

"Who are these friends?"

"Some people I met in the self-defence class."

"Not from the Scriptorium?"

"Some of them are."

"Oh." That seemed to comfort her a little, even if it was also a lie. Yes, there *were* people from the Scriptorium in the class, but not the ones he'd met up with.

"Are they… what do they study?"

"I don't know. They're not in my class and I didn't ask. We talked about the training."

"So they're all good people?"

"Of course they are."

"From good families?"

"Mother…"

Of course, that was what it was all about. Making sure he didn't mingle with *unworthy* people. Those who worked in the shops or in the markets, whose mothers who had to work to make ends meet and abandoned their children all day. And whatever else didn't meet with her approval.

"At least I hope you've had fun."

"Yes. I'm going to bed now."

He left the kitchen and went up to his room.

Ravi didn't know what he'd call the meet-up, but fun was probably not it. Disappointment, a deflation of his expectations. If that was how people went out—just getting together for a drink while ogling girls and making irrelevant conversation, then he wasn't sure that this was his thing.

He'd expected so much of it, and he'd felt so... useless. Almost as if Keran was there just to drink himself stupid, and Neba really didn't want to be there either.

And Fali only wanted him or Keran to sign up.

Ravi didn't want to sign up. But he needed a better excuse than he had given to Fali. He also needed something else in his life. A job. Normal people had jobs. They worked in shops or offices. They paid things for themselves. They didn't have to ask permission for everything they wanted to do. They didn't have to answer questions about their friends' families.

Who would give him a job?

He didn't know anything useful.

Except perhaps for working in a library. Maybe at the Scriptorium... or in the town hall... or the doga.

Yes, if he had a job, then he would earn some money and he wouldn't have to ask for it. Or squirrel it away from money his father gave him to buy other things.

But how could he get a job if he wasn't allowed to go anywhere?

He lay awake at night thinking about the different possibilities, the places where he could work. He'd have to ask his father, because there was no point doing this without his approval. But his father would just say that if he wanted money, all he needed to do was ask... and he would then question Ravi's need for those things he wanted to spend money on.

Ravi wanted his own money so that he could, if he wanted, pay the girl to show him all the things, and probably feel disappointed about it for the rest of his life, because that was the way his life usually worked out for him.

So, no, the need for money was not going to sway his father. He would argue that working gave him experience for the future.

He'd say that acquiring the experience was important for his learning.

He'd say that he should learn to find his own job.

It was important that he got his arguments right.

RAVI FINALLY MUSTERED the courage to go into his father's office the next day.

It was after the midday meal. His father had gone to a doga session in the morning, had spent most of his time in the dining room ranting about it, about the senators and their affairs and raunchy parties and the usual topics, and had retired to his office.

He had his nose buried in stacks of notes when Ravi entered the room.

"Yes, son." He didn't even look up. Ravi wondered if his mother had told him about last night. Probably not. Because his father would have asked her why she didn't stop her son from going out.

"I was wondering if I could ask you something." Ravi hated how timid his voice sounded.

His father looked up, a surprised look on his face. Judging by all the stuff on the table, he was quite busy.

Ravi sat down on the edge of the seat that stood on the other side of his father's desk. The seat where visitors sat.

"You know I've been studying for more than two years..."

"Yes?" To be honest, his father's voice sounded a bit annoyed.

A sheet of paper on his desk held lists of numbers, probably to do with some item they were voting on. Below the list, his father had written a name: Parvi. Senator Parvitus was a rival of his father's, a hardline, petty man who had made an example out of his two daughters by marrying both of them off to much older men.

His father despised the man.

Ravi was very close to making a hasty retreat out of the room. But he plunged ahead.

"Well, I was wondering... if I could... you know... do something that gives me more experience with all the things I've been studying?"

Now his father paid him full attention. He put his pen down.

Ravi felt like sinking through the floor.

"You mean—work? Who do you think would take you on with as little experience as you have?"

"It was only a thought."

All his carefully prepared words had vanished, like they always did when facing his father, because his father always had *thoughts* and *comments* that sounded like orders, and Ravi was always too timid to respond, because when his father said he had no experience and didn't know anything, he was right. He didn't have experience and didn't know anything.

But then he found a seed of resolve to hang onto. "I can't get experience if I can never work."

His father met his eyes squarely, but didn't say anything. He didn't say yes. He didn't say no either. He just left Ravi sitting there in this awful silence that felt like molasses, while he mulled over the comment like one lets a merchant wait for your decision if you're going to buy the expensive thing or not.

"Hmmm," he said finally. "What sort of thing would you like to do?"

Ravi's hope surged. "Anything. I can do all kinds of work. Whatever I can find."

"But you want it to be relevant to your studies, though."

Drat.

Yes, he did kind of want that, but in reality, he didn't care where he worked. He just wanted to be a normal young man, who could do what he wanted, and who made a bit of money so that he could spend it on—no, not on the dancer's sweet fruits. Something else. Something that was fun and something *he* chose to spend money on.

His father continued. "I think it could work, as an idea. Yes, you should do some work to gain experience. I might just have the thing for you. I'd been looking for an assistant to help the doga deal with correspondence. You could help in there."

Ravi didn't want to say no, that was not what he wanted, because he did want to do something, just not *that* thing, because he'd been in that office before. "Helping out" didn't mean getting paid for it, and it didn't mean independence or experience because his father's office was nextdoor and so he wouldn't have the freedom to do or say anything. Not that he wanted to do wild things. Just… things that he wanted to do, without his father looking over his shoulder.

"Yes, I think that could work quite nicely for you." His father seemed rather pleased with himself. "How about we go there for a look?"

"What? Now?"

"Why not? Your tutor doesn't come until later. Unless you're busy preparing."

His father gave him a stern look. Ravi *should* prepare for the tutor, because the tutor was never happy with anything Ravi did, and he'd been so excited about going out with his friends that he hadn't done a lot, but admitting that to his father was another issue.

"No, it's fine."

His father grabbed his coat. They left the house a bit later and walked through the busy streets of the city to the main square, where the doga complex, and the library and the Scriptorium took up one side.

People streamed in and out of the stately building, greeting Ravi's father with polite nods.

In the marble-lined foyer with its stately doors and statues, his father met another senator and introduced Ravi as *my son, who's coming to work for us.*

Then they went up the sweeping staircase.

A barrier with a rope attached to posts cordoned off half the width of the stairs. Behind the barrier, watched by a couple of poker-faced doga guards, stood a line of people. They were dressed well. Most were older, and some were very old.

They all started yelling at his father as they walked past.

"Senator, please. We need you to lower the business tax. Our businesses can't survive like this."

"Senator, the road into Fairlight is worse than bad. We need it to be fixed."

"Senator, no one in our district wanted the huge army camp. Why did it still go ahead? We gave you plenty of alternatives."

Some people held out paper petitions in their hands and leaned over the rope barrier.

His father ignored all those people as if they were part of the furniture.

"Stay behind the barrier!" one of the guards shouted. "Don't bother the senators or we will remove you from the building!"

The people briefly fell quiet while Ravi and his father continued up the stairs.

The line of petitioners waiting for an audience with the Proctor was a legendary fixture of the doga building. People always waited here, sometimes for days, until the Proctor agreed to see them.

Just because the people waited here didn't mean that they would see the Proctor. The Proctor chose who he was prepared to see. And a lot of these people would be waiting here for nothing.

What would make an old woman desperate enough to travel all the way from Fairlight to ask the doga about the condition of the road?

Once Ravi and his father were in the foyer, the cries and shouts of their pleading voices faded.

This large oval room held the desk of the receptionist who controlled who went in and out of this inner sanctum of the doga. The office of the proctor himself was behind a door to the right. A guard stood on one side and on the other side was a line of velvet-covered chairs, all of them empty. This was where the selected petitioners sat before going in.

The receptionist at the desk greeted Ravi's father before going back to his work, which included taking pretty printed folded cards from a box on the desk and inserting a sheet of paper in each.

His father led him down the corridor into a room with a sign next to the door that said *mail room*. In this room, more boxes of cards stood on tables.

There were a number of people in this room, a couple of young women and two men, one of them very young and the other much older.

Yes, Ravi remembered this place. It was quite spacious and sunny, with open doors that led to a balcony—this would be one of those balconies at the facade of the building.

The people inside were all chatting and laughing and fell silent as Ravi's father came in.

"Good afternoon, Senator," the older man said.

"This is my son, Ravinius," his father said. "He wants to get some experience of work in this important office. I'm sure you can find something for him to do."

"Most definitely. We're just sending out the invitations for the start of the political year gala event. We've almost finished, but there's been a bit of work that we haven't been able to do for the last few days. We can always use a helping hand."

Ravi's father turned to Ravi. "See, there you go, son. When can he start? He is still studying, so any work will have to fit around his study commitments."

"And my fighting training," Ravi added.

"Oh yes, that, too. I would have thought you were rather looking for a reason to not have to wield swords and crossbows and reload powder guns anymore."

"I promised I would continue to come. I don't mind the training. One of the tutors said I was quite good."

His father smiled. "They all say that. If you don't want to do it, I'm happy for you to spend that extra time here."

"Is this going to be a proper job?"

"It's proper work. You'll see that there are people doing this work every day."

"Does that mean I'll be paid?"

His father met his eyes, as if only now realising that this was a very important part of the reason why Ravi asked about a job.

"Well…" He shrugged. "You'd have to get some experience."

"How long?"

"Eh…" His father looked around the office, very obviously uncomfortable and not prepared for this question, certainly not having to answer it in front of these people, who were all looking at him.

None of them dared say anything. Maybe they were too scared. Maybe they didn't want Ravi to be paid either.

Not so long ago, he would have been sorry to have asked, but no more. After spending time with Fali, Neba and Keran, Ravi realised just what a strange life he led, and how much more freedom other people had. Which was part of the reason he'd asked for a job. A question that now looked like backfiring on him.

"I'll talk to you about that later," his father said.

Well, at least it wasn't a no.

His father asked the people to introduce themselves. The older man who seemed to be in charge was called Marlo. The younger one was Siman. Both of those were worker names.

The women were all a bit of a blur to him. Most of them were young and shy, and they all looked the same to him. Girls from the worker classes who would only stay for as long as they were not married.

But one girl stood out because her name was Dana and that was definitely not a worker class name. She didn't give her family name, but she didn't look like a worker class girl either.

She was quite tall and skinny, with pale skin and black hair. She wore it uncharacteristically short and a bit messy, like a boy. Her eyes had a very unusual dark blue colour. Her pale arms were quite muscular, for a girl and the fact that she showed so much skin was also quite unusual. A bit like Neba, who had no time for *modest* clothing if it got in the way of sword training.

This Dana girl regarded him with an intense expression. Ravi didn't know where to look.

Marlo explained the job, which was not complicated, so the rest of the afternoon, Ravi spent inserting leaflets in invitations—they had the participant's name written on them—and then inserting the invitations in envelopes, packing those in boxes and taking the boxes to the courier's office downstairs. For that, they had to walk past the queue of petitioners again, and that queue didn't seem to have grown any shorter. Ravi vaguely recognised a few people in the queue.

"Does the proctor not see any people today?" Ravi asked Marlo when they were back upstairs in the mail room.

"It's mostly the secretary who deals with these people, and he has been very busy with the start of the new year."

That meant no?

"So the proctor just leaves them standing there?"

Marlo gave him a strange look. "They do this to themselves. There is no need for them to stand here, because they can send their petitions by mail, but this is what they choose to do."

"But why, if there is no point?"

"Because some people just like to be seen in this building, and they talk to each other and to the minor senators, and they get paid for passing information back to whomever is happy to pay for it. Local administrators and merchants and people like that. Petitioning is an industry. An artform, some say. Hang around for long enough, and people will respect you, and give you jobs. Some of the senators started as petitioners. They learn how the system works."

Oh, right. Sing the praises of those above you and hope they'd throw you some crumbs. Where had he heard that before?

CHAPTER 13

Following the raid, the people of the Gathering hung around the temple, waiting for further news.

Tylve wanted to go home because she was tired from having worked long days at sea, but her family was one of the foundation families of the Samiran Gathering and while she welcomed the new people, she didn't want to leave the protection of the temple to them. They didn't have the deep ancestral connection with the building that looked out over the town like a guardian. The building that had been a constant in her life even after her parents died. That had been a source of protection against old men who wanted to "save" her when she became orphaned, who wanted to "help" her. Pandor and his predecessor had said that if she didn't want these men, they had no right to force themselves on her.

And there had been times when Tylve had come up to the temple to shelter in the safety of its hall.

Now the temple and Pandor were in trouble, so she should help.

The newer people didn't understand that. Those people hadn't been shunned for most of their lives for being part of the Gathering. They knew nothing about lightstream and lacked the unspoken connection that people who could shape lightstream shared with each other and with the dead.

So she waited in the temple hall.

A young man reported that he had seen that the guards had taken Pandor away, presumably for questioning.

As the night grew darker, people speculated about what was going on with him. That the guards interrogated him under force. That they would take him to Tiverius to jail. That they killed him.

But there was no evidence for any of it, and Pandor himself put an end to the rumours by ambling into the temple yard later.

He said the guards had questioned him. They had not forced him to reply, and there were many questions he said he hadn't answered.

They wanted to know about the Gathering and who attended.

He said they were looking for someone—a criminal—but they remained vague about who this was when Pandor asked.

They let him go without giving him orders, a warrant or charging him. He didn't know why they picked him up, probably because he tried to stop the guards from coming into the temple with their shoes on.

Tylve finally went home long after midnight, but she glanced over her shoulder all the way through town.

It started raining during the night. The sound of water lashing against the bedroom window woke her up a few times.

Just as well she had come into port the previous night. This weather was atrocious for fishing.

She had a few errands to run in town. The pantry needed restocking, and she needed to pick up her shirts from the tailor who had them since before her last trip to fix buttons and fix and turn collars.

So she started on those things the next morning.

The weather was still blustery—unsuited to sailing. She went to the harbour and cleaned the cabin in her boat.

She picked up the shirts. She went to the grocery store to buy supplies for the coming month and lugged them back to her house in the rain, while rivulets of water ran down the streets and most sane people kept inside.

In the afternoon, the weather looked like it would settle for a few days, so she went to find someone to fix her nets.

This required going into the bars in the harbour where the harbour workers hung out.

Because of the weather and the lack of ships coming in, they had little else to do except get stupidly drunk.

Tylve disliked these rowdy places, but she had built up enough of a reputation amongst these men that none dared bother her.

But the snide remarks still followed wherever she went.

She should be used to it, but the made-up accusations she overheard being said behind her back were infuriating.

That the people of the Gathering had brought the raid upon themselves because they were a secret cabal using evil forces that spoke to the dead.

That they had brought in bands of criminals who now called the town home.

Arguing against this nonsense was pointless.

If the bars were the equivalent of parts of the human body, these were the opening of the arse. The populace had feasted on a diet of hatred and lies for years, and what came out resembled a stream of putrid shit, and this wouldn't improve until the people of the Gathering found their way into more than just the occasional council post.

But these men had no principles and no morals, because even if they professed to hate people from the Gathering, they would do anything to get her money. Even if they knew she could shape lightstream and she did connect with the souls of the dead.

They called her a witch, but they took her money anyway.

The only thing she didn't understand about the influx of adherents of the Gathering into town was why it hadn't happened earlier. If this was how the members of the Gathering were treated in Samira, she could only imagine what they faced in other towns.

To top it off, the Tiverian guards were still in town.

The guards lodged in the inn at the market square, and the townsfolk had set private guards around the building to keep an eye on what they were doing.

Tylve heard that the men hadn't just bothered the Gathering, but also several respected townsfolk, including the mayor's wife.

The villagers were angry and wanted to make sure there weren't any further raids.

Tylve walked past the inn on her way home.

Those visiting guards had to realise they were being watched. The townsfolk were not exactly secret about their sentries.

Everyone was watching and gossiping about everyone else, talking garbage in bars, spreading rumours in the street.

Tylve hated it and wanted to go back out fishing, but the weather was still blustery and the sea was rough, weather in which she would spend more time tending to the sails and staying her course than casting the nets.

Neither had she been paid for her previous catch. She visited the harbour master's office to check on the progress with that, only to find it closed.

As it was, the harbour master stood outside the guest house in the company of a couple of important businessmen from the town.

They were talking, and opened their circle when Tylve approached. They nodded politely.

Tylve knew these men thought little of her, since she belonged to a founding family of the Gathering, but her father had been a respected member of the local council, so they kept a thin veneer of respectability.

"I heard you were at the temple raid," a man said to her.

His tone was semi-casual, even if he would know exactly where she had been during the temple raid. He was a warehouse owner and stood with his hands in the pockets of his sea-lion felt coat.

Tylve replied in a similarly casual tone. "I saw the raid, but I wasn't inside the building. I didn't see whether they found anything."

"We don't know what they were looking for."

"They said they were looking for criminals from the city." Why did these men always play innocent? Had they even spoken to Pandor? Did they think she was stupid?

"That's what they said," another man said, his voice angry. "But I'd like to know what they planned for my cousin's daughter."

That caught Tylve's attention. "Your cousin's daughter?"

"Yes. When they came to my cousin's house while searching for whatever they're searching for, they found her in the vegetable garden. Two men took her behind my cousin's shed and did unspeakable things to her. She is barely fifteen."

Tylve shuddered. Fifteen. She'd been two years older, and a lot more prepared, including the fact that the man had ambushed her in a kitchen full of weapons.

Still, she wasn't sure about the man's story. Guards from the doga sometimes came for inspections or visits or to solve disputes in the district. They were harsh, but she hadn't known them to misbehave. For one, their supervisors were very strict. "Do you know for certain that they were these guards?"

The warehouse owner said, "We saw them. They dressed like guards."

"It seems inappropriate behaviour for them. Their superiors in Tiverius would never allow their men to lay a hand on local women."

"That doesn't mean nothing ever happens."

True, but for it to come out into the open was another thing. Usually—and she shuddered again—those guards would know to hide their tracks. If this was what had happened, they would either take the girl with them or kill her.

The warehouse owner gave her a pointed look. Twenty years of history passed between them. History that covered the reason Tylve had never married or taken a man from town. She could still feel the wet sliding of the knife into his chest. And the heavy thud as he dropped, lifeless, onto the floor in the kitchen. The young man, trying to have his way with the fiery young woman she'd been, had been the son of an established family. Not one of the Gathering, because otherwise the situation would have been dealt with, and reparations would have been paid. But because she was of the Gathering and he was not, the whole thing was covered under a cloak of secrecy that persisted even today.

And because the situation grew too tense, and neither wanted to talk about this subject, she walked away.

Without having asked the harbour master when she could expect payment for her fish. Well, damn.

Because she couldn't go out sailing again, Tylve returned to the temple to help clean up. Partially because she had nothing else to do, and it was too early to go home, and partially because she was curious if she could find out anything else about the men who had searched the building, and what they had been looking for.

Pandor was inside, directing a few other townsfolk. Tylve accepted a broom from him, and went to sweep the tiles, which were already meticulously clean. But it was important that all traces of evil were banned from this building. The temple was a place where people could speak their minds, and it needed to be free of contamination. It needed to be free from dust so that the winds would listen and would direct sense over the village.

That was necessary, because they certainly didn't have much sense right now.

Tylve swept the tiles in the building for the rest of the day, and encountered nothing terribly interesting. She came across a few clumps of hair, but whether they were from humans or animals, whether they were from the fight or had been there all the time, was very hard to tell. She returned home in the evening, where she had left the strange neck band and the fragment of see-through material on the kitchen table. She made some tea and sat there looking at those items, wondering about the man who had died—or been killed—on that cliff in the last two weeks, his bones pecked clean by birds.

About the debris on the shoreline that—now she thought about it—looked like it had fallen from the cliff rather than washed onto the rocks by the ocean. That could explain the lack of a boat, but it still didn't answer the question of how the man had arrived there.

The army had hot air balloons, but she understood they worked poorly out at sea, because of the wind, the lack of landmarks, the lack of safe places to land and many other things.

But in theory, people could come to the Island of Skulls in a balloon.

Why, though?

And why leave a dead guy with this strange thing around his neck?

And where had the other occupants of the balloon gone?

Were they adrift on the ocean and needed help? Were they

murderers? Perhaps these ill-behaved visiting guards were looking for them? Or they were looking for the dead man? And if they looked hard enough and stayed long enough, they might find that Tylve had his jewellery.

Well, damn it.

While she sat there, it grew later and later until the time arrived for the evening's Gathering.

She walked back and sat in the newly cleaned temple, on her usual bench.

The attendants usually divided into two distinct groups that each stuck to their own side of the temple hall.

On one side were the old locals, the people she had grown up knowing all her life, like Pandor and his family, like her cousins, like old friends of her own family.

On the other side were the newcomers: those who had joined the community in the past few years.

The harbour master and other non-Gathering locals had circulated rumours that these newcomers harboured thieves and murderers.

As far as Tylve could see, they were just people from surrounding villages. There were times that life on the farms was hard because of poor weather, locusts or crop diseases, and that people flocked to the towns hoping to find jobs and a better life for themselves.

She wasn't sure what had driven all these people to come now, but here they were, and the Gathering taught that all good-hearted visitors should be made to feel welcome.

Tylve only attended gatherings whenever she was not at sea. It had been a while since she had attended two in a row.

Why had she never noticed how all these new people all sat together and no one of the old villagers spoke to them? That was not how she was raised.

Tylve was also not the kind of person to raise her voice in the Gathering except on her name day, when she had to speak to the community. Trouble came from being too outspoken.

But she made sure to speak to some of the new followers after the ceremony.

Quite a few people she already knew reasonably well. A young man worked for the bakery. Another she had seen unloading ships in the harbour. An older woman had hired a stall in the markets and sold homemade clothing there.

Those people were all hard-working, honest citizens. They had come because life had been hard, and the people of the Gathering had been kind to them. She'd heard their stories already. There was no reason to distrust them.

When she asked about it, they had all, without exception, received a knock on the door from the visiting guards, asking questions and demanding to search their houses. There was an older woman whose daughter had been attacked, and she didn't want to speak about the nature of the attack.

"Those men are not proper soldiers," a man said. "I tell you, because I served in the army as a young man. Soldiers would never be allowed to behave in this way."

This had also been Tylve's suspicion.

Which left the question: who were these men and why were they here? Especially since they had not stolen anything, didn't seem to be after money, and if they were looking for a criminal, as they said, they didn't make a convincing case for their behaviour.

Tylve left the temple in the dark, her mind full of questions.

Other than a fisherman, her father had been the town's official administrator, looking after the official affairs from the capital.

He used to say that people in Tiverius took advantage of people in the smaller towns. They preyed on the ignorance of the folk who farmed the fields and their unfamiliarity with the many rules of district administration. The smaller the town, the worse it was.

Tylve had no interest in rules and after her father's death, had not kept up with any communication from the capital.

There had been some recently. Apparently, they wanted young men to sign up for the army because of a distant conflict that had nothing to do with the coast. She had advised the young men of the Gathering to ignore it all. Because people from the city only wanted to use the townsfolk for their own aims. The young people shouldn't take part in anything unless they knew what those aims were.

She'd been to Tiverius. She knew how much richer people in the city were. Those people in the city didn't do anything out of the goodness of their hearts.

And now they were trying to set two groups in Samira up against each other?

Bah, she really hated this. All this gossip and sniping. The politics.

She wanted to go fishing.

She walked past the harbour office to look at the weather forecast. It was not good, with bad weather to continue most of the week.

That didn't put her in a good mood. She walked back home, her hands in her pockets. She didn't want to hang around here while these guards upset everyone, with the gossip and the baseless rumours. She couldn't go fishing.

The weather was gloomy and started spitting rain by the time she arrived home.

Her packs still stood against the wall in the living room, where the light glittered on the strange neck band that lay on a cloth on the table.

She stopped at the table while looking at it.

When she held her head at a certain angle, it was as if the stone was a bottomless hole. It sat snugly in the metal encasing and couldn't move. The metal felt cool under her touch, but when she slid her finger along the edge, a tiny spark of lightstream lit up. That surprised her. Was that a remnant from her trip out there? It didn't usually linger that long. Or was there a flare?

She walked to the window. In the front corner of the room stood a metal rod as long as her forearm. It had come from her father's old boat, where it sat in the cabin. He would use it to guide lightstream, to let it keep him, his family and his boat safe through the spirit of their ancestors.

She opened the window. A fine spray of rain and cold air hit her in the face. Urgh.

Tylve stuck the rod out into the weather, waving it through the air.

After a little while, she pulled her arm in, shut the window, used a tea towel to dry her arm and slid her dry hand along the length of the rod.

Tiny sparks of lightstream dripped from her fingers.

"I need your help to know if I need to keep, or hide or use this object," she whispered.

She let the sparks fall onto the metal neck band. The thing grew warm, and the stones briefly glowed within before winking out.

That was kind of… disappointing.

It meant this strange object behaved normally for something made out of metal. She had expected… something else. Something magical to happen, but the thing wasn't going to give up its secrets in this manner.

If only she knew what the significance of the thing was.

Hmm. She knew what she could do. There was someone she could visit to talk about this thing. As a bonus, it would take her out of town.

CHAPTER 14

*J*aves and Mindo and the two camels stayed at the shelter for the next day.

Even if Javes was keen to get back to civilisation, he had undertaken this trip so that he could study this ruin site and be paid for his time while doing it.

He had made this arrangement with none other than King Isandor of Peria and could not—and didn't want to—go back on it.

He'd been looking forward to this part of the trip too much.

He tried to explain to Mindo that he could rest in the shelter, or sleep or eat—it didn't matter, there was enough food. Or he could look after the camels and brush the knots out of their fur.

He didn't think Mindo understood.

Javes was part of a group of people, which included the king, who corresponded regularly about discoveries of old artefacts they made. This arrangement dated from the time he was a student, when he would correspond with a fellow student Lana, and she with Tamer-ane, who was the king's wife in the City of Glass. Which was how that contact had come about, because Javes had definitely never been to Peria.

He'd felt out of place in a group of such powerful people, but they all shared a deep interest in ancient history and now that King Isandor was taking a step back in favour of his son, he had taken up his old interest. Having lots of time and money led him to pay people like Javes to do the work. And he paid well, because Javes was familiar with the history and understood the work and could interpret what he saw.

Twenty years ago, he and Lana and Tamerane had solved the mystery: *What is the world?* by putting their observations together.

Now they joined forces to solve the mystery of the ancient civilisation that had left traces all over the continent, but especially in the very south and very north.

In the north it involved sites like these, that required him to travel deep into the desert he loved so much.

In the south…

Javes had received a beautiful book sent by the king with observations and diagrams that showed the City of Glass was a giant ruined site with ancient tall buildings of stone and glass. The city was even built on the footprint of the ancient structures, and people in the inner city lived in them.

The ruins in the City of Glass were very different from those in the desert of northern Chevakia. The desert held no remnants of ancient cities, only sprawling settlements with structures that were a mystery to everyone.

But none of the known histories went back far enough to know who these people were and where they had gone, and what was the purpose of some of their installations. Some of them formed a shield against sonorics. That's what they had established years ago. They had repaired the shield, and the world was safe once again, but the other buildings, like these bowls on pedestals?

Looking at the sky, huh?

He'd never considered that might be a possibility. Looking at what? Just the stars?

The only thing left of the installations were the ruined buildings and other items that could not be removed.

Javes had travelled all over the desert and had catalogued all the items he found. In times past, the windwalker desert dwellers had plundered many of these sites, taken the artefacts and sold them at markets, sometimes to collectors in Chevakia, and sometimes to Arania or even to Peria.

Over the years, what remained of the history had spread far and wide. But no one had ever catalogued and mapped the buildings.

Javes spent most of the day walking around the valley, drawing up maps. Mindo predictably hadn't understood that Javes was happy for him to sit in the shade, and he tagged along. He studied everything with a pensive look on his face.

He helped, and seemed to understand what they were doing, even if he probably didn't know why. Or did he?

With the language barrier, it was hard to figure out what the man was thinking. He was intelligent, but strangely disturbed by things like the sound of the wind whistling through the installations. He spent a long time trying to figure out where that came from and trying to recreate the sound.

Javes showed him how to make a noise by clamping a leaf between his thumbs and blowing through the tiny hole. It was a strangely nostalgic experience. He used to do this with the fat grass leaves that grew on the banks of the creek near his house.

The camels hated the shrill sound of the leaf-blowing and made their displeasure known.

Mindo laughed. There was something childish about him. Was this truly the first time he blew on a leaf?

Javes spent most of the evening repacking the camels' saddlebags so that each animal had an equal amount to carry. With both animals having to carry a rider, they couldn't cover quite as much distance as he could on his own, which meant they had to take a longer route, since it led through a tiny hamlet where he'd be able to get supplies and let the camels graze.

They left the ruins early the next morning.

Mindo had become much more comfortable with the camel, although Javes didn't think that handling animals was in Mindo's culture.

Several times, Mindo took out his paper and scribbled something on it. Javes didn't see what he was writing and would probably not have understood it anyway.

He was still trying to piece together the puzzle.

The possibility of a land beyond the horizon, from where people travelled by balloon. There had long been talk about this, since he and fellow students found out that the world was round and that there was another side of it where no one had ever been, save for people from Arania being sent to face the Mother and they didn't survive to tell what they saw.

Did Aranians still send people to their deaths like this?

Lana, his fellow student at the Scriptorium, now lived in the Citadel in Kadrish in Arania. It was a long time since he had heard from her.

In order to get to the tiny hamlet of Whitesands Creek, they needed to cross the tallest part of the plateau. It was harsh country, devoid of any vegetation, where it grew so hot in summer that not even the camels liked going there.

The wind was hot and bone dry, and they avoided speaking, instead covering their nose and mouth with a shawl.

By the time they made their way down the slope, the sight of even a barely alive straggly bush was welcome.

The hamlet lay on the banks of Whitesands Creek, which, of course, only flowed after rain, and then never for long.

The hamlet's telegraph box stood on the closest creek bank. Javes stopped there briefly to send through his weather station measurements.

Mindo studied the single pole, the wire that went to the next pole, and the one after that.

"We use it to talk to each other," Javes said, cupping his hands in front of his mouth.

Who knew what Mindo would make of that.

There were about twenty houses in all, scattered over the valley. People moved here primarily for two reasons: because they hated other people or because they were in trouble with the authorities.

Javes only felt comfortable enough with the owner of the house that doubled as waystation. This was a woman who had settled here after an acrimonious fallout with the windwalkers and her windwalker partner. The woman herself came from Ysherra. She lived with her half-windwalker daughter and the daughter's flock of camels.

Those camels all stood along the fence of their paddock, curious to check out the arriving beasts. They were beautiful animals, windwalker beasts, and Javes would sometimes bring his own windwalker camels for breeding. These camels knew each other.

The "food and accommodation" part of the business was the courtyard out the back, with an old wooden table and benches in the shade of an old olive tree and a patch of dirt on the other side of the unpaved road past the property where visitors could camp. This plot was also the home of a couple of ancient olive trees and their knobbly trunks and roots.

Javes noticed that two of the female camels in the next paddock were particularly interested in his male. He had trouble keeping the beast still. The female went straight to the food trough to see if there was any hay—there wasn't—and then she nosed around the plot, while Javes and Mindo set up camp. They took the saddles and packs off the camels and tied them up. They strung the oiled cloth from the branches of an olive tree. He sent Mindo down to the creek bed to get some water from the well for the camels.

By the time they had done all that, Saree had noticed that she had customers, and she came out of the house.

"Hadn't expected you back so soon," she said.

"Yeah, I had a strange experience on the coast. I found a lost man."

"Yer kidding. Out there? How did he get there?"

"That's just it. I'm not sure. He can't speak in any language I can understand."

She looked around. "Where is he?"

"I sent him down to the creek to get some water."

"You'll be wanting some dinner, I guess?"

"That would be nice."

"And some hay?"

"That, too."

"Well, it so happens that two of my cows are in heat. Maybe your boy would like to do his duty?"

"I'm sure he'd like that very much."

She grinned. "I'll catch them and bring them around after I put on dinner."

Saree turned to go back into the house, but at that moment, there was a commotion down the road.

A woman yelled out.

"Huh. That sounds like Trini," Saree said.

But it was Mindo who came running up the road, carrying his bucket with water sloshing over the side. Trini, Saree's daughter, followed him, carrying a rake which she hefted threateningly above her head.

She yelled, "How dare you set foot in this place?"

Mindo scurried across to the tent, dumped the bucket on the ground and vanished inside.

Saree looked from him to Javes. "Is he with you?"

"He's the man I was talking about."

Saree again looked from Javes to the tent where Mindo had disappeared.

Trini had arrived in the yard, still holding her rake. Her face was red and her eyes wide. She was thin and tall, like windwalkers and, like windwalkers, her skin had patches of white. One covered the top right half of her face and eye, which was blue, while the rest of her skin was brown and other other eye was dark.

She was also about six months pregnant, which was probably what had slowed her down.

Huh. Javes didn't know there was a man in her life.

"What's he doing here?" she asked, still panting, her voice sharp.

"Do you know him?" Javes asked.

"Not him, but his ilk."

"Trini. You don't know that. Javes says he saved this man all the way over on the shore."

"I know he's one of them! I know! I don't want any of them on my land, looking at my camels! Eating my food."

"He's with Javes, and they're paying customers."

"I don't care!"

She stared at her mother, breathing hard. "I never thought you would protect one of them."

She turned around and stomped across the road into the yard.

"I'm sorry about that," Saree said. "This has nothing to do with you."

"But it might," Javes said. "I don't know who this man is and I don't know where he's from and how he ended up where I found him. He just seemed… desperate and hungry, and I thought I should help him. He didn't refuse any of my help. What does she think he did?"

She blew out a breath. "A few months ago, a group of men came into town. They were outsiders. From the city we thought at first, but I don't know anymore. Tiverius doesn't care about us. They don't even care enough to send spies. Anyway, these characters who came into town spoke to the young folk. Were they happy? Did they think life was fair, that sort of stuff. They held meetings in a shed every evening."

Saree shrugged.

"Trini went because the other young people went, too. They called it the Gathering. It seemed to bring people together, you know. People here can be funny. Most of the older folk don't like each other and it's fair enough that the kids were sick of that. Most of them have at least one windwalker parent and the windwalkers are very close."

She shrugged again and didn't say anything for a while.

Trini had disappeared into the house, Mindo was still hiding, and Javes' male camel had located the source of the female smell. He was making faces at the females, moving his lips about. His male tackle dangled free for all to see, pink and glistening and ready for action.

"I better bring one of the girls across," Saree said. "He can have the other one tomorrow morning."

Javes walked with her to the pen.

She continued. "The young people seemed to enjoy these gatherings from what I understand. Every evening, one or two members got to have their say and they would talk about those things. But they also started talking about leaving town to spend time on the road together. Trini wanted to go, and I was like yeah sure because she said it would only be for a few months and then she'd be back to work."

She climbed over the fence, and grabbed one of the females by the rope around the neck. The animal protested a bit, but came with her to the gate. Javes followed on the other side of the fence.

"She came back after only two weeks. At first she didn't want to talk about what happened and why she came back, other than that she wanted nothing more to do with those people. Then she told me that most of the young people who went were girls. They went to this camp and they would have big parties every night and sleep until well into the day. But my girl Trini doesn't take to drink very much. It makes her awful sick, so she just pretended. And one night after a big party, the men went to all the girls and put things up their private parts. You know…"

She shrugged.

"They were raped?"

"No. At least not that she said. Just that they felt them up."

Saree tied the female camel to an olive tree, keeping the rope really short so that the animal couldn't move very far.

"But she's expecting," Javes said after a while.

"Yeah. She swears the men did not rape the women. She says the men were always very proper. They never even took their shirts off."

How those two things lined up in the same story was probably too painful to talk about. Javes remembered his own Tali, how she had never understood what had happened to her at thirteen, when the Aranian soldiers had *hurt her*, which had resulted in the difficult birth of Renko nine months later, and how she both deeply wanted Javes to marry her and she had been too scared to allow him to take his clothes off in her presence for years. Renko was now an adult young man. Lissa was only five. He didn't think there would ever be any other children.

"How does Trini decide that Mindo belongs to the same group?"

"Don't ask me. You might ask her if she decides to come to dinner."

Javes untied his camel and walked the beast over. Actually, the camel walked *him* over at a trot. He jumped onto the female's back and did his thing with his usual groaning and bellowing. The noise brought Mindo from the tent.

He watched with wide eyes. Javes didn't think he'd ever seen two camels in the noisy act of procreation before.

CHAPTER 15

Ravi had to study the next day, and in the afternoon, he went to training.

Fali was gone, as he said he would, but Keran was in the class. As a merchant's son, Keran also didn't have a military career mapped out for him, so during a break, Ravi asked Keran what plans he had for the future.

Keran shrugged. "I might sign up. As long as it's not working in the business."

Keran complained a lot about his father's business and Ravi didn't think Keran's father either did all that well or liked his son very much, nor cared much about him. But at the same time, he required his son to help him.

They both agreed that parents were the source of a lot of trouble.

The combat school had taken on a new class trained by Neba and they came into the courtyard when Ravi's class took a break.

Ravi greeted her, but she was really busy and didn't greet him back. That seemed a kind of impersonal thing to do after the previous night, but Neba could get like that. Very focused on her job.

She started with the same lessons that Ravi had also started with. She made the same rude remarks. The younger men in the class laughed at her. They ogled her backside. The same things had happened in Ravi's class.

He realised: It was all a game to her.

Neba had seemed serious and professional last night because she *was* still working. The night out had not been about friendship. He had thought it odd that tutors of classes would be interested in going to bars with students. And felt kind of honoured that a tutor wanted to go out with him.

No, the fighting classes—offered for free to all who wanted to come—had to be a front for something else.

The army. They were constantly telling people to sign up. Even Keran was repeating the suggestions.

Was that it? The doga wanted people to sign up for armed duty and they employed training tutors to tell young men and women that they were good and should sign up. They acted like friends, but Fali and Neba weren't real friends. Look at how restrained both had acted last night. It had been Keran who'd gotten drunk. They had just wanted to get Ravi and Keran to sign up.

And now that neither Ravi and Keran appeared to show great enthusiasm, Neba no longer wanted to pretend to be friends. She had different people to try to recruit.

He felt ill.

Was there a place in the world where people weren't trying to take advantage of you?

Was his path in life truly going to involve finding a way to beat himself out of this mire of exploitation schemes?

Ravi rejected Keran's invitation to go out again.

The tutor had given him a lot of homework, but at night he just sat staring at the pages without reading anything.

Tomorrow, he was going to work in his father's office again. He still didn't know if and when or how much he was going to be paid, but he'd go anyway until he could see a way out of this situation. What had his father done to get ahead when he was young?

He got married.

Ravi had no money for that.

The people of his parents' generation in their big houses with lots of servants weren't going to move to make way for him and his friends and the wives they didn't yet have. Those houses belonged to the family. He would eventually get his parents' house, but the idea of having to listen to his father's rants about politics until he was well into his forties or fifties didn't appeal to him. If he married—and that wasn't on the horizon—he didn't want a young woman having to listen to his father either.

He also didn't want his parents to die.

This was why so many young people signed up for armed duty: to get out of the house.

But through his reading of history, he could see that the doga wanted this, just to repress the rebellion in the north and to exert its influence over whatever groups they didn't like within the country.

Like all the unhappy young people.

If things weren't going well—and they weren't—governments needed someone to blame.

Arania used to be on the receiving end of this kind of blame, but Arania had been quiet and quite civilised in the last fifteen years. They'd quit raiding the border villages for women. They'd quit threatening to invade Chevakia. The Aranian queen was even half Chevakian. Lana han Chevonian, the daughter of the exalted proctor Sadorius han Chevonian, who had led the country through so much trouble. She was a cousin twice removed of his.

All Ravi knew was that he didn't want to be stuck being the pointy end of someone else's plan. He also didn't want to blow with all the winds like Keran, and spend his money on drinks. Or fight in an army for things he didn't believe in.

In the morning, he walked with his father to the doga office.

The queue on the steps had not shrunk one bit. In fact, he recognised many of the same people he'd seen two days ago.

When he and his father walked up the stairs, the petitioners yelled their questions at his father. The guards reminded them that they had to stay behind the barrier, as they did every day.

It was a game.

It was a game to all of these people.

The proctor was in his office, because Ravi could hear his voice drifting out of the room. The secretary was also inside. The row of seats next to the door was again empty.

They turned into the hallway. A man came the other way and wanted to talk to his father, who said to Ravi, "You know the way. You can keep going."

Ravi continued into the mail room.

He found the workers surrounding a table with a mountain of pieces of paper.

Marlo turned around when Ravi came in.

"Ah, I thought I heard you in the hall. Come in. Let's get started on this."

"What are we doing? Are these still invitations?"

The folded papers were mostly envelopes. Some were very neat with beautiful writing. Ravi spotted one that said "to the honourable senators of the doga". Another looked like it had been in someone's back pocket for a long time. The writing at the front was messy, and a few drops of water had made circles on the page and made the ink run.

"We finished the invitations yesterday," Dana said.

"Then what are all these?"

"Petitions."

"You mean—from the people outside?"

"Yes, at least the ones who are happy to put their issues in writing."

"Then why are they still waiting outside?"

Marlo said, "Those are different people. Some people send us their grievances. Sometimes they're individuals, but often it's the district administrator who sends the questions. We open the letters, look at what the complaint is about, sort them into broad categories and pass them onto the relevant senators dealing with the subject in question."

"And the senator responds to the people?"

"That's up to the senator in question. That's out of our hands."

Marlo pushed the pile of letters into four roughly equal stacks. Siman and Dana each gathered one and found a desk.

"You can have that desk," Marlo said, indicating a work table near the door. "You will find everything you need there. Take a stack and open them."

Ravi gathered one of the remaining piles. There were rather a lot of letters, and the stack was awkward to carry.

When he dumped it on the table, two letters slid off and fell onto the floor. One of them was a pretty blue envelope with neat writing. The stamp that proved postage had been paid said that it had come from Samira. That was on the east coast, right?

Well, he might not be paid in this job for the time being, at least he'd refresh his geography.

Ravi sat down and pushed the pile to one side to make room for opened letters.

The desk held a glass jar with a number of writing implements. There was also a bronze letter opener in the shape of a sword.

He asked, "How do I know what subjects to sort the petitions in?"

Marlo said, "We sort them by departments. I believe you know what the departments are?"

Ravi nodded. Well, he knew the basic ones.

Marlo added, "Ask me if you're not sure."

Ravi picked up the first letter and slit the top open with the—very blunt—bronze miniature sword.

The envelope was made of nice smooth white paper and the paper inside was of the same material.

In neat writing, it said,

Dear Proctor and senators of the doga,
I'm writing to you today to draw your attention to the fact that
the railway bridge in Ensar needs urgent repairs. The recent
floods have hollowed out the creek bed underneath the bridge
and a number of pylons have shifted to the point where the
structure is under constant strain, made worse by the weight
of passing trains.
The local district administration does not have the funds for
the very significant repairs that need to be done urgently. We
ask for your attention to this matter.

Most sincerely, the district administration of Ensar.

That was easy. This went under the department of transport.

Ravi put the letter on the corner of the desk.

He took the next envelope from the pile. It was made of a similar paper and the writing was similarly neat.

The complaint was about repairs needed for a school in Solmeni where part of the roof had fallen in after a bad hail storm.

Ravi guessed that one would go to education.

The next letter was a messily-written note by someone with a barely functional grasp of grammar. The writer, a man called Erro, apparently without a family name, asked the proctor to assist in finding his son and daughter.

They be seventeen years, and good kids that know how to work hard. They went with the bad crowd. Me and the wife haven't heard since.

Ravi looked at it for a bit. The paper was dirty, the envelope had clearly gone through many hands. Probably sent through the cheapest mail.

He doubted the proctor would busy himself with a missing persons case. Probably in the time this letter had taken to be delivered, the kids had turned up.

Where could he even send something like this? Those people should have gone to the local guards.

He made another pile for the department of crime and justice.

The next letter was another neat one.

The piles on his desk grew.

He had opened a few more letters before a pattern became really clear to him. There were a lot of letters that used similar paper, similar neat handwriting and even similar wording. It was always clear what was being asked, and he never had any trouble deciding what department the subject fell under. Usually, the requests came from district offices.

"Why are these letters all the same?" he asked when Marlo declared it was time for the midday break.

"The local offices hire professional petitioners," Marlo said. "There are two major petition-writing businesses that send their clients to us. They use a set format."

"Really, people pay for that?"

Marlo shrugged. "It's cheaper than paying for someone to travel here."

Ravi guessed that was true, but…

"What about the people outside on the stairs?"

"There are some people you'll see in that queue every day of the year. They're hired to stand there. Obviously, that will cost a lot more than for someone to send a letter."

"But…" Ravi thought about what he'd learned at school about petitioning. That if you had a problem that could not be solved in usual ways, you had the option to address the proctor directly. That was a very naive definition, of course. "Are any of those people here for themselves?"

"There are some."

"But not many?"

"No, a few, but not many."

"And they all complain about bridges and roads?"

"A whole range of things."

"How many does the proctor see every day? How fast does the line move?"

"No, you don't understand. We decide the selection of petitions from which the proctor chooses who he will see. He spends a morning most weeks."

"Wait—one morning per week?"

"Yes."

"Then why are these people waiting here all day?"

Marlo spread his hands. "Publicity? Sometimes important citizens get upset when they meet with the proctor that they're heckled on the stairs, or someone catches their interest. Those people not waiting to see the proctor. None of us makes them wait that long. No, they wait in the hope of gaining influence or a job, or money."

Well… that was… quite a punch to the honourable intentions that he'd learned about at school. And had believed in.

He asked, "And you said *we* determine which petitions to give to the proctor to choose from?"

"I determine that. I look at things we've addressed in the past, and petitions that intersect with doga focus points. When the proctor sees someone, he wants to make sure it's in his power to address the problem, and that the doga is in a position to do something."

That seemed fair enough, on the surface. The proctor's time was limited. Everyone understood that.

But also, it was political. To make the senators look good, so that they got re-elected.

He wondered if the proctor had any say in the types of petitions he didn't want to see, but he didn't think it was wise to ask that question.

Marlo showed him a register with petitions the proctor had dealt with for most weeks of the past year. These were mostly requests from regional offices for repairs, extra staff, or similar things.

Very rarely did the proctor see any of the private petitioners, those who wrote messy letters full of spelling mistakes. Presentation was important, his father would always tell him, and Ravi could see how his father was right.

And if your teenage child had run away and was missing, a petition to the proctor was not the best way to deal with it. Even he could see that. Those people should go to the local authorities, because the doga was not set up to deal with that type of stuff.

But during the afternoon, he came across three private petitions that asked to help find missing children. All three appeared to be from peasant folk with very little comprehension about how to present their case—or even how to spell. Two were short, but one was quite long, a messy, rambling, incoherent letter. Ravi couldn't comprehend all of it, but he made out that the writer of the petition outlined the entire bureaucratic process he had been through in order to get the guards to take the issue of his missing daughter seriously.

Poorly written as it was, the story felt genuine and it chilled him.

The man had, as his father, only one child, and she had gone off somewhere with friends—the man called it a "gathering"— and had not come back. Ravi even looked up the address in a town that was unfamiliar to him. The man lived in a hamlet outside Twin Bridges, which was in the central part of Chevakia, an area considered safe and civilised.

When one of the last petitions left on his desk was yet another poorly written quest to help find a missing young adult child, he went to see Marlo about it.

"I'm seeing a lot of these types of requests," he said. "I don't know what to do with them. It's not clear where to file them, and it feels… I don't know… kind of bad to treat these in the same way as the requests for money to fix the bridge or something."

"People should go to the guards for missing person reports," Marlo said.

"This man says he's done that, but he also says that the guards couldn't help him because his daughter willingly went to this meeting. They called it a gathering."

"A lot of the young kids go to gatherings. There is nothing wrong with those," Dana said.

Whoa, what was up with her? She'd barely said anything all day.

"I didn't say there was. I don't know what they mean by gathering."

"It's a movement where people come together to discuss their problems and help fix them together."

"You mean like a political party?"

"No. It's for everyone. That's the point of it. Everyone talking to each other, not just people who think a certain way, talking to other people who think the same way. The principle is from the Samiran coast. My sister is very active in it."

"Dana…"

Marlo's voice sounded like a warning.

Dana flicked her eyebrows up. Very nice eyebrows they were, too.

Ravi looked from one to the other.

Marlo glared at Dana, and she glared back. There was clearly some prior history between the two, and Ravi didn't want to put his foot in it.

She was such a strange girl. So fiery, so different from other girls he had met. Which, admittedly, weren't that many. Just the students in his class, who were mostly silent and polite as their high-class families had taught them to be, or fighting girls like Neba, who came from worker families, swore a lot but didn't comment on politics.

CHAPTER 16

Over the next few days, Kotori regretted the visit to the markets in more ways than one. His bowels took almost three days to settle, which made that teaching was a rather interesting affair.

On the matter of the prince, Kotori wavered from thinking the prince would betray him to his mother, to thinking he might be keen to have a mothers' house. He had already tried to find rumours about the boy's interest in girls, but mostly came up blank. However, Harek was growing into a strapping young man, so of course there would be girls.

He learned that Harek had become much enamoured with learning to fight properly and Kotori did hear on the grapevine rumours that the young prince found a role model of sorts in Prince Denori, who had been murdered in the struggle for the throne when the king decided that no, he wasn't going to choose one of his adult sons as successor, but it would be the child yet to be born with his new wife, and that child was Loriane, who had the blood of all three countries in her veins—and who wasn't interested in ruling.

Harek was young, but he could be made to be interested, and to rule as a proxy king in the vein of the old ones, strong and decisive, intolerant of power jockeying in the lower ranks of the Citadel or the army. That would keep the army quiet for as long as Harek could give them the hope that mothers' houses would return. Which the prince might never allow, but by the time that caused trouble, Kotori would be long dead.

Kotori was rather pleased with himself for getting that idea.

He went and watched the prince as he trained in the barracks next to the Citadel, where he would spar with old-fashioned weapons with much older partners, where the sweat gleamed on his exceptionally well-toned body. Yeah, Kotori found it hard to believe that the young man wouldn't have an interest in girls, nor that he hadn't already tried a few.

He wanted to know what else the young man did and needed to employ an informant. He couldn't ask Pertak, because although he'd returned from his trip to the border regions, everyone in the Citadel knew Pertak and knew he was a spy.

So he hired a few youngsters who worked in strategic places in the Citadel and got them to report on what Harek was up to.

Which amounted to not much. He loved to practice his fighting skills—Kotori already knew that. He didn't frequent bars and none of the youngsters spotted him talking to girls. He liked horses, though, and he also appeared to be interested in sailing, especially on the new steam ships. The army had also taken delivery of a balloon, and Harek made sure he was invited to a demonstration.

But he said nothing untoward, not even to the very shapely female officer in charge of said balloon. How very boring.

Kotori even called in a friend of Pertak's, who had served in the royal guard when a few months back, Harek and Loriane and a few other young men and women had travelled to Chevakia to a meeting of mutual understanding—as they called it—of the youth who would have to work with each other once their generation took over power.

The attendants had included both Harek and Loriane, the sons and daughters of Chevakian senators and Prince Selinor of Peria.

And while the meeting of rich and high-powered Chevakian and Perian youngsters was ripe with possibility, the informant had no juicy stories about Harek either.

No, Harek might be enamoured with the stories about Denori, but the young prince wasn't like Denori at all.

He also didn't respond to Kotori's earlier offer to set up a discreet mothers' house with some well-chosen country girls whose fathers were writing letters to Kotori offering their daughters.

It was all very frustrating, and it was not as if Kotori had a lot of time to devote to this issue. The first lot of student exams were coming up, and while the administration of the exams was mainly in the hands of his assistants, Kotori was still in charge of coming up with the questions. And then dealing with the complaints that the questions were too hard.

Well, tough, he only wanted good students in his class.

In the old days, if you failed the class, you were out. Now he'd been asked to do remedial lessons for students who wanted to pay for them, and also students from the country, because their prior education was lacking.

And in addition to this, the annual update of the star map was due, and he spent many late nights and early mornings on top of the astrology tower.

He didn't like this as much as he used to, because after a lifetime of stargazing, he found that the nightly sessions left him feeling tired for a week.

And also because there was so much work that he hadn't yet completed that he had planned to do later in life. But that was not how things had worked out.

Instead of studying his favourite projects, like interference between star signs during certain times of the year, he'd had to rewrite the entire study book when he'd finally been forced to accept that the southern woman was right about the position of the world in the sky, that it went around the Mother and that the Mother and its many other children went around the sun. This very reluctant acceptance necessitated many changes to the descriptions and maps of the sky.

And now, Kotori was due to give a tutoring session in the observation of the stars.

Stargazing was one of the classes he still enjoyed giving, even though the schedule messed with his dinner time, which he found very important nowadays.

Kotori was setting up his equipment on the top of the tower in the dark, while the students came up.

He could already hear their voices in the stairwell, and to his annoyance, most of the students appeared to be female. Damn it, he hadn't looked at the list of attendees.

And indeed, when they came out into the open, there was a big bunch of girls which included, to his horror, the crown princess.

A few days ago, when he had met the students in the courtyard, he had told them to come to the session. He had never expected any of them to do as he said.

Loriane's face displayed the disdainful expression that she seemed to reserve especially for him. He wondered if she had come here specifically to laugh at him, or whether she hadn't realised that getting a class in stargazing would mean that she'd be taught by the court astrologer.

Well, he hadn't bargained for that.

There was always a chance that her mother had given her a talking to about studying subjects other than music, because the rumours went that her mother was equally despairing of the crown princess' lack of interest in serious subjects. But although her presence was a good development, right now it filled Kotori with despair.

He'd spent most of his younger years navigating the difficult waters around the royal family, and he wasn't keen to start this process again.

Loriane had come to the class with a group of her friends, and while Kotori searched very hard for a reason to refuse them from his class, reasons that included inappropriate dress or the absence of textbooks, he found none.

The Princess, of course, had never been to any of the previous stargazing sessions, and had attended only half of the lessons.

Because there were always *reasons* and he couldn't fail her for not attending, either. Because she was the crown princess.

He had often looked for other ways to fail her, but had also not been successful… She was one of these people who scored annoyingly well in study while appearing to do very little for it.

So he gritted his teeth, and continued to set up his telescopes while the students each found a seat in the small circle of benches surrounding the star map he had set up on an easel.

Of course, Kotori needed to make a light in order to see the map and talk about it.

The group contained eleven students, all of them from the older years. More than half of them he'd never seen on the top of the tower before.

During the first part of the lesson, he explained—in more detail than he'd do if only his regular students were in attendance—about all the star signs and other objects in the sky, the direction and speed that they moved, and he explained why it was necessary for him to redraw the star map every few years. The stars moved. The distance differences were very small, but they were big enough to be noticeable.

When he finished his talk without much in the way of questions from the students, he divided them into a couple of groups so that they could each peer through the telescopes.

The two boys wanted to be together, and he could sadly see no reason to separate the princess from her giggly friends.

He had given the students objects to search for, and they each had to draw their own map. Of course, the star map was not completely exhaustive, and he gave them the task to discover additional stars signs that they might want to mark.

Then one of the male students asked what defined a star sign, and he had to tell them about the register and how one could make a mark in astrology by discovering a new star sign.

Astrology was, after all, a highly interpretive business, and if you could discover a new star sign and have it properly named, you could have your name inscribed in the hall of fame of astrologers.

"Have you named any star signs?" the boy then asked.

"Twice," Kotori said. "I've named the rabbit and the bridge."

"I know the rabbit," one of the female students said. Kotori had seen her before in the stargazing sessions.

"You can just make up any star sign you like," Loriane said. "There are thousands upon thousands of stars in the sky and you can group them together in any way you please."

"No, you cannot. The meaning and intention of the star sign has to be divined. This is a long and complicated process and has to be done many times."

"Stars are flaming balls deep in the sky. They have no intentions. The just *are*."

There was that disdainful look again. And an extraordinary irreverence for an ancient art practiced by astrologers for thousands of years.

How dare she?

But she was the crown princess, so he turned away before he said anything that would get him into trouble.

"All right, class, let's get on with your observations, otherwise daylight will come before we're done."

While the students went to their spyglasses and studied the sky and drew the maps, Kotori circulated between the groups.

The night was rather chilly, and he wore his heavy astrologer's robe to keep him warm.

While he was talking to the group with the two young male students who were making all the mistakes that Kotori had seen before, another group started talking in excited voices. They weren't laughing and giggling as he half-expected—because they were girls—but were actually taking turns to look at the sky through the spyglass.

He went over for a look. The princess was in the group. The glow of the oil light danced over her book, where she had made an entire page of notes with calculations.

"Is anything the matter?" Kotori asked.

"We have just discovered something interesting," another female student said.

Kotori had seen her before, a lot of times in fact, because she was one of his most diligent students. And for the life of him, he couldn't remember her name right now.

She continued, "There is a little speck like a falling star that travels through the sky and makes a small blinking light."

Oh.

That.

No, seriously.

Kotori felt his heart sink.

He had first seen this strange phenomenon before the princess was born.

Over the past more than twenty years, he had developed a chart of when it would and could not be seen tracking through the sky. It was a highly regular occurrence, and he had as yet been unable to determine what it was.

He had no idea. Absolutely none at all.

Theory after theory had kept him busy, but none had made sense.

He'd tried the library, he'd tried casting his stones, he'd tried asking people in Chevakia or Peria. But it seemed he was the only one who saw it and knew about it. Or, he suspected, cared about it.

People in Peria would care, but he was sure that where they were, on top of the world axis, they couldn't see the blinking object in the sky at all. And the Chevakians were too busy arguing with each other. These days, the once-exalted Scriptorium just churned out lackeys who repeated statements by their predecessors.

Of course, Kotori didn't want to face the questions about the phenomenon before he had answers. He was supposed to know everything. But he didn't, and none of the feasible explanations, that it was a falling star, that it was a moon or anything like that, fitted with the object's behaviour. It moved too quickly to be very far away, it moved in the wrong direction to be a moon, and the blinking light puzzled him to no end.

And, what was more, it galled him that he had completely forgotten about this when scheduling this observation session.

He usually planned the class observation times when this particular phenomenon wasn't in the sky. And it had totally slipped his mind.

"Let me have a look." That was all he could think of saying, while his mind frantically searched for something to say that would satisfy the students.

He peered through the spyglass and found the object easily.

"What is it?" the girl asked.

"It is probably a falling star."

The focusing mechanism of the spyglass became slippery under his fingers from his own sweat.

Now the boys had also turned their telescope on the unknown object. One was even attempting to calculate where the falling star would come down.

That would lead nowhere. Kotori had tried that, much as he despised the calculations.

Then a student in another group shouted, "Oooh!"

"What? What?" Voices went up.

"Oh, did you see that flash?" the second male student said, looking through the spyglass. "Ooooh, look at that! It's now… Wait! There are two things!"

Kotori scurried to his own spyglass and struggled with trembling hands to point it at the object as it whizzed through the sky. He could see the original blinking object as it described its usual trajectory through the sky. And a second object, much smaller, tracking in an arc away from the original object.

As he watched, the blinking object flashed again, and another speck separated from it.

Kotori's heart thudded.

"Oh, it did it again! What is that?" someone called out.

"Did you see that astrologer?"

Yes, Kotori had seen it, and no, he didn't know what it was, and he didn't want to speculate about it. The regular speck of light kept going and would soon disappear behind the hills, but the smaller dots had slowed a lot. The latest dot had disappeared over the horizon with the object, but the first one was still visible in the sky.

He thought… no, it *was* slowly drifting down.

Possibly a piece breaking off the main object. But that would cause a bright flash, like a flashing star, and would travel much faster.

This was drifting down, like a balloon.

He had never mentioned anything about this thing, because he was supposed to *know* everything. And he was still hurting from being proven wrong by that southern woman, and he would certainly be wrong about anything he said. But also because the thing he suspected deep in his mind was too scary to contemplate. He'd not mentioned that to anyone except in his diary of observations.

And this very scary thing would also cause people to ask why he hadn't said anything before, and that would just lead to too many questions he couldn't answer. Because he was supposed to know everything and he didn't. He had staked his life's reputation on knowing the right things.

And he knew nothing. He'd made wrong prediction after wrong prediction. The people still listened to him, but they would soon find out how much of a fraud he was.

He was always wrong about everything, and one day, people would notice.

He had reached the age of eighty while pretending. He was very good at pretending.

But while the students were packing up to go to their dorms—and Kotori was very much looking forward to his bed—Loriane came to him with a sheet of paper ripped from her book.

"What's that?" he asked.

"Calculations. You can tell by the speed at which the blinking light travels through the sky how far up it is. If you know the angle where it broke off, you can calculate where it's likely to come down." She pushed the paper in his hands and followed her friends into the stairwell.

Kotori took the paper over to the light. By the glow of the dancing flame, he deciphered her loopy writing.

Everything about the calculations was perfect.

CHAPTER 17

The young man Lana employed to spy on Harek reported to her every day.

Harek spent a lot of time training with various weapons: swords, crossbows and even powder guns. He also visited friends in town, usually in an eating house. Lana asked if he drank spirits, and the young man said he wasn't sure, but if he did, he definitely hadn't drunk too much, if that was what she was asking.

As to who these friends were, the young man gave her names. They were very proper young men from decent families, and at least their fathers didn't support the old princes, most of whom she had managed to promote to regional posts or convinced to retire. Almost all of them, apart from that despicable Colonel Betaro.

The young man also reported that he had seen Harek at the markets meeting up with Kotori.

"What? Kotori? The astrologer?"

"The very one."

"What is he talking to him about?"

"I don't know. I couldn't get close because they walked to the harbour and spoke to each other in front of the wall of names. They only spoke for a short while and then they walked back. They didn't give each other anything. They weren't angry at each other. Kotori didn't take out his casting stones or cloth. Harek seemed to be surprised about something the astrologer said."

"Have you spoken to Kotori?"

"About this? No. I can hardly admit that I spied on him. I have no other reason to talk to him."

"Could you… find a reason to win his trust?"

"Maybe, but it would take time. He's not someone who trusts easily."

She heard the question he didn't ask in his voice: do you want me to continue following the prince or follow Kotori?

Kotori, who was full of trickery and would use the first available opportunity to sideline her, once Orik wasn't looking, or—she shuddered—if Orik died or became incapacitated.

She pushed away uncomfortable memories of Orik's older sons. Denori, Nayek, Sferuk and other violent and rude princes who called women fuckholes.

"All right. Just concentrate on my son for the time being." That was the important part, after all.

As for what to do about Loriane, that was both easier and harder.

Lana knew just who to ask to talk to her daughter about the importance of statecraft.

Along the strange path that Lana's life had taken, from the Proctor's daughter, a student, to a prisoner in the mothers' house in Kadrish, to the queen of Arania, she had met many people she respected.

Her father, the longest-ever serving proctor of Chevakia, had been one. Sadly, he was no longer alive.

Her mother, too, midwife and breeder, having fled from Peria and having learned many lessons in life the hard way.

But she had also died.

Lana had used her father in particular to teach her children in statecraft and diplomacy when he was still well enough to travel.

She had sent her children, and continued to send them, to events of importance where people from all three countries were present. In fact, Harek and Loriane had returned from a trade fair in Chevakia not that long ago. Now that Harek was fifteen, he showed signs that he was beginning to understand the importance of relationships across the border.

Loriane went to music-related events all the time, and she had many contacts, particularly in the City of Glass. She had been invited to play at a big concert there.

In the City of Glass lived someone she could use.

King Isandor of Peria had announced that he would step back from public duties and he would support his son, Prince Selinor. Like Arania had never had a queen, the Perian throne in the weirdly beautiful but cold City of Glass had not seen a king since the evil King Caldor, whose influence on the throne had died with his grandson.

She should ask Isandor to help her daughter, because Loriane would clearly no longer listen to her.

So she wrote a letter to the king, which she then went to the Citadel's mail office to deliver. These days, the mail office kept a few Perian gulls, along with the pigeons they used for fast mail to Chevakia. The slow mail went on the train. And it was slow because the freight needed to be unloaded and put on the ferry at the border and then onto a different train to Tiverius.

There was no train to Peria. The slow mail used boats.

The poor gulls didn't like the hot days in Kadrish. The two birds in the mail room were rather scruffy, even if also full of life, which they made known, loudly.

The mail boy said that they'd probably release both of them with Loriane's message, so that Peria would send some fresh birds.

After this rather relaxing detour to the mail house, Lana went back to her office. She had to attend a meeting of the king's council, a body inspired by the Eagle Knight council in the City of Glass. Because before she came, the king used to have absolute power and would rule alone, and not only did this mean that the citizens had no say, it was also far too big a job for one person, so this meant lots of worthy areas were neglected.

The council consisted, like the Chevakian doga, of representatives of the districts, but also the army, the library and the hall of commerce.

She counted herself lucky that she had managed to keep out that annoying astrologer, although many people said the astrology department should be represented, but she saw no place for men with fancy pieces of cloth and dice to have a say in the running of the country.

Orik used to come to this meeting, but having ruled as absolute monarch, he had little interest in meetings about minutiae, and these days, his failing health was a good excuse to let her run the show.

When she came to the room—which used to be an audience chamber—about half of the attendees were already there. She was pleased to see that Harek was also there. She had given him observer status recently. Whoever else he spent time with when he wasn't home, at least he'd see what responsible government looked like. She'd wanted Loriane to come, but as happened so often recently, Loriane was nowhere to be found.

She took her place at the table.

Harek in the corner held a notebook open on his lap.

He looked so much older than his fifteen years. Lana tried to remember what she did at that age, and didn't get much further than studying and talking to her friends about nonsense. Boys, probably.

The remaining people came in and she started the council meeting.

There were a range of issues to deal with. Sections of the harbour wall needed to be replaced after many years of faithful service.

A stonemason was found, and the business had given a quote. The work would take rather longer than anyone had envisaged because of "problems with the supply of the best quality sandstone from Chevakia."

The stone came from a quarry at the edge of the floodplain of the Aramys basin. There was, the stonemason had said, a shortage of workers because of some dispute over working conditions. And this affected the availability of good quality stone.

Then the military officer reported. This was a grey-haired but sharp-witted Major by the name of Ralek, who had held the position for years.

He reported that the military had contracted a business in Kadrish to make balloons for them after the delivery of an impressive proto-type. The military officer reported on the progress with this project.

"We got the initial balloons from Chevakia through a roundabout process by posing as a private operator, but these are civilian transport balloons and didn't have any military capability, such as to drop explosives from a height, and the machinery to calibrate when to drop the load. We had to develop that technology for ourselves. I've engaged some informants embedded in Chevakian military camps."

"That would be a difficult and dangerous task," Lana said.

"Not half as dangerous as you think. The Chevakian army is poorly disciplined and the soldiers are short of supplies most of the time. So if you offer what they need, whether that is food or clothing or tents or fuel, they will do business with you and let you into their camp."

"The Chevakian army is poorly supplied?" she asked.

"From what we can gather, they are, yes."

"But why? They used to run the biggest army in the world?"

"They found that once they defeated us, and since Peria became more interested in trade than in lobbing magic over the border, they had no need for a large army. It costs a lot of money. Also, maybe they found that once they had balloons, they didn't need so many troops on the ground?"

Another council member snorted. "I think it's plain old deca-dence. They still think they own the world."

Ralek interrupted. "Well, it may be that, but it's also for a good part because the internal fights have become nasty."

"Not nasty enough for people to pick up weapons," Lana said.

A chill went over her back. This was now the second time she heard about internal conflict in Chevakia. Her father would never have stationed poorly supplied troops near the border. Had they become so complacent?

"I've heard rumours otherwise," Major Ralek said. "I can't yet confirm any of these rumours with facts—"

"I can," said a clear, young voice in the corner of the room.

They all turned around.

It was Harek who had spoken.

Lana frowned at him. "You have information?" She stopped short of asking him if he was serious. She had allowed him to come because he should engage with the council and the people who were in it, who were all much older than he was.

"I have Chevakian friends. These are all people of my age or a bit older, old enough to be in the army. They say that there are people who support the proctor, because he lines their pockets, but there are also people who want more power to the regions. The doga doesn't like those people and is powerless against them, because many of them are young people, who haven't been listened to for many years. They want to have a say in running the country, and as punishment, they're being sent to army camps to do the doga's jobs so that they can't organise—"

"Chevakia has a national service," Lana said sharply. "They've always had a national service. Young men and women have to spend time to perform a duty for their country. They're not *being sent*."

"I know, but my friends are telling me that the terms are extended without agreements. The normal service is about a year. That's for common people because those with money can buy themselves out. You either go into the army, or you learn a craft or another skill. Then you get work and you get paid. But they're not doing that anymore. Now you have to work another year for free, and the young people are just not getting anywhere, because everything is so expensive, and places to live are too expensive, so they're poor and they're angry, so they join groups, like rebels or other things. And the doga sends the army to spy on them and report back to the proctor on what they're doing. That only makes them more angry. Then the military sends more people." He shrugged.

"That's a lot of speculation."

"It's not speculation. It's what they're doing. We have reports from trustworthy sources."

The people of the council eyed each other. No one quite knew what to say. Lana didn't want to dismiss this, because if he had this from people he'd met while he was in Chevakia, well, that was exactly why she'd sent him.

And she also did not want to give any space for the question *Is this a good time to send troops across the border?* to exist. She didn't *think* these men of the king's council would be interested in waging war, but to be honest, you never knew with Aranian princes who had lived through the times when they used to fight each other for the throne. And she didn't want to have anything to do with that.

"We need more information," she said.

They all agreed.

Major Ralek said that he would try to recruit more spies.

"We need information from places where there may be unrest. If we're following only what happens in the doga, we might miss a lot, if it's purely composed of the political class."

She didn't want to say "old guard" because many in the king's council were "old guard" too. She needed to keep the unity, even while Chevakia slid into chaos. *Especially* because Chevakia slid into chaos.

"I might have friends who can find out about this stuff," Harek said. "But to be honest, most of them are going to be scared, so they would need good provisions."

"Engaging spies costs money," Major Ralek said. "That's no surprise. We're prepared to pay."

Harek gave him a sharp glance, his eyes wide, his face beaming. "So, can I tell them?"

"If you're convinced these people will have value," Ralek said.

"They will."

Lana walked back to the family's royal quarters with Harek. Every time she stood next to him, she was reminded of just how much he had grown and how much he resembled Denori.

"It was useful that you met some friendly Chevakians while you were travelling," Lana said.

"Isn't that why you sent me?"

"It is, but no one knows how a meeting is going to turn out and who you'll end up talking to."

"No, it's not like that. If I go somewhere to find Chevakian friends, I will find Chevakian friends."

And there it was, just as she was starting to feel proud of him, the sign, if she needed reminding, that he was mingling with people who planted old-fashioned hardline ideas in his head. And he was past the time where he'd listen unconditionally to his parents.

He would never be happy to stand behind his sister. He would grab the throne, and slowly, the country would slide back to a place with feuding princes, where women lived in mothers' houses.

Even if her young spy could find no evidence that the prince behaved inappropriately in any way.

CHAPTER 18

When Tylve got up the next morning and ambled out of the kitchen into the living room with the porridge breakfast bowl in one hand, her normally pretty view over the town and harbour had morphed into a wall of white.

She could just make out the roof of the shed that stood in the backyard of the house behind hers, but everything else had vanished in the thick mist.

Boy, she was glad she wasn't out at sea today, because even though much of the fishing was done by following the currents, navigating in this weather could be interesting.

In this area where the warm water from the Aramys River met the cold current that brought plenty of fish down the coast, mist was often thick and hung around for days.

Tylve ate her breakfast and went back to the bedroom where she packed a small bag for a short trip. Then she went into town to the courier depot, owned by a family friend, where she borrowed a donkey. The beast was dopey and stood looking morose and dejected, with its head and ears down, while a stable boy decked the animal out with a waterproof cover and a saddle.

There were also two camels in the stable, sitting in that weird way with their back knees poking out. People called these *the ship of the desert*, but she preferred real ships. Or donkeys.

Not much later, she sat atop the donkey while it plodded along the main road out of town. The road was wide, nicely paved and well-maintained. It snaked up the side of the ridge amongst rocky outcrops and meadows, where small flocks of scruffy sheep with black legs and heads grazed.

The constant salt-laden wind from the ocean made it that no trees grew up here, and from the top of the ridge, you had a magnificent view over the wide mouth of the Aramys River and the ocean to the east. But not today, with all that mist.

Today, the view stretched little further than the fields surrounding the town, which were yellow with ripening grain. The farmers who lived on the outskirts of town had pretty houses painted white with blue gutters and windowsills.

On a sunny day, the fields would be bright green and the flowers by the roadside vivid with colour, but the misty weather rendered everything in shades of blue and grey.

Tylve crested the ridge and went down into the next valley. The mist cleared. There were more farms here, mostly with sheep and a few donkeys. Some farmers grew crops or had orchards full of apples.

All morning, she travelled through the valley.

The donkey's plodding pace was slow. The occasional truck passed her, usually filled with agricultural produce on the way to market. Drivers greeted her. They were all locals.

At the point where the road climbed out of the valley, she turned into a smaller track that went up the flank of the next ridge, covered with small stands of pine forest interspersed with orchards.

The further she climbed, the wilder the country grew, until the narrow, potholed and rutted road ended at an overgrown wall with a broken gate.

The magnificent house in the yard beyond had stood there for many years. It had seen better days, but in her life, she never remembered it other than derelict and in want of maintenance.

Maintenance that its elderly current owner wasn't interested in providing.

The fences were sagging, the paddocks were overgrown, and it was a long time since there had last been any livestock in the fields, so pine saplings grew in the grass and mostly hid the house from view of the road. A long driveway led to the house from the main road, a set of tracks that were well used, because the owner came into town.

The man owned a truck, one of the few in the region. That vehicle stood off to the side in a shelter with open sides that it shared with bales of hay that had lain there for years and were all overgrown with weeds.

The house was also connected to the telegraph network, and the line of poles that led to the house from the road was the only thing that looked well-maintained.

By the time Tylve reached the house, Nari had come to the veranda, a tall man with grey hair, startling brown eyes, wrapped in a long coat against the biting wind.

His eyesight was not what it had been, and he squinted against the light, shading his eyes with his hand.

He came down from the veranda when she dismounted from the donkey and landed stiffly on the puddle-dotted driveway. Ouch, her backside.

He came down the veranda steps. "Well, well, I didn't think I'd see you again so soon. Do you need another thing for your boat? I'm not travelling to Tiverius any time soon."

The last time he'd visited Tiverius, she'd given him money to buy one of those fancy new compasses for the cabin.

"No, I'm here for something else."

"I know. To bring me some good fish."

"I didn't bring any fish, either. I delivered the catch at the harbour, and haven't been paid yet."

She would often bring him fresh fish in an ice box, but that hadn't even crossed her mind.

"Oh?"

"I've come to ask for some advice."

He raised his eyebrows, and then his expression went serious. Nari, or Narinius han Samirian, had served as a senator in the doga in

Tiverius. He had been the local representative for many long years until his retirement. No one was sure about his precise family lineage, whether han Samirian was his real name, or whether "uncle", as Tylve knew him, was a Tiverian noble who had fallen in love with the district and had adopted the regional name later.

As town administrator, Tylve's father had welcomed him, and treated him as an uncle, and that was what mattered.

This had all happened when Tylve was too young to realise. When her mother was still alive.

After tying up the donkey and providing it with hay, Tylve followed him up the veranda into the house.

The house was like a museum of times past, full of knick-knacks Nari had collected over his long and unmarried life. He preferred beautiful things over beautiful people, he had once told her. You could never trust beautiful people, but beautiful things spoke of a rich history that you could relate to future generations.

As usual, he spent most of his time on the back veranda of the house, overlooking the valley and peeping between dips in the ridge, to the ocean.

The wind was cold here, but he didn't seem to mind. In her experience, old people came in two types: those who were always cold, and those who never were.

Of course, before they could go outside, tea needed to be made in the old kitchen with its granite benches, racks full of implements and spices and jars of produce from the garden. But eventually, Nari and Tylve sat on the back veranda, draped with rugs on his sturdy hand-made bench, facing a metal container that glowed with a lusty fire. At their side lay firewood stacked up to the ceiling.

The grove of orange trees out the back was well and truly overgrown, and the birds were feasting on the oranges that had fallen to the ground.

Nari would just wander around every day and pick some oranges and make juice out of them for himself.

A bunch of chickens scratched at the bottom of the steps.

Steam rose from the tea.

Tylve told him of all the things that had happened in the past few days, from her discovery of the dead man to the visit to town by the guards and the raids and rumours of other misbehaviour. Nari raised his eyebrows several times during the story about the temple raid, but he said nothing, so she finished. After that, she dug the neck band and the other strange device from her pack.

He whistled slowly by breathing air into his pursed lips. "Where did you find this man again?"

"On the island where I go to read the barygraph. It's called the Island of Skulls. That name only means something to fishermen, though. I don't know that it has an official name. It's very small and rocky and full of noisy, pooping birds."

"Why skulls?" he asked.

"Sea lion skulls. My father always told me that when his father came to the beach, there would be a bunch of skulls left over from a bad fight between the males."

And she told him how she had found the man and the crates with the little tubes and the sail that lay ripped on the rocks above high tide level, that looked like it could be part of a balloon, because there was no sign of a boat. Also that she couldn't believe the man would have been alone. With each word, his frown deepened. He shook his head when she suggested the man might have fallen down from a wayward balloon.

"I get the reports from balloon flights in this area. There have been none as recent as in the last two weeks. Remember that only the Chevakian army uses balloons and to be honest, this coast has never caused any issues that justify sending the army, and Tiverius is in far too much turmoil right now to worry about us."

"Turmoil?"

"Argh." He lifted his hands. "Just stupid machinations of politicians that are unimportant for us here. The decadent systems eating each other. People worrying about scandals and corruption rather than governing the country."

Nothing new, then. "What about the Aranians?"

"If they have balloons, which I doubt, they would have had to come all the way around the coast. We would have heard about it. Inefficient as they are, Tiverius would never allow that."

"But then if he didn't come in with a balloon, how did that guy get all the way up there?"

"Could he climb?"

"Yes, but not from that side. There is only one access point to the barygraph, and it is from a beach around the corner. It's a narrow path and you have to know where it is. Supposing he washed ashore where the sail was, there is no way he could have walked around the island to get to that beach."

"Could he swim?"

"You'd be smashed against the rocks in the calmest of weather. The weather hasn't been calm. It's just been… normal, which means it would have been rough. I never come close to those rocks in the boat. It's that treacherous."

"Did he have anything else on him that gives us a clue of where he's from?"

"Nothing except this collar and this strange thing. It flashed when I pressed this button."

"This one?" He pointed.

"No, don't touch it. I don't know what it does."

He picked up the device and studied it, a frown on his face. He turned the device over, weighed it in his hand, and ran his finger along the side.

"A flash, you said?"

He held a slender index finger, clean-skinned and much more sophisticated than her rough hands, over the button. He pushed it down gently.

Nothing happened.

"Hmmm." He pressed again. Nothing again. "It's very well-made, but it doesn't appear to work."

Tylve felt uncomfortable. "It could be related to lightstream."

"Could be. The sonorics levels are really low here."

That's what he thought. But Tylve could feel the prick of lightstream in the air even here, but she had known all her life that not everyone could feel this. And it was best not to talk about it.

He picked the neck band up, weighed it in his hand and turned it over. He studied it for a while, and then he shook his head and put both items down.

"I haven't seen anything like this. It's very well-made, but I have no idea who made it."

"I thought it might be some of that really old stuff that people find and collect up north. That the collectors pay lots of money for? That maybe this man was working for the collectors and maybe they found some valuable things and didn't want anyone else to know."

"I don't know. I've seen some of that stuff and this looks more recent to me. Newer, more modern. Those things that we find and we put in collections, they're usually not as complete and flawless as this, and nobody uses them for anything in daily life. If there are dials or buttons, they're usually rusted and don't work."

"But there were the lightstream machines in the south. The ones that the doga copied to make the lighstream shields."

He gave her a disturbed look. Yes, there were those. The network of machines along both coasts of the continent that kept the land safe from the harmful effects of lightstream. The Chevakian ones were very new, having been built less than twenty years ago according to an old design, because the original machines had been destroyed long ago because no one understood what they were for until the feeble defence mechanism failed. There was a machine in Samira, but it stood on an island immediately off the coast, because the building and the area around it were dangerous.

"Maybe this device was left behind by the Perians who made those machines when they were last here."

"That's possible, but not likely. I've worked with them, and they didn't have things like this."

"But what about the ancient things that people find in Peria? This man could have been one of these people who collects these things. Maybe even he was looking for this." A thought occurred to her: "It could be that there are secret places on the offshore islands where people find these artefacts."

"Could be." He fingered his lip. "But I don't know. I would think that locals would be in the best place to find stuff like that. If there are artefacts to be found on that island where you go, then your family would have found them, right?"

Tylve shrugged, looking at the thing on the table. "I never looked for anything like this. I wouldn't know where to start. The salt spray destroys everything that's in the open and on the island, there are no places to hide out of the weather. I had to get a pretty special barygraph cage to make sure the machine could do its job."

"See? That is important local information."

Tylve didn't know what to think, but it was clear to her that Nari didn't know what to think either.

They contemplated what the purpose of this thing might be, but didn't come up with any useful answers.

While they were talking, the sun went down over the mountain ridge. For a brief moment, the sky turned brilliant orange.

Then it quickly got dark, and they went inside to prepare the evening meal. Nari was a meticulous and excellent cook, and his land provided everything he needed.

During the meal, Tylve spoke about the guards visiting town, and Nari agreed that their behaviour didn't match what he knew about the men who came from Tiverius. And having worked in the doga building, he had a lot of useful experience.

"The Tiverian guards don't behave like that. They're taught to be respectful, to always have official documentation before searching private houses. Of course, there are occasional exceptions, but no patrol leader would condone the type of behaviour that you described from this unit without doing something about it. They definitely don't attack people, let alone take girls into the backyard and have their way with them—"

"I don't know the full truth about that story. I don't want to discount it, but I also haven't been able to verify it."

"No, but still. Something inappropriate likely went on there, and proper guards would not even have given anyone the suspicion that something like this happened."

"So, are you saying they're fake guards?"

He hesitated.

"Fake is a big word I wouldn't use without seeing them, but at the very least, I'd question their orders and their leader. Were they all in proper uniform?"

"Yes. There seemed to be men from two different units, though."

"What did their uniforms look like?"

Tylve described them as best as she remembered.

Nari shook his head. "Definitely not proper guards. By the sound of things, only half of them were wearing proper attire. The grey shirts are only training wear. They would never wear those while questioning citizens."

"They did all have insignia on them."

"So they would, but no, those grey shirts are not official wear. To me it sounds like they could only get their hands on a certain number and certain type of uniform, and they didn't know the significance of each outfit. If someone would raid the uniform depot, they would find a lot of those grey shirts because the soldiers wear them a lot. Just not outside the barracks."

"So why did they disguise as guards? Could they perhaps be looking for this dead man?"

"Maybe, but if these people are smart enough to have this technology, why didn't they know they have to look at sea?"

That was a very good question. They just didn't know enough about what this thing was, how old it was, and where it came from.

While they sat at the enormous table eating dinner—with more than half the table taken up by half-finished carvings out of olive wood that had occupied much of Nari's time recently—he told her of people he knew who might know more about her strange find. These people were studying the old civilisation that had built the light-stream machines that kept the world safe. There was a man named Javes, who was an administrator up north, who had a vast collection, and one very important scholar was King Isandor of Peria. He gave her ways to contact both.

The sky after sunset was deep red and orange, a sign that more bad weather was on its way. Tylve was glad that she had brought her rain coat.

After sitting by the fire with a glass of excellent wine, Tylve went to sleep in the guest room. She was still not sure what she should do, or whether she even wanted to become involved. In her experience, any time she put up her hand, she ended up shunned and ignored by authorities because she was a Samiran of the Gathering. People wouldn't believe her. They wouldn't take her seriously. She was just so tired of trying. She just wanted to go fishing and not have to worry about annoying people.

CHAPTER 19

*R*avi had never heard of this Gathering youth movement, and yet it sounded like something everyone knew about. That was one of the disadvantages of not being allowed anything. That things that all the kids did passed him by and that he looked dumb as a result.

When it was time to leave the office to go home with his father, he put the three letters about the missing children on a separate pile and gave them to Marlo.

"I think someone should at least investigate what's going on with this," he said.

Marlo leafed through the documents. An expression of distaste ever so slightly flickered over his face. "It's not in the doga's power to do much about. I doubt the proctor is interested in replying to those petitions himself."

"But children are missing. Should the proctor not prefer to address the petitions with the greatest urgency rather than the ones that…"

He was going to say *make him look good*, but that would be uncharitable.

To him, worrying about young people going missing, especially if there was a pattern, became a matter of urgency.

But clearly, the established politicians didn't care much because *there were plenty of protections*. True, but only for people with money. And also, *Young people always find ways around the rules to do what they want*. Which was also true.

But he still didn't like it. Those letters were genuine in a way the correspondence from professional petitioners was not.

Later, at training, he asked Keran if he knew about the Gathering movement.

"Yeah, all the younger kids are in it. They like going to the gatherings because it gets them out of the house."

"What do they talk about?"

"Doing things differently, you know... Getting a chance to do something with their lives. Their parents own everything and everything is expensive. It might be different for you..."

"For me? Why?"

"Because your parents obviously have money."

Was it that obvious? Yes, he led a sheltered life, but even he could feel frustration at having nowhere to go. "It sounds like it would be an interesting kind of movement."

"Yeah, no wonder people leave their families behind."

"Leave their families behind?"

"Yeah, kids go to join the camps, but they're not always asking their parents for permission. Or their parents don't give it, and the kids leave anyway. It's common."

"How do you know about that?"

"You just told me."

"There were only three cases. I don't know if this is what's happened, that they joined this movement." Although the long and messy letter had suggested it.

"It's pretty clear, though. I know of some others. The young kids leave because there is nothing else for them to do that seems to have any—you know—point to it."

"Seriously, you know of other people who have disappeared? Here in Tiverius?" The letters had all come from the regions.

"I wouldn't call it disappeared. They chose to leave with the organisation. They organise travelling camps or something. Kids I know who went asked their parents, and they were fine with it, but maybe those people you heard about didn't tell their parents because their parents didn't agree or would never let them go. It's only for a year, they say, so yeah, the people I know left, but there wasn't a big—you know—stink about it because their families knew."

That conversation kept repeating itself in Ravi's memory while he walked home.

Barely a day went by where he didn't consider his own futile existence that did nothing except prove to him and his father that he was *just a young guy* who needed *honest experience*, without being paid for it, of course, while not being able to do all the things his father had done at the same age: move into a house of his own, get married and get a decent job.

Heck, anything that offered a way out seemed attractive to *him* and he was supposed to be educated and rich.

He wondered what those people did while they were away. He must ask Dana. She seemed to know a lot about it.

In the library the next day, he looked over all the other students who were there. Young people, at least thirty of them, studying politics and history. Since they started the course, no one had spoken to them about the types of things they'd do when they finished their studies. Whether there were even things to do for them when they finished. They just innocently assumed they'd be given jobs. Well, they might be, but were they going to be paid for it? His father still hadn't mentioned payment when they came home last night. Ravi was sure his father would rather forget about it. So if there was a group that offered something better in this slow-moving, empty husk of a city that offered nothing except bureaucracy and working for free, why wouldn't young people take it?

Did the generation of his parents know that many younger kids were taken with this group?

What did they call it again? Gatherings?

Something bothered him about that name in the back of his mind. Dana said this new movement was a resuscitation of the reclusive Samiran sect.

And there was something eerie about this group.

Not too long ago, he had written an essay about the life and habits of the fishermen in the wide inlet that was the mouth of the Aramys River. It had mentioned that many of them belonged to this sect.

He knew where in the library to find the very heavy and thick book with beautiful illustrations of the different costumes and building styles of the smaller communities in Chevakia.

The library was a valid reason for him to be out of the house, so he went in on his way back, and climbed up to the second floor where the rare volumes were held.

He leafed through the heavy pages until he came to the one he remembered.

Samira.
The fishing village Samira at the mouth of the Aramys River services both the fishing ports along the coast and the agricultural hinterland. A well-developed road leads from Samira inland.
The village's claim to fame is that it is the origin and currently only known home of the Samiran Gathering sect and the home of its only dedicated temple. This ancient Samiran culture dates back from before the formation of Chevakia as a country. The fishermen would go out to sea during the day and would gather in the temple at night to discuss their affairs. The gatherings are places where truth should always be spoken, and where those who are on the receiving end of complaints always be given an opportunity to respond.
The Samiran culture is so old and so reclusive that a few of the original families—although it's not known how many there are left—retain the ability to shape sonorics rays, an ability they have likely inherited from their forefathers in Peria. They call this lightstream.
The Samirans believe that lightstream is a manifestation of death. They believe lightstream connects them to the after world. Their culture includes ceremonies where they deliberately contaminate a victim with the rays so that they can speak with the dead with this person as a conduit.

The doga considers the Samiran culture as a marginal group. They have directed several schemes at the group, including an employment scheme that seeks to scatter the group over the country. They consider the group a low-level threat against the country.

Was this really the same movement? The way Keran and Dana spoke about it sounded much more attractive.

How long ago was this written?

Dana had said that there had been a revival of the sect, but hadn't said anything about sonorics. That was because, thanks to the protective network of machines, they didn't have to worry about the harmful rays anymore.

Years ago, sonorics killed a lot of people when there was a large explosion in the City of Glass in far southern Peria, and a poisonous cloud had come over the border. All children learned about this terrible period in history at school.

So, the fishermen of the coast could shape the rays, like some Perians could? That might be because they were the only ones who could go out on the ocean and come back alive, especially in the old days, when the network of devices that repelled sonorics was not strong.

Ravi had an afternoon class to attend at the Scriptorium—it was all about the history of the Aranian wars—and the tutor gave the students lots of homework.

Then Ravi had to go home to prepare for his Aranian tutor and he barely had the time to think about anything other than his upcoming exams.

Walking out of the Scriptorium, he saw that the recent exam results were up on the board.

His mark for his assignment about the fishing village came back really good, so clearly he was not half as stupid as he'd felt the last few days.

But Aranian was another matter altogether. There were just so many verb forms that depended on the gender and status of the speaker. The book his tutor used to teach from was really old-fashioned. It still spoke of Aranian women belonging in mothers' houses. Ravi was pretty sure that the forms of language taught were also on the conservative side. The tutor was older than his father. That might have something to do with it. Also, he understood that many older men had fled Arania after King Orik abolished the mothers' houses—fearing retribution and scorn from the women. So yeah, probably his Aranian tutor was cut from the same cloth as his father: happy with the old ways and in no hurry to hand over power to the younger generation.

THE NEXT DAY, Ravi worked in the doga's mail office again.

For once, the proctor appeared to be in the office when Ravi came up the stairs, past the long line of waiting petitioners. He could clearly hear the proctor's voice drifting from the room.

A man sat in one of the row of seats outside the door. Ravi had seen this man in the building before. He was an assistant from the treasury department.

As Ravi came up the stairs, the secretary crossed the foyer with a stack of documents and went into the proctor's office. While crossing the foyer, Ravi caught a glimpse of the proctor's softly carpeted office with its wood panelling and velvet-covered chairs.

For the rest of the morning, Ravi worked in the mail room with Siman, Marlo and Dana. Some responses to the invitations to the official opening of the year had come in, and Marlo dealt with those.

But he also learned that overnight some scandal had blown up about a senator of the Ensar district who was said to have given his wife's family business the first choice of government contracts for road maintenance. Several other building contractors were very unhappy about this and they had encouraged people in the district to write about this.

This meant Siman, Dana and Ravi had more mail to open and sort.

Oh, joy.

All morning, Ravi opened and read petitions.

As before, most correspondence followed clear formats and standard language that made it clear the petition had been sent in by a hired petitioner.

But he came across four more letters that mentioned missing children or *an evil group drawing our children away from us*. The other three letters which he had opened two days ago still lay on the long bench that lined the wall as he had left them, but the secretary had been in to pass the other stacks to the relevant departments.

However, as Marlo said when Ravi asked about it, the justice department would only act on citizen requests if the citizens went into an office. Petitions were only for departments that did not have offices. You could report a crime to the local guards, and they would act. There was no obvious place for citizens to complain about the state of the local bridge.

So, why hadn't they, and why did he now have seven letters that mentioned missing children, all of them adolescent or young adults?

He could only assume that the people *had* reported it, and not enough was done. In fact, two of the responses specifically mentioned this.

So he asked Marlo if he knew anything about the Samiran movement or Gatherings, as some people called them.

Marlo gave him a puzzled look. "That's something for people of your age."

The fact that he knew what it was meant he *had* heard of it.

"I'm hearing a lot of stories of people who have left and not contacted their parents."

"Young people do that, sometimes."

Yes, but… "Do the parents usually write a petition about it?"

"Sometimes, they do."

"And what do you then do with those petitions?"

"We can't do anything, as I've already said—"

"Even if the letters all appear to point in the direction of the same group?"

Marlo stared at him, several emotions crossing his face. Annoyance, that Ravi was keeping him off his work, disbelief that something like that would really be happening, indifference, because *young people do that all the time.*

And Ravi was suddenly consumed by an overpowering rage. He didn't know where it came from. The frustration of being made to do so much *work*, without payment, without recognition, without promise of a future reward, while the older generation sat on the wealth, the houses and the opportunities, and they didn't even understand what was happening. They didn't understand why young people felt pressed to leave their families and do... goodness knew what with these mysterious groups that... who knew what was behind them. And they didn't care, because it was *something that young people did.*

"Right."

He pushed himself up from his desk. His legs trembled.

While the others in the room stared at him, he picked up the four letters he'd put aside. He went to the long bench against the wall and added the other three letters from two days ago to the pile, then he strode out of the mail room.

There was no one in the corridor, but people were at work in the offices and many doors were open.

"Ravi," Marlo called behind him. His voice sounded mildly alarmed.

Ravi strode into the high-ceilinged foyer.

"Ravi, what are you doing?"

He could sense that people had come out of office doors to look at him. Maybe even his father was watching.

He didn't *care.*

The secretary at his desk in the large foyer looked up. "I'm sorry, what is going—"

Ravi strode past him.

Two men sat on the row of chairs next to the proctor's office. Ravi had seen both of them in the building before. Old men, who played by all the stuffy rules.

"Excuse me, young man, what are you doing?" the secretary called behind him.

"I have something the proctor should see."

"The proctor is busy—"

Ravi opened the door to the office.

He had never been inside the proctor's office. It was a large circular room with its own ceiling dome. A large desk stood in the middle of the floor, and a couple of velvet-covered chairs stood near the hearth to the right.

The proctor himself stood by the window in the company of a man Ravi didn't know, but who wore a military uniform.

A tray with tea and cakes stood on the table.

Both men looked around when Ravi burst in, the military man surprised, the proctor irritated.

"What's the meaning of this? Wait—aren't you Gerinius' son?"

"My name is Ravi, and I work in the mail office for work experience." He found it necessary to add that last bit of information, lest the proctor think that working in the mail room was his life's ambition.

"And why are you disturbing our meeting?"

"Because you have to read these letters that say that young people are leaving their families and have been going to a movement they call the Gathering, and this has been happening all over the country. People are dismissing it as just young people doing what young people do, but I don't think anyone has any idea what is happening to young people in Chevakia."

"What is happening? Do you think that is worth disturbing my meeting about important military matters?"

"Yes, it's important, and also for the military. The young people have no hope. No hope for decent positions and for living independently. Everything we do is a lesser version of what you did when you were young. We're told to study, but there is no money, or will, to properly pay us when we've finished. People in town are making use of that despair to get young people to sign up for the military. What for? To put down rebellions in other parts of the country? Governments don't use their own military against their own people. No one wants to do that. So what do the young people do? They find other groups, like this Gathering. And their parents don't agree because they don't understand what's going on. That we have no hope. No jobs to go to. Not enough money to start out on our own. That's what's going on. It's not about a few people who went missing, it's about all those who have lost hope and sign up with the first group, violent, foreign or otherwise, that comes to their door. It's about the future of Chevakia. We used to be a nation of builders and makers of things. Of inventors who would employ workshops full of engineers. But what can we do? Work for free to *gain experience* or sign up for the army to fight our own countrymen."

Ravi's voice had risen while he spoke and now needed to catch his breath.

Now not only the proctor and the military man but also the secretary and a group of other people, including his father, had come to the door and watched him with wide eyes. His father's expression was horrified.

The proctor's face was red. He slowly turned to Ravi.

"I think, young man, that you have entirely too high an opinion of yourself. Work experience, right? You know that it is an extreme privilege to work here? That many kids would be lining up for the opportunity you've been given?"

"The opportunity to not pay me for work I do? To use me to open the mail. I could have done that straight out of school. I wouldn't have needed to waste years at the Scriptorium for that. But I don't ask much. All I ask is that the doga takes the disappearance of these young people seriously, and tries to understand why young people are all signing up for things like this, like the army, like anyone who offers them something useful to do. That's all I ask."

"I think, young man, you need to be taught the value of respect for your elders."

CHAPTER 20

Trini didn't come to dinner.

Javes, Saree and Mindo sat at the table in the courtyard where Saree brought out dinner and they discussed the local gossip.

About the impending expansion of her family, Saree was pragmatic. The world belonged to the new generation, and she didn't particularly care for institutes like marriage and official families. She said she hoped it was a boy, because living with just women in the house was boring.

Javes didn't think Trini was so down to earth. He thought he could hear her crying inside the house, and when he left and walked past a window, there were the distressed and disturbing sounds of repeated vomiting.

He went back and asked Saree to check on her daughter, but she remained pragmatic.

"She'll be fine. No, she don't want this child, but once it's outta her, she'll be fine."

He and Mindo slept in the tent. Mindo had shown no sign of having been here before, and Javes was pretty sure that Trini was mistaken. Whitesands Creek was a long way from where he had found Mindo. There was no way Mindo had been strong enough to walk that distance without animals.

Javes didn't sleep very well, because his mind churned. Those strangers coming to town, holding gatherings with the young people, that also happened in Ysherra. He wondered if those young people, too, were told to go to these camps and if those girls, too, were violated by the men there.

Tali's son Renko had once mentioned the movement, but had never followed up on it. Either he had decided he was too busy with the camels—Javes had promised that he could keep money he earned from the animals he looked after—or they had decided he was too Aranian for them, because Renko looked painfully like the Aranian soldier father who had raped Tali when she was just thirteen and whom Javes had never seen.

Either way, Javes should perhaps have looked into this group, and he hadn't.

He must have fallen asleep eventually, because he woke up suddenly to see that the light had turned pale blue and that Mindo's mat was empty.

Well, damn.

Javes scrambled from the tent into the cool morning.

It was still some time before dawn. The sky was pale blue and skeins of mist hung over the sides of the valley. Not a leaf moved on the olive trees.

All the camels, including his own and Saree's camels, were still asleep.

He couldn't see Mindo anywhere. He'd probably gone to relieve himself. But then he noticed footsteps on the ground cover of the scattered dew-covered plants, leading away from the house, down the hill towards the other houses in the hamlet.

Well, that was certainly interesting.

There was no sign of life in the house, so Javes followed the dirt track past the neighbour's house. At this point, the road crossed Whitesands Creek, an expanse of sandy bogs with some rocks and vegetation, considered by some to be the head of the great Aramys River.

Javes had never come here when there hadn't been at least a tiny bit of water, but a great river, it definitely wasn't.

On the other side of the sandy creek bed, across the ford, stood the town's telegraph box. Mindo had opened it and was doing something inside.

Well… that was interesting.

Mindo wouldn't try to use the telegraph box if he didn't know its purpose, and he wouldn't try to use it if he had no one to contact.

After a while, he shut the box and walked across the ford, stepping carefully from rock to rock across the water. In the middle, he stopped and flung a small object—a rock or piece of wood—into the water.

Javes hid behind the wall of a shed when Mindo came back up the bank. He didn't look happy.

While Mindo trudged back up the road, Javes ran through the field and came up on the other side of the tent when Mindo returned. Mindo didn't attempt to explain what he'd tried to do. Javes didn't tell him what he'd seen.

He would have to ask about this in Ysherra, because the Whitesands Creek line was a recent extension of the Ysherra telegraph line. Could the telegraph office see everything that came through? He thought so.

Now he doubted everything Mindo had tried to tell him. Damn, he wanted to go home to Ysherra and let the district law enforcement take this man off his hands.

Saree provided a breakfast of flatbread and jam in the yard of the house under the olive tree.

Javes asked about Trini, but Saree said her daughter was still asleep.

The sun was fast rising, and they had a long day of travel ahead, and there was still some camel business to be done.

Javes and Mindo were underway again when the sun angled low over the landscape.

It was several days later in the evening when Javes, Mindo and the camels returned to his hometown of Ysherra.

"Here it is," Javes said when they crested the ridge, which offered a view over the town. "It's not much, but the place grows on you."

In fact, the town was already much bigger than when he'd first come here.

Ysherra was a proper regional town now.

Javes was always happy to come home after being away in the field, seeing the familiar blocky houses surrounded by olive groves and fields of golden grain or stubble, depending on the time of year.

The last part of the trek home had been as uneventful as it had been frustrating.

After having seen Mindo use the telegraph box, Javes had been reluctant to share anything else, because this man had a secret, and Mindo hadn't volunteered any information about himself other than that he couldn't speak the language, and, well, Javes just didn't believe that anymore.

Javes had in fact contemplated whether, once they arrived in Ysherra, he should put Mindo on the bus to Watya or whether he should take him to the guard station to be investigated for potential crimes.

Javes' house lay on the top of the hill overlooking the town, surrounded by paddocks, in which his breeding stock of camels grazed happily.

He was glad to see that the young animals were coming along fine after he had separated them from their mothers. Some of these animals were almost ready to be sold at the markets. They were nice animals, healthy looking and plump.

He spotted one of his stable hands rolling out bales of hay. Everything was going well at home, and yet he couldn't shake the uneasy feeling that had plagued in the past few months. The world was changing, and he wasn't quite sure whether it was for the worse or the better.

A child's voice rang out. "Daddy!"

Lissa came running down the driveway with her arms spread wide.

Javes swept his daughter up in a hug. But her eyes widened when she saw Mindo.

She turned to Mindo. "Why did you bring back that man?"

"It's a long story. Let's go inside and I'll tell it to you and mama. Is Renko home?"

"Yes. He sold a camel yesterday, and he was very happy. He promised to take me on the train to Watya. Now he's got money."

Javes let himself slide from the camel's saddle. They walked up the long driveway.

Renko was in the camel shed. He waved.

"Where is mama?" Javes said.

"Inside. There is a man in the kitchen talking to her."

Turning into the yard of his house, he noticed the truck that stood parked in the yard. It belonged to the district administrator, who made a regular trip from Watya in the vehicle. Half the time Javes thought he only used the vehicle to show off, but the kids in town enjoyed looking at it and maybe one day the town would have a fuel station or a place where these vehicles could be maintained.

The man himself, and a couple of travel weary and dusty companions, sat in the large kitchen of the house.

Tali sat at the end of the table, with all the books on the table. She was very capable of dealing with town matter matters in his absence but Javes didn't miss the relieved expression when he entered the room.

"We were just talking about you," the administrator said.

"Well, I'm lucky, then, because you might have made bad gossip." It was a thing that townsfolk said.

He came into the kitchen while Mindo remained at the door.

"Who is the visitor?" Tali said.

"It's a strange story." And he told them in a few sentences where he'd found Mindo.

"And he doesn't understand any Chevakian at all?" Tali said. "That is just so strange. Even the kids in Arania learn some. Especially those who study."

"That's what he says." He left the unspoken—that he doubted it— hang in the air. Tali would understand.

They all sat at the table with the others.

The cook went around with tea and sweet bread, and for a while, talk was about the town's administrative matters. The northern district council had notified Javes a while back that they planned to send a team of technicians to maintain the telegraph line. Those people would soon arrive and the town would need to provide the materials for them to use as well as accommodation.

Throughout the discussion, the administrator kept glancing at Mindo, whose face remained blank during the discussions. He looked out the window, where over the years, Javes had built a courtyard with nice pavers, a place to sit in the cooling evenings by the light of oil lamps whose smoke kept the insects away. Through the bushes on the other side of the courtyard, a small path led into the olive grove, which Javes had planted, and where the trees were now big enough to deliver a healthy crop.

Then the meeting was finished, all the items dealing with the upcoming telegraph line maintenance dealt with, and the visitors got up, ready to go back to their vehicle.

In the hallway, on the way to the door, the administrator said to Javes, "It's a very strange situation with this man. What do you plan to do with him?"

"Part of me was hoping he'd figure that out for himself, to show us where he came from so that we can send him back, but…"

The administrator looked at him, and he looked back, and nodded. "Tell me if there is anything I need to know." Javes jerked his head at the kitchen, where Mindo had remained at the table. "Has there been news about an escaped criminal?"

"No, but I've had a bit of news about young people enticed away from their families. The older folk are pretty unhappy about this, because often it involves the next generation working on a farm."

Javes' mind immediately went to Trini's story. "Any reports of mistreatment in those groups?"

"Not that I've heard."

Javes then told him about Trini.

The administrator let a heavy silence pass. He was clearly worried about something. Then he said, "Thank you. I'll get into contact with Whitesands for more information. Until we have a formal complaint, we can't do anything. She said your stranger was one of those people?"

"She did, but I don't know how he would have been involved, seeing as at the time, he was starving and desperate many days' travel away from Whitesands."

"It takes months between a violation of a woman and the birth of the resulting child."

True.

That thought chilled Javes. Had he unknowingly brought Trini's violator back to her? No. She had never said that Mindo *was* the man, just that he belonged to the same group.

Now he regretted not asking Trini more.

He'd pass it onto the guard station, but he also doubted that they could do much, because they usually had their hands full with other stuff: neighbour disputes, camel theft, fence line creep and things like that. He doubted they'd have time to travel to Whitesands to talk to someone who might not want to talk.

"What do you want me to do with him?" he asked.

The administrator shrugged. "Without evidence, we can't investigate or charge him with anything. He might simply have forgotten who he is. That happens sometimes."

"Can he work?" Tali asked behind him.

Javes said, "He seems to get on well with the camels, but I don't think he has ever worked with animals before. I could offer him some work on the farm for the time being, or until we know what else we can do with him. But someone would have to watch him."

"I can do that," Renko said. "He can eat with us. He can work in the stables. I'll tell everyone to keep an eye on him. There is enough work to be done to keep him busy."

"Keep him away from the house and the office and keep him on the farm. Don't let him go into town without company and keep him away from Lissa."

"We don't have the facility to stop him from doing any of those things," Tali said. "I'd prefer if you could take him to the guard station. I don't want him anywhere near Lissa."

"The guard station can't take him without a formal charge," the administrator said. "But, I assume you're planning to attend the northern council meeting in Watya. You could bring him and we'll take him off your hand then."

"That's weeks away. You could do it now."

"Yes, I could. It'd be crowded in the truck, and I'd want to bring a guard. I think it would be better if you found a solution locally before that time. He'll probably start talking and might remember what happened to him and where he lives. He's more likely to come from here than Watya. I'm sorry. If you're still at a loss about what to do with him when you travel to Watya, and he shows no sign of wanting to return to wherever he came from, bring him. We'll give him a house in the Aranian quarter."

Javes nodded, and then the administrator walked back to his vehicle and left. Javes and Tali watched the vehicle putter down the driveway.

Javes sighed. "I'm sorry," he said to Tali.

"You did the right thing," she said.

Javes sighed. "I don't know what else I should have done. He would have died out there. I don't know if he did anything bad to anyone. I feel stupid for having taken him through Whitesands. Trini should not have felt threatened about something I did."

"You're a good man. I'm sure that if people want to judge you, you'll be judged on the goodness of your heart. You didn't know, and we still don't know who he is and what he did. But he is a human being and deserves to be treated as one."

They went back into the kitchen, where Tali asked Renko to take Mindo to the workers' quarters and give him everything he needed to be comfortable. He told Renko to treat Mindo as if he understood Chevakian, and if by chance he didn't understand, he'd learn pretty soon.

They shared an evening meal and put Lissa to bed. She was very excited because she would start school soon and her paper and colourful pencils lay on the table in the corner of her room like prized objects.

Then Javes and Tali shared a drink in the courtyard. They sat on the cosy bench under the trellis where juicy grapes grew on the vine.

Javes said, "I'll visit the telegraph office tomorrow to check if he sent anything from Whitesands, and if so, who he sent it to, and I'll also write to Saree to ask for more detail of what happened to Trini. Who these people were and where it happened. Then I'll really need to start preparing for the northern council meeting. If we're to secure money for a market hall in Ysherra, I need to make a really good case."

"Other than it would be nice to shop in the shade? I'm sure we can find all kinds of other benefits." Tali's eyes twinkled.

In the flapping light from the oil lamp, she looked so gorgeous. Sunbeaten, mature with a few greying hairs at her temples, but still gorgeous.

He reached up for the grape vine, pulled a fat grape off, and put it in her mouth. She licked his fingers.

"Are you all right?"

She wasn't normally so affectionate.

"The world is changing," she said. "I don't like the stories coming out of Watya. Of a blockade of the road and soldiers coming up from Tiverius as if they expect us to declare independence at the council meeting. They will cause trouble just by being there and strutting around town. I also don't like people trying to lure young people away from their families. It's like they are secretly recruiting for an army. I wish you didn't have to go to Watya."

"Me, too, but it's best that I go and keep up with the events."

"I'm glad I have you."

"Yes, I'm happy to have you, too."

CHAPTER 21

$\mathcal{I}$t took Kotori a few days to go through the pages of the princess' calculations. They described the path the object took through the sky in great detail. She had drawn a half-circle that was the surface of the continent, showing the piece falling off and hitting the ground.

If one assumed that the blinking object was a moon of some sort, then the piece that had broken off and floated to the surface would have come down somewhere in the Aranian highlands, close to the border with Chevakia.

He checked her calculations. He had to spend a decent amount of time doing this because it was not his area of expertise. His expertise was in star signs and their meanings.

But after filling three pages with numbers and repeating the process just to be sure, he knew the princess was correct.

The central highlands of Arania were a particularly wild area, with rugged mountains and deep crevasses. It was semi-arid and had no large rivers that offered easy options to travel or enough flat land to grow crops.

Anything that fell down there might well remain undiscovered forever.

Kotori asked Pertak if he had heard of any reports of rocks falling from the sky, but he had a hard time explaining what this would have looked like, and Pertak said that his contacts looked for what happened in the towns and villages, and wouldn't report *a sound like thunder in a clear sky* to him. To top it off, it had happened at night and, being farmers, most people would have been in bed.

But several of the students who had been on the astrology tower asked him about the blinking moon in the days following the observation.

They were just curious, Kotori reminded himself, but oh, he worried about this. Because if the princess told the queen, and the queen came to ask him about this mysterious thing, there was no way he could hide from her that he'd been looking at this phenomenon for many years. And she would ask him why he hadn't said anything previously, and he didn't have an answer that wasn't going to sound like: I'm stupid and have no idea. And he would have to admit to not having an idea for twenty years.

Kotori had a strong tendency to take the blame of the universe on his shoulders. He knew that. His brother and his friends in the Citadel reminded him of this. But he had a lot of reasons to feel shame about not mentioning this blinking light to anyone. Because he had no idea what made it blink, and, over the past twenty years, he had entertained thoughts about this when he lay in bed at night that strayed to possibilities he dare not speak. Things too big for him to comprehend, too scary to consider. If he spoke about this, he knew what would happen: everyone would expect him to come up with a solution. Because that's what the astrologer did.

But he had no solutions.

And he could cast his stones all he wanted, but no one had asked for a casting, and this late in life, he'd stopped believing that castings either made a difference or had any value at all.

Instead, he'd hoped that the blinking thing would disappear or stop blinking of its own accord, but of course, that was just wishful thinking.

And now someone else had discovered it, and there would be serious questions over why Kotori had remained silent on the subject for so long.

Why indeed?

Kotori spent a lot of time in his room at the top of the astrology tower. It was only in this room, that safe haven of the top of the tower with all the books and paraphernalia he'd collected over the many years and had inherited from the previous court astrologer, that he felt remotely safe.

He sat at his desk, and stared at his book of observations about the strange phenomenon, and the copious notes he'd taken over the years when scouring the library for information. But the act of staring at it did not give him any more ideas than it had during the past twenty years, and now there was an additional thing to worry about: the speck that had fallen to the surface. Somewhere on the highlands. And the princess knew about it.

And sooner rather than later, the king was going to ask questions about why he had kept quiet.

Back then, he had, perhaps mistakenly, assumed that his time was over, that with the coming of the foreign Queen, he would be offered retirement and the phenomenon could be for the new astrologer to worry about.

He'd dreamed of that time. His life would be peaceful, and he would no longer be used by members of the royal family to make any castings against each other. That he would no longer be asked to do horrible things because people in the royal family wanted them done.

He thought that in his old age, King Orik had gone soft.

But a crow does not really change its call, doesn't it? You can dye the feathers, and in some regions people caught crows and dyed them in outrageous colours in the spring festival every year just to prove that you could, and the land would be occupied by strangely coloured crows as the feathers one by one fell out and returned to black, but as soon as it opened its beak, it would still be a crow.

So after all those years, his job was still about protecting the favoured successor to the throne, and now that Prince Harek was old enough, he needed to be manipulated so he didn't become a danger to the king, the princess and the kingdom.

Kotori could understand. Oh yes, he could. He had not been in favour of women getting power in the Citadel by disbanding the mothers' houses as places where women waited for the king and the princes to visit them. You needed a permit to visit the mothers' house these days, and the women would be taking or teaching lessons, and they would be reading and writing and doing calculus.

Kotori didn't like that at all. He preferred the mothers' houses to be full of innocent women, and he preferred to go in there to make a casting for the girl that the king or one of the princes had chosen to come in his room that evening. He even preferred to make castings while the woman was about to give birth—heaven knew he'd seen enough children being born.

Instead, the king and the queen now occupied an apartment, and she was always with him, as was the crown princess, and the less said about her, the better.

But at the same time, it did happen to be the safest and most peaceful years of Kotori's life. And to go back to the time of the murders and the betrayal was, to be honest, something he had not prepared for or seen coming.

And there had been so much study, but none of it solved the problem of his mysterious blinking light.

He looked again at the star map and the constellations he had added and dice on the fabric that he cast every day.

Yes, he had added two constellations in the course of his life. He was proud of it, too, but it had not really solved anything, had it?

He rose from the desk and stood in indecision in front of the bookcase. It was all he knew how to do, to go back to knowledge for the answers in his life.

He was standing there when there was a knock on the door. He quickly shut the book with his observations that still lay open on the desk and put it in the drawer in his desk before telling the visitor to come in.

To his horror, it was Prince Harek.

"Good morning astrologer," he said.

He sounded so much like his half brother Denori, whom he had never known. The same deepening voice, the same arrogant attitude that suggested that he knew everything, and since Kotori had last seen the boy, he had even shaved most of his head, tattooed red patterns onto the skin where his hair used to be that looked like flames about to devour his face.

The only thing missing were the tattooed eyeballs, and he would probably do that as soon as he could locate someone who still specialised in the art, and that was getting rare.

"Good morning, young prince."

Harek stepped into the room and shut the door rather more forceful than necessary.

"I want you to stop addressing me like that," he said. "I'm taller than you." It was a fairly polite request, but the tone, oh how Kotori recognised that sweet threatening tone.

Where had he learned to do that?

"How can I help you?" Kotori said.

"There are two things," Harek said. "I'll tell you in good order. The first thing is that I want you to make me a casting."

"You…"

"Is that a surprise? I have turned fifteen, and I want you to do a casting for me. The books tell me that I'm old enough to request a casting without having to ask anyone for permission."

"Yes, yes, certainly. What is the second thing?"

"All in good time. I'll tell you after the casting."

"Sure. Let me get my things."

Kotori scrambled for the star map and his stones in his drawer.

Harek had never asked for a casting, nor had his mother ever asked for one since she moved into the palace.

Kotori would have liked to hope that the prince saw sense and had been told by some military person that he should ask for a casting as those men often did, but he didn't trust the boy's motives.

At any rate, he had best put forward his best effort.

He had two star maps: one that was old and a bit worn, but he chose the other one that was new and that had the star signs embroidered rather than painted on the velvet surface.

He spread it out on the desk. It was so big that he needed to shift some books aside, and then he had to remove those books and place them in such a way that the prince couldn't read the titles. They were about phenomena of the sky and other things Kotori had been checking—as he had already done so many times before. Strangely enough, no amount of checking brought up the answer to what this strange blinking light could be.

Kotori took out the bag with his stones and upended them in the palm of his hand.

"Now what do you want the casting to be for?" he asked.

Harek raised his eyebrows as if he wanted to say, *You're the astrologer.*

"Isn't it normally for my fortune in the future?"

"Yes." Kotori swallowed a snarky remark. He couldn't blame the boy for his mother's poor manners. "Only the person who is the subject of the casting can ask for one, and the quality of the outcome is greatly improved the more information I have."

"I said I'd tell you after the casting."

Well, let's take back the thought about his mother's rudeness. The boy had obviously learned from her.

"It is improved if I know more specifically what the casting is for, which activity, which relationship with which woman…"

Harek didn't reply. The silence lingered for a long, uncomfortable time.

Then, because he could do nothing else, Kotori cast the content of his hand over the cloth.

The coins and stones rolled over the velvet, catching the light that came into the window.

Then they came to a rest.

Kotori stared.

He couldn't believe it. This was exactly the same casting he'd made for his mother all those years ago when she first came into the Citadel as a prisoner.

Two of the coins landed on top of each other in the Eagle, and the venerable emerald lay in the sign of the Shield.

The Eagle was a rare star sign… and the boy was born in the sign of the eagle. So that made that the coins that landed in the star sign a super powerful omen for him. Whether it was good or bad depended on the rest of the casting. But like all those years ago for his mother, the outcome could be taken either way.

He cleared his throat. "By far the most powerful sign in the casting is the Eagle, which is also your birth sign. This means that the other stones carry comparatively more weight in their predictive qualities. This usually means that I advise caution. The birth sign is a powerful multiplier."

"What do the other stones say?"

The boy was too young to start astrology classes, but he seemed to have picked up some knowledge.

"This is an auspicious or inauspicious casting that is almost the same as one I did for your mother when she first came to the Citadel. Your mother is also born in the sign of the Eagle. There are not one, but two coins in the Eagle. When I cast for your mother, the emerald was over the Great Wanderer. Yours is in the Shield star sign. The Great Wanderer is in the Shield at this time of the year."

"What does it mean?"

"The Eagle points to a dramatic occurrence. It can be good or bad. The Shield is a sign of protection, as the name suggests."

"That I'm protected, or I need to protect something?"

"Both, depending on circumstance. This is why I asked what the casting is for. If I have no details, it's very hard to say any more than this. I would have to leave the interpretation over to you, and you will probably make rash decisions or draw the wrong conclusions."

"What are *wrong conclusions* in a subject that is mostly inter-pretation?"

That, of course, was a very good question.

"I think, young prince, that you and I are dancing around each other like swans on a lake. You don't want to tell me why you want me to cast your fortune, and therefore I can't tell you what you want to hear."

"That brings me to my second reason for coming here. You mentioned this house to me—"

"Ah, you want the casting for starting a mothers' house?"

"No. I want to see the house."

"You mean…?"

"The actual house that you said was available. Can I see it?"

"Yes, yes, sure. I can contact the administration for the key."

CHAPTER 22

The beautiful sunset clouds had delivered on their promise of rain by the next morning.

Tylve woke up in Nari's guest room, hearing the rain patter on the roof, and dreading the day she would have to spend riding the slow donkey all the way back to town in this weather. Sure, the weather along the coast was predictable, and she had prepared for this, but that didn't make travel in the rain any more pleasant.

Nari had already prepared a breakfast that put her to shame. Living alone, she often bought pre-baked jam rolls at the markets and ate those—no cooking required—but he had cooked eggs and fresh bread with orange juice and apple sauce.

"I don't know how you do all this just for yourself," she said.

"If I don't do it for myself, who else do I have to do it for?"

That was a good question. She just preferred to keep things simple and would rather be on the water with her boat than in the kitchen.

He wanted to know whether she had proper rain gear, and she said she did.

"What do you think? I spend most of my days on the ocean."

"I don't understand how you do that all by yourself. To be all alone on the water would frighten me."

She grinned.

"It's people that frighten me. You can learn about the ocean and you could learn how to navigate away from dangerous situations. You can learn how to recover or take shelter. You can't predict what evil people are going to do."

"That's true."

And then they were silent for a while. Tylve had never asked him what had driven him away from Tiverius, and it seemed a sore subject at the time, so she had never pressed him on the matter. Because "just retirement" was not the whole story. He'd have family in the city. There would be brothers or sisters, nieces and nephews, maybe even children.

After breakfast was done, he gave her a pack of produce from the farm. Some cheese and raisins and a jar of olives, a bag of dried orange slices and biscuits. It was as if he spent all his time cooking.

She made sure her supplies were all packed in oiled cloth inside the leather saddle bags and then she took her pack out in the rain to the donkey, which stood in the stable next to Nari's truck still munching on hay.

He came out in the rain to say goodbye to her and gave her a little note book while they stood in the stable, with the instruction to keep it in its leather pouch to keep it dry.

"What's that?" She slid the book out. It looked quite new.

"I copied some of my notes on the subject of ancient history. I'd give you the originals, but I'm rather attached to them and hope to find the time to study them later. So I copied the important bits for you."

"Thank you."

"You'll find all the contacts I have in there. Mention my name to them and they will be happy to talk to you. The learned community is only small and we're all in contact with each other."

Tylve flicked through the book and landed on a page that had information on how to contact King Isandor of Peria.

He gestured at it. "Do write to these people about the objects you found."

"I will try my best," Tylve said.

"No. Not try. Do it."

"But surely the king of Peria is not going to want to hear a simple sailor's story."

"I can assure you, he will be very interested. He's not king anymore. He passed that responsibility off to his son and devotes all his time to learning about the ancient civilisation. He will be interested. He will also be able to tell you whether this item is from the old civilisation. They have plenty of those artefacts in the City of Glass. You should travel there to see for yourself."

"Hey, yeah. Once I don't have to catch fish for a living anymore."

Some people really didn't understand what it was like, not being able to rely on vast family fortunes.

But the City of Glass was one of the places she had dreamed of visiting. Going there wouldn't even be hard. She could just take the boat out to sea and turn south and keep going. The weather would be bad, but she could handle that. What she couldn't handle was losing her spot in the fish delivery schedule, and her customers being angry with her.

It was a strange kind of life that she led, seemingly free, but not really.

Nari made her promise yet again that she would contact the old king and also somebody called Javes in the north of Chevakia in another place where Tylve had never been, the small desert town of Ysherra. Although she heard that it had grown considerably since the time that she learned about its desolate location on the edge of the northern desert when she was at school.

She saddled the donkey and tied the packs to the saddle and then climbed on and set off in the misty and grey morning.

The rain was not extremely heavy, but it was dense and steady.

Patches of haze hung over the countryside, and when they opened up, it was to show a leaden grey sky. There was very little traffic on the road.

People would think twice before travelling in this weather. It was cold, and the animals hated it, the road might be slippery and trucks would have trouble getting their engines started.

It also looked like rain would settle in for a couple of days, so she definitely wanted to get home before puddles grew too deep and creeks ran over the road.

For most of the morning, she plodded through the valley, not even taking much time to stop.

She gave the donkey an oats bag, so that it could keep moving, albeit very slowly, while they walked.

She got cold and walked next to the donkey for a while.

It was mid afternoon when she finally came across the next ridge and could see the houses on the outskirts of Samira, hazy in the rain.

The road wound along the hillside into town, and on this road she spotted a couple of people on horses coming the other way. That caught her attention.

The people in town didn't usually ride horses. They preferred the much more hardy donkeys, so these had to be visitors.

What was the bet that this was the group of "guards" leaving town to go back to Tiverius or wherever they had come from, or continuing to look for the thing that they were looking for, or continuing to rough up innocent citizens?

Tylve didn't want to be noticed by them yet again, and definitely didn't want to face them alone, especially not after what she had heard had happened to other women. So she steered the donkey into an old abandoned shed that lay at the end of a muddy driveway.

It wasn't a very good hiding place. Evidently, the shed had lain abandoned for a long time. The roof had partially collapsed. The remaining ceiling beams, half rotted through and the uneven floor made it quite dangerous inside and the remaining parts of roofing offered next to no shelter, but the wall that faced the road did have a small window where she could stand and watch what happened out there.

The group travelled slowly. Tylve could hear their voices long before she could see the horses. They were men, and by the sound of things, they were drunk.

When they came into view, Tylve confirmed her suspicion that this was the group of fake guards.

On second thoughts, she didn't know that even people in Tiverius would use horses. All the patrols that had come into town previously always used trucks.

Why use horses for such a distance when you could use a truck that could cover the distance twice as quickly?

For the fact that the men pretended to be guards, they were doing a poor job, laughing and yelling like a bunch of drunken louts. They must hold the townsfolk for fools.

But the joke was on them, because none of them spotted Tylve, while they continued up the road, still talking to each other.

She waited until they were out of sight before steering the donkey away from the musty bale of hay and continuing into town.

By this time, the rain had intensified, and the poor old donkey was so pleased to be taken back to its owner and its dry stable that it trotted the last of the distance.

Tylve took her pack and went home through the deserted streets in the increasing darkness. She was thinking about going to the temple for the gathering, considering what she'd say.

As little as two years ago, she would have shared all she had heard and learned about the dead man and his strange devices, but … it wasn't so much that she didn't trust the new people. They were hard-working and honest. But she didn't know who they spoke to when they went home and whether perhaps her stories would travel further than she intended. Stories of death and murder tended to do that.

But as soon as she came to her house, she knew that something was wrong. There were deep booted footsteps in the moss-covered grass in the front yard. The front door was closed, but the handle was bent, and splinters of wood had broken off the door frame.

She pushed the door open fully, pushing something metallic across the tiles.

It was the bolt, which had come straight off the wood.

She stopped and listened, but couldn't hear anything.

Heart thudding, she took the poker from the hearth in the central hallway and went into the rooms one by one.

In the small sitting room, she found all the contents of the book-shelves on the floor. The intruders had opened all the drawers in the desk and all her administration papers lay on the couch. They had made dirty footsteps all over the room. Big, male footsteps.

In the kitchen they had opened all the cupboards, and had taken out her knives and shoved aside all her food supplies, but as far as she could see, they hadn't actually taken any. They hadn't even touched the money jar that sat in the back of the pantry.

In the bedroom, they had upset the bed and looked under the mattress and then her clothes cupboard.

Again, she couldn't see that they had taken anything, but it was such a mess that it was hard to tell. She didn't even know where to begin. Why would anyone break into her house?

As she stood there, dumbfounded and not knowing what to do, there came a small knock on the front door.

She took in a sharp breath.

Then a voice said, "Tylve?"

That was the wife of the carpenter who lived nextdoor.

Tylve rushed to the door.

The neighbour stood there with two of her young children.

"I'm so sorry. I tried but I couldn't stop them. I told them you'd be back soon, but they just kicked in the door."

She enveloped Tylve in a soup-scented hug.

"Who were they?"

"Those Tiverian guards who came to town a few days ago. They were not nice men at all. I had to protect the children. I'm so sorry that they did this to your house…"

"It's all right. I can fix the door and it doesn't look like they stole anything."

But somewhere deep inside, she was certain that they had been looking for the strange object that she had taken with her to show Nari.

She felt cold.

The men looked like guards, but she was pretty sure they were not. Not official guards, at least. She didn't think they knew much about this area at all, and she didn't think they were really looking for a criminal. They were looking for this thing. Maybe they were looking for the man who owned it, the man who was now dead.

Maybe, when they finally found him, they would think that she had killed him.

The only person she had shown the device and neck band was Nari. He wouldn't tell anyone about her find.

Well, not voluntarily.

Under force, you could get any kind of answer out of people.

The men had been going in the direction of Nari's house. They might not know that she'd visited him. Or they might. She had told the owner of the donkey where she was going. Everyone in town knew that she visited Nari to bring him supplies.

After telling the neighbour repeatedly that she had done the right thing, Tylve walked around the house, trying to make herself believe that she was wrong about this, making herself believe that she would just go back to her usual life and be safe, but the more of her possessions she picked up off the floor and packed away in the cupboards, the more she realised that they really hadn't stolen anything, and that the chance was high they would have been searching for this metal neck band, probably guided by the flash it had emitted when she accidentally pressed the button. Maybe they had even followed her on her recent trip.

What was she going to do?

There was only one thing she could do, and that was to get out of here, even if only for a short time. Her father had always told her that there might be times that as an adherent of the Gathering, she would be persecuted. When all the extra followers of the Gathering came into down, she had believed that this was less likely to happen. But even if she had felt safer, but she had never packed away her bag of emergency supplies that she kept in the back of the cupboard.

Just in case.

The intruders had found it, but tossed it into the corner of the room.

They had opened it but found only clothes and some supplies inside.

She checked the contents of the bag, but again, nothing was missing.

They had been looking for the dead man and his devices, she was sure of that.

Right.

That meant she needed to find out what this thing was. It was no good pretending she didn't have it or didn't know about it. These types of men knew how to get answers out of people. There was not much point tossing it into the ocean, either, because a few people knew she had found it.

Part of her wished she had never noticed the dead man, but another part wanted him not to have died alone and abandoned in vain.

Much as she disliked it, she was now part of the man's story.

She packed Nari's supplies into the bag. She was not leaving his efforts in her house for the mould or the mice to find.

Then she added the neck band and strange device to the bag and the little book Nari had given her.

She added as many supplies from her kitchen to the bag as she could carry, and then set out for the harbour. It was now almost dark, and the weather was still atrocious, but she crawled under the sail-cloth strung over her boat's deck to keep the birds off, and made herself comfortable in the little cabin where she slept when she was out at sea.

Of course, she couldn't sleep. Every slap sounded like a footstep. Every groan that sounded like a voice made her jump.

At the earliest light, she took the covers off the boat, hoisted the sails, which weren't doing much because there was very little wind, fished up the pulley cable from the water and cranked the boat out of the harbour. Once she had passed the lighthouse, the main sail filled with a faint breath of wind that allowed her to put the oars away.

Normally she would go straight out to the ocean to the fishing grounds, but now she set the boat on a course further south. If anyone was looking for her and found her boat missing, they would expect her to be at the fishing grounds. She couldn't go about her usual business, but there were a few islands off the coast. Some were inhabited by fishing families, but one contained only an abandoned house.

She'd wait there while deciding what to do.

The land lay, dark and foreboding, on the horizon. Rugged mountain ridges jutted out from the coast. There were a few islands, too. The lighthouse flashed its regular glow over the ocean. Only a few lights burned in the streets of the town. At this time of the day, the oil reservoirs on most street lights would have run out.

A few pinpricks of light dotted the shoreline to the north and south of Samira, but also on the hills behind the town.

But wait, what was that? A fire burned on the ridge behind the town.

Her heart thudding, she watched the flames leap into the air. Was that Nari's house? She didn't know of any other houses on that ridge.

In her mind, she saw Nari taken by fake guards, dragged into a wagon, tied up and beaten and taken to their den. Certainly not to Tiverius.

For what?

So that he would tell them about the mysterious thing she found?

No, scratch waiting at the island. She owed it to Nari to take this thing to someone who could help her decipher its meaning. He had given her some names and one was more accessible to her than others. She would have to take it to the City of Glass.

CHAPTER 23

Ravi and his father came home after having walked through the streets in complete silence.

His father preceded him into the yard, up the steps to the house and into the front door.

"Office," his father said in a curt tone, as soon as the front door shut behind them.

There was no escaping it now.

Ravi went into his father's office and sat down on the couch.

"Who says you can sit?"

He got up again, while his father walked around the desk and sat down, fixing him with a severe look.

"What did you think you were doing with this stunt?"

"It was not a stunt. It's true."

"You wouldn't know what is true if it hit you in the face. What did you want to achieve with this idiotic behaviour that is not going to disrespect all the work I've done for you, all the opportunities I've given you?"

"I do not disrespect you."

"Yes, you do. What do you think my boss will say to me tomorrow? That I can't even control my own son, in front of the proctor. Why, Ravi, why?"

"You don't understand. No one understands."

"Then explain it to me. I'm listening."

"The young people, people of my age, they have no hope."

"We've lived the best lives we've ever lived. You call that no hope?"

"We want to make things better."

"Yes."

"We want to be valued."

"And you say you're not?"

"We want to have choice."

"What choice is there that you're not having?"

Ravi glared at his father.

"Really, tell me."

"The choice to make our own lives. That's why people sign up to the army, to get out."

"Is that all you want, after all your education?"

"No. Not just those things."

"Then what do you want? Because to me, it seems like you're a spoilt brat and I'd love to know what I've done wrong to have you end up like this. And then to embarrass me in front of the proctor. You disappoint me deeply."

Ravi was engulfed in a deep, all-consuming rage. He had no more words, because his father did not and could not understand.

He said through clenched teeth, "You don't understand. I can explain, but you don't really listen."

"Then go and think about it and come to see me when you have figured out how to explain it to me. Meanwhile, I think it would be better for all concerned if you remained home."

Ravi left the office, having to restrain himself not to slam the door. He strode through the hall. His mother had a visitor, because he could hear their voices from the living room.

He took the steps two at a time and ran through the corridor to his room.

He stood inside the doorway, looking at all the pieces of his life. His study books on his desk—he swiped his hand over the surface and pushed them all on the floor. The clothes he had worn to the

Scriptorium—he pulled them off the chair and threw them on the bed.

All he could feel was rage.

No one took him seriously. No one understood how people of his age were overlooked, ignored, and how the "choices" their parents offered were not real choices. They were the older generation's wishes. The scraps they were willing to throw out for the kids to fight over. So that they'd sign up for the army, to fight useless conflicts about granting railways to the north, or something.

He sat down on his bed.

At a deeper level, he knew that his father was right about never having a better time, but his father was talking about material things. In the time his father grew up, there was the threat of war, and the threat of rising sonorics. In those days, people had gone into the army to fight Arania to stop raids across the border. They had worked like crazy at the Scriptorium to find better materials and better protection from the harmful rays. They had even figured out how the network of old machines protected the continent.

Then they had provided sonorics suits to outlying villages so that the invisible force didn't kill the citizens.

In Tiverius and elsewhere, learned people studied sonorics, and had figured out how to keep the harm at bay. They now knew what to do and life was safe—but this also meant there was very little left to do for the younger generation except enjoy the safety, and it was just that... older people expected gratitude for having created the safe land, and in the doga these old men did nothing except pat each other on the back for having saved the land.

Old Sadorius han Chevonian, the old proctor who had finally retired at the ripe age of eighty-four and had died a few years ago, bless his soul, had understood, having led the country through all of it, and worse, but this current lot of senators had no idea that the country had sat on its hands doing nothing, and that its young people withered away while older generations said *do this* because they did it, but they didn't understand that at the end of each study, each course, the sense of purpose that used to exist in his father's day had vanished, because all the positions were already taken.

And that talking about it only met with anger and disbelief from the older generation, while those people argued over the affairs and corruption of senators, while making it clear no one would ever be bold enough to extend the railway to Ysherra and make those people feel part of the same country.

So, what now?

He heaved a deep sigh and went to the window.

Going back to the mail room would be out of the question. Self defence training was probably also off the cards. He didn't have any lessons until tomorrow, but his parents wouldn't know that.

He changed into the robe he usually wore when he went to the Scriptorium. The door to his father's office was closed. Either his father had gone back to the doga, or he was inside at work.

He couldn't hear his mother's voice anymore, so the visitor must have left.

Ravi crept down the stairs.

He glanced into the living room, where his mother was setting up a new canvas on her easel.

"I'm going to the library," he called into the room.

"That's fine, dear."

Instead of walking past his father's office again, Ravi turned to the kitchen and left the house via the laundry door.

He walked through the yard, past the side of the house and out the front gate.

He turned in the direction of the centre of town, but he didn't know where he was going. Not to the library, although his tutor would be furious if he did poorly in his exams.

A deep part of him didn't care. Or better said, he desperately wanted not to care, because his Aranian tutor terrified him.

For a while, he walked aimlessly through the streets.

Of course, his father was right. Life in Tiverius had never been better, but its institutions were decadent and rotten with laws paid for with favours by people in business.

There were only so many times you could walk the same route before people started to notice, so he turned into a different street that brought him past the ulli hall.

The building was of the same type as the market hall, with many doors along the sides to allow people to come and go freely and to let stuffy air out of the building when it was busy.

And it was surprisingly busy inside.

Ravi stopped and looked over the long tables, one for each game. The surface of the table was covered with smooth felt for the metallic marbles to roll freely. Unused tables would have a box of these marbles sitting in the middle, ready for use. There were eleven, and the magnetic wands to move them around lay in a basket at the head of the table.

A large group of younger people stood around a table, but the game must have finished because they weren't playing.

As Ravi was about to leave again, he recognised one of the people: it was Dana from the mail room.

"Ravi!" She beckoned enthusiastically for him to join her.

It was a bit strange. He didn't know her that well, and she acted like he was her best friend.

But he had nowhere else to go, so he went into the hall.

She stood with a group of about twenty young people around a table. One young man, probably a fellow student, was distributing balls across the felt-covered surface of the table.

He joined Dana. "Hello." And because that sounded too awkward, he added, "Have you finished work already?"

"You're so funny. Don't you know what time it is?"

Well, he guessed, while he'd been arguing with his father, it had gotten quite late. He hadn't looked at the time, but now that he thought about it, yes, it was late. Close to dinnertime, maybe. Would his mother expect him back soon?

"I thought it was very brave what you did today."

Was it? "I don't know. I just got angry. It was a bit stupid, I think. I don't know that it achieved anything."

"No, it probably doesn't."

"It sounds like you have experience?"

"A bit."

They were silent for a while. This all felt very awkward. Ravi was not a natural in making small talk, especially with other young people who had so much more freedom than he did.

"Look… I better go. I don't want to keep you off your game."

"We're not here to play, really."

"Aren't you? This is the ulli hall."

"We just use the game as an excuse."

"For what?"

"To meet up. Get out of the house."

She laughed, and he laughed, too, because he had expected something serious.

But then she added. "We hold Gatherings here most evenings."

Wait—what?

"Samiran gatherings?"

"It's not really exactly the same as the old tradition, but yeah, a lot of young people get involved."

"So it was not just your sister?"

"Oh, no, but I can't say anything about it in front of Marlo. He's so old-fashioned."

They laughed.

Then Ravi asked, "What do you do at these gatherings? Do you have incantations and blessings and magic? What do they call it again? The song of Peace and Everlasting?"

"Oh, no." She chuckled, a bit uneasy. "That's the trouble with people like us who know about the history and study the books. It's not like that at all. Our gatherings are usually very informal, but each day one person gets to have their say about something they find important, or something they've noticed, or whatever takes their fancy. We talk about the doga a lot."

"I'm guessing it's not good talk?"

She laughed. "What do you think? We're all young people. No one is going to defend those old prunes sending all of us off to fight in conflicts we haven't asked for. I don't care about whether there is a dam at Watya. I don't care if the north has more autonomy. Heaven knows they've been treated badly enough." She stopped and gave him a sideways look. "I'm sorry. I guess your father is one of those people."

"Old prunes," he repeated.

They looked at each other and both laughed. Her cheeks had gone red.

An awkward silence followed.

"It's all right," he said. "I agree with you. Why do you think I'm here and not having dinner with my family?"

"I'm sorry. I'd love to say I have no idea what you're talking about, but sadly, I do. Oh yes, I do." She sighed. "Families."

"What is your family? I'm sorry if you've told me, I've forgotten." He was certain that she *hadn't* told him, because he would have remembered, being attuned to remembering things like that courtesy of his mother.

"Oh." She looked aside. "I'm from an old family. Very traditional. They want me to marry for money and influence."

"In the doga?"

She shook her head. "Much older and more traditional and nastier than that. Old nobility. It's about ownership of land and property."

"Urgh."

There were old families like that. She was right. They did not usually sit in the doga themselves, but controlled those who did. Those were the han Veleskians and di Fabrioli and families like that.

"And you work in the mail office?"

"Shows you how far I've fallen."

They laughed.

"Dana is not your real name, then?"

"It is, kind of. It's an abbreviation of sorts."

After another silence, he said, "And when you finish having your say in these gatherings, what do you do then? Do you act on anything you talk about?"

"Sometimes we decide we can do something about a subject. Not always." She shrugged. "Mostly not. We'll say things like we'll talk to our parents and everyone agrees—Yeah right, they'll never listen."

Another awkward silence followed.

Then he said, "We're really powerless, aren't we?"

She nodded.

They watched the others in the group. They'd gone back to the ulli set, laying the balls out on the table, ready for a game.

Dana watched with that intense, expectant look. She was nothing like any girl he had ever met. She didn't wear pretty dresses. She wasn't pretty in the usual girlish way, although he didn't think she was plain or ugly either. Her face was angled and boyish, accentuated by her short hair. She wore no jewellery except for a single gold loop in her right ear and a tiny jewelled stud in her nose. Those dark blue eyes of hers were quite unusual.

Then he asked, "I read about the Samiran Gathering that they believe that the lightstream comes from the afterlife and is their way of communicating with the dead. Do you believe stuff like that, too?"

"No, we don't do that. That belief goes with the fact that some of the older Samiran families come from the coast and have the ability to shape sonorics like the people in Peria."

"Yes, I read about that."

"We can't do that. We're not officially recognised by those people. We've just based our movement on the gathering."

"What are you? A political movement?"

"Not really. Just a place where people listen to each other."

"Who is going to talk today?"

"I am."

"Really? What are you going to talk about?"

"Stay around and listen."

Ravi did just that. Dana introduced him to some of the others in the group. There were kids from a lot of different types of families. Not many he had seen at the Scriptorium. If fact, a few people referred to study at the Scriptorium as *a waste of time*.

A few were getting heavily into a heated game at the table. There was a lot of shouting and at one stage, a magnetic ball jumped clear of the raised table's edge and bounced on the tiled floor with an almighty clatter.

Ravi watched, laughed and shouted with the spectators.

Then Dana came forward, and the group fell quiet.

She started her talk with, "I think the wind is turning. I witnessed something today that proves this is so, this fellow student here who has come to the same conclusions we have discussed so often between us in this group. He tried to convince the proctor, but the proctor isn't listening yet. But many people are starting to listen."

Everyone was looking at Ravi. His cheeks burned.

Dana went on to talk about the mail office, about the prepared petitions, and the companies that prepared petitions for the small town administrators. That there was nothing genuine about this process. And that no one talked about young people. They could go and study, the older people said. But the land had lost purpose. Look at Peria, she said. All the rich people had gone there because there was so much going on. The rebuilding of the City of Glass, now that people from Chevakia and Arania could go there. She said, look at the provinces north of the Aramys River, those the doga considered troublesome and were once desperately poor. Those people were farming ever more land, building irrigation channels and greenhouses, breeding herds of camels, travelling deep into the desert to study history.

"We in Tiverius pretend we know everything and there was a time that we did, but even Arania has overtaken us now that it's acceptable for the women of Arania to work. And because they were stopped from learning and working for so long, their hunger is great. We have become lazy, thinking that life is easy. We have it so good, the older generation says, but what they mean is that *they* worked hard and *they* have it very good. But we are supposed to thank them for all their work, but no one has any idea for what we should be doing next."

This was precisely what Ravi had also been feeling. He agreed with everything, but what he wanted to know was this: did this group propose any solutions for it?

He asked Dana when they walked home. It turned out that she lived close to him. Her family owned a number of businesses in town and her father managed investments across a wide range of business interests. Her mother was mostly interested in marrying off their two daughters.

"I have to marry someone who will take over the business. It's more about what sort of business manager this person is going to be than whether he will be good for me."

"That sounds awful." And he meant it.

"Yes. Right? They're all too old and boring."

The thought that parents could just send you off with some random man who then had the right to perform the most intimate act on you, without your permission, horrified him.

The fact that he might one day be paired up with a girl to do that to her terrified him to no end. What if she didn't want to? Or if she cried. Or what if his body wouldn't cooperate?

And yet, his parents had never even spoken about marriage for him. But they *had* to think about it, right? Because they would care about the family's wealth and that it fell in good hands.

"Ravi?"

He gasped, having been lost in his thoughts.

"Yes?"

She laughed. "You looked like you were daydreaming."

"I was thinking about my tutor, who's going to be mad at me for not studying my Aranian lessons for tomorrow. What were you saying?"

"Do you want to come to our next gathering?" She stopped and jerked her head at a side street. "I have to walk this way."

In the late afternoon, her eyes were almost black.

She was so stylish and so fresh-faced.

"The gathering is tomorrow, right?"

"Yes."

"All right. Is it at the ulli hall again?"

"No, we're meeting at the north bank park."

"Where the horse market is?"

"Yes, exactly there. We meet somewhere different every day, so it's not so obvious what we're doing."

"Don't you have to do homework for your tutors?"

She laughed. "Yes. But I think they've already given up on me. My sister is much smarter than I am, even if she's also younger."

"I think you're smart."

She laughed. "Thank you."

And she met his eyes in the gathering darkness.

"Well, bye then."

She turned and walked away. He watched her walk down the street.

At home, his father had told his mother of the incident with the proctor, but like most things in life, she couldn't get too excited about it because *if young people are not allowed to say radical things, then who can say them?*

His father clearly thought that no one should be able to say radical things to anyone from the venerable institution that was the doga.

After dinner, Ravi went to his room—to study, he said.

But he lay on his bed thinking about the meeting, and thinking about Dana.

And suddenly, he was walking home through the dark streets next to this unconventionally pretty, self-assured girl. And then he saw himself standing awkwardly in a bedroom facing her and she was so terrified of him that the required body part would not cooperate.

And her brothers—because this girl had many brothers who were big and strong soldiers—all laughed at him.

The girl looked suspiciously like Dana.

She laughed at him.

Ravi woke up with a shock with his pyjama pants tangled around him. The crotch felt wet.

CHAPTER 24

Kotori got up from his desk and took the cloak from the wardrobe, even if he was doubtful he'd need it.

Then he followed the prince out the door.

Prince Harek went first down the winding staircase to the bottom of the tower where the prince's guard waited: two stone-faced men barely older than the prince, but towering over Kotori by more than a head.

They left the building and set off across the courtyard. Harek and his guards let Kotori go first, which both flattered him and alarmed him. What were these silent mountains of flesh up to while he couldn't see them?

But of course his imagination was running away with his perpetual desperate need to cover his backside, resulting from years of having to watch his back in the Citadel. Things really weren't like that anymore.

Except—by telling the prince about this house that he could turn into a mothers' house, he was goading the prince to return to the old ways.

Because…

Because Kotori couldn't stand being sidelined, and because he didn't want to become a servant to women.

Well, the women could have prevented this by doing a good job, right?

Even though that southern woman was all right.

It was all about her daughter, being obsessed with music and… giggling with her friends and… not being interested in any of the important things.

That behaviour forced him to act, right?

But now, as the prince was taking his bait, he feared for what would happen if he was found out.

Not if, *when* he was found out.

He'd not worried about the secureness of the position of his head on his shoulders for a very pleasing length of time. He didn't *think* the queen supported public executions, but then he'd been wrong before.

Very wrong.

Very often.

Feeling sweaty and dizzy with the implications of what he was doing, Kotori led the group through the courtyard and out the main gates.

The main entrance of the Citadel was in a fairly narrow and busy street lined with shops. At this time of day, close to midday, many people ambled down the street.

The appearance of the court astrologer and the prince in the company of two guards didn't raise many eyebrows. The days that people would bow and clear the street were also in the past.

After walking a short distance down the hill, still well within view of the Citadel, Kotori entered the courtyard of a traditional house in the style dating back to the time the Citadel had been built. These houses used to be for people who worked in the Citadel. The closer houses were for the people with higher functions. The workers would live in cottages further down the hill.

The house's many rooms looked out over the courtyard which contained a fountain that had gone dry. The basin had filled with the leaves that had fallen off the tree that stood in the corner. The paving was dusty and covered in a desiccated layer of black moss that grew in shady spots, looked dead but miraculously came to life when it rained. Heaps of leaves had also blown into the corners. The windows were dull with grit and dust.

This particular house had lain empty for a number of years. It used to belong to the Citadel's armourer, but after the man had passed away, his family had spent many years arguing over the house. They'd arrived at the conclusion to sell it, but their arguing amongst each other had racked up such a legal bill that the price necessary to cover those costs was more than the value of the house.

On top of that, the house needed a good amount of maintenance.

When the Citadel had bought it to end the dispute, the two merchants living in the houses on either side had ganged up against any potential expansion of the Citadel's perimeter, not that anyone inside the Citadel had entertained such plans.

All this meant that no one had used the house.

"The Citadel owns this house," Kotori said. "I'm sure you could very discreetly transfer ownership in your name. There is enough room to lodge a good number of girls from the country. Take them in a group so they won't feel lonely."

He opened the door and led the prince into a hall where the air smelled mouldy and stale. Ahead, sunlight slanted in through grimy windows into a large, high-ceilinged room.

"This would make a nice communal room where they can host guests and hold plays."

He left it unsaid that Harek's activities would mean they'd also hold birth ceremonies here, and oh, he could almost hear the music and feel the excitement.

Harek's eyes moved as he scanned the room. He said nothing.

Hosting guests and holding plays was not the right angle to take with the boy. He wanted to train and fight.

Kotori moved to the next room, which, back in the day, used to contain the armourer's office.

"This could be something more intimate—a library... or since it would be unwise to have the women visit you in the Citadel, you could turn this into a sumptuous bedroom, to... eh..."

Harek again made no comment about this.

"Or it could be a room for displaying trophies from conquests."

Now Harek turned around and gave him a sharp look. "Are we at war with anyone?"

"Well… uhm… your highness, we're not, but conquests could feature adventurous trips to remote locations, navigating the coast and penetrating the Mother's Veil, setting eyes upon the Mother and surviving to tell the tale."

"I'm sure you would like me trying to end or shorten my life like that."

Kotori took in a sharp breath. "No, not at all. It was just an example."

And another bad move on his part. Yes, it was true that many of the people who had set eyes on the Mother—said to be a huge striped ball that occupied the sky in the ocean obscured by the veil of clouds —might survive if they wore protective clothing, but many of them still grew lumps on their skin and died before their time.

"I mean, your highness, if you travel to exotic locations, you bring back mementos—gifts, I must stress. You need to display them appropriately."

"Ah, you mean like the gilded box with my father's excrement that the Chevakians displayed in the hall to their place of government? Did you know that it's still there?"

Why was it that with every word he said, the boy took him deeper into the morass? Really, at his age, he should know better and hold his tongue.

The next room was the kitchen, and then they saw a few much smaller rooms for servants.

The women would need servants, Kotori said, because they couldn't be expected to work. The bathroom, also on the ground floor, was huge and a dressing room off the bathroom could be made into a birthing room, since there would only be a few women in the house at the start and they wouldn't need a large ceremony room.

Kotori couldn't stop talking, because he felt a need to fill the awkward silence, a silence that would invite uncomfortable questions, such as whether the queen knew of all this and approved of it.

Harek took all of this in without saying anything.

They went upstairs and inspected the bedrooms.

Kotori knew he was getting ahead of himself, but he could already imagine this house full of soft music and beautiful women on the cusp of motherhood, who would entertain the young prince and keep their families in the regions happy at the same time.

They were on the stairs back down when Harek said, "What do you know about women?"

"What do I—what?"

Kotori stopped on the stairs to stare at the prince, who walked behind him.

"Know about women," Harek repeated. "You seem to talk about them all the time."

"Well, I... I used to come to the mothers' house often to make castings. I saw the mothers at their seductive tricks, I saw them bloom into motherhood, I saw them birth the king's children. I was one of the few men who got to see that. It's beautiful, even if it's hard. The other women are very caring for their sisters when that time comes. You haven't lived until you have seen new life emerge from a woman's body."

"Hmmmm."

And then he said nothing, so Kotori kept walking, overcome with powerful memories of princes whose births he'd witnessed, at all times of the year, day or night, often in the main ceremony room with all the cheering and the music, but sometimes in the upstairs lounge or in the bathroom, on the stairs, or in the hallway outside the room. Those many, many princes who had gone into the army and who had never returned from distant wars.

Or some of those princes, like Denori, who had built their own mothers' houses, where they also invited Kotori as revered guest.

He thought of all the beautiful strong women who used to live in the mother's house. When the house finally closed, Selwa—dear Selwa, mother of the king's oldest sons—had returned to her family on the south coast. And while the queen had given birth to princess Loriane on the stage in the large ceremony room and Kotori had been present, Harek had been born in the King's private quarters with the attendance of only the midwife.

Kotori remembered hearing about it in the morning, after the fact. The queen didn't even want him to do a casting for the young prince.

Harek's voice jolted him from his memories.

"I have been told that you have never shown an interest in women."

"I… ehhh? I've just told you I care greatly about these women."

"That you have no interest in having women. Not the king's, that you shouldn't be interested in, not the women in the women's house, and not the women that you could have if you wanted, outside the Citadel."

"What kind of question is that? What do you want me to say to that? I'm the court astrologer. That's my life."

"It was not a question. Some men don't care much for women."

"Well…" Kotori put his hands in his pockets. "As the court astrologer, I'm not supposed to—"

"Supposed to and actually doing it are two different things. Being the court astrologer never stopped Sizek."

No, it hadn't. Some of the rumours said that the previous astrologer had more children than the king, although none had come forward at the time of his death.

"Not for me. And if you will excuse me, young man, this kind of talk is highly inappropriate." The boy was *fifteen*, by the Mother's Breath.

"I don't think so. Why are you so keen for me to look at this house?"

"Because it's empty?"

"No, I don't think so. You take me here, because you want to be surrounded by women who adore you, and you want to fill this house with them, or any house, really, as long as you can return to the old ways where they invited you to special occasions and they listened to every word you said."

"Uhhh—uhmmmm?" Kotori had nothing more to say to that remark, because it was so painfully true, and to deny it would just make things worse, as everything in this conversation had already been used against him.

Harek continued, "Whereas I just want to look at the house. I don't have to tell you what I want to do with it. I don't need your suggestions about it. In fact, you might keep your sordid suggestions to yourself, because there are people in the Citadel who won't like hearing them. I am not interested in stoking those sentiments, but well, walls sometimes do have ears."

Kotori swallowed. And swallowed again.

"Well, young prince…. That's a bit…"

He wasn't suggesting that he would…

"Blunt? Maybe, but that seems to be the only way you understand things. But let me put it this way, if I wanted to resurrect this sordid tradition of mothers' houses, I wouldn't need to start with the house, I'd start with the women."

"How do I know whether you don't already have those lined up?"

Harek gave him a startled look and said nothing for a while. Ha.

"Ownership of this house requires a use for it. If an owner can't state a use, people will talk. The walls may have ears, young prince, but the cobblestones in the streets and the tiles in the kitchen have mouths."

He met the boy's eyes and could see in them that Harek realised that this game was up. If he wanted the house, then he would have to tell *someone* what his purpose for it was or risk gossip or his mother's anger, or both.

Ha! Kotori might be old, but he was not stupid.

CHAPTER 25

Over the next few days, Javes turned his attention to the many jobs he needed to catch up on as administrator for Ysherra. Most of it was rather mundane stuff that required him to sit in his office and read correspondence and write responses. The volume of this stuff building up over just a few weeks never ceased to amaze him.

The window of the office gave him a view across the farm, where he would see Renko work with the camels, looking after Mindo.

For all that the man was strange, he was a decent worker. Javes watched him carry bales of hay, fill up water troughs, cut down thistles or other prickly plants and help another farm hand build a stone wall to line the draining channel that would carry water from the typical sudden downpours to the town's holding ponds.

In the afternoon, Mindo would accompany the farm hands to the corner of the farm where that channel met up with another coming from the neighbour's property. A pool of water collected here, protected from the harsh sun by sheer rock walls. The locals often swam here.

Javes could hear their laughing voices and echoing splashes from the room of his office.

On the second day after having returned from his trip, Javes visited the local telegraph office. He had to send a few messages—including his acceptance to attend the northern district council meeting—but he filed a request to see correspondence from the Whitesands Creek telegraph line for the day he had travelled through there with Mindo.

Javes was a bit annoyed that the employee told him he would need a few days to look at it, but the man said they were busy because a lot of northern district council documents were being sent, so that was fair enough.

Javes also occupied some of the man's time for the purpose of this meeting.

He received the meeting's agenda, which included full documentation about the location of Tiverian army troops around Watya.

To be fair, he had not given the issue much thought, but now that he saw those maps, he realised with a chill that he should have given it more attention. Much more attention.

Troops from Tiverius always trained in the area, people said, and that was true. But just how many soldiers had they stationed south of the broad and rambling stone-covered river bed where a low bridge —that always flooded after heavy rain—provided the pivotal link from the northern districts to the capital? The map showed at least four camps where there only ever been one.

What were they doing there? What were they afraid of? Arania had been very peaceful and well-behaved for years.

Or was it the tiny camp of building workers who were constructing the sorely needed dam that would service the town and the surrounding fruit tree groves and grain fields, and that would stop the massively wide bed of the river overflowing and keep the bridge open?

Because Tiverius didn't want the dam, that much was clear to him.

The Aramys River was the lifeblood of Chevakia, feeding the central agricultural district. They said a dam would risk water supplies to that area.

For twenty years, Javes had seen the correspondence of the northern council with the capital about a potential dam pass his desk.

It had gone from *Give us the dam* to *If you give us money, we'll build* it, to *If you're not going to give us money to extend the railway, the dam would be a good alternative* to *If you're not going to give us anything, we'll build it ourselves, keep the extra produce to feed our own people first, and charge good money for the rest.*

It was ridiculous that the district needed to trade railway promises for the dam, while other districts in the country got both.

To say that the relationship of the northern council with the doga in Tiverius was tense would be understating it. But it had always been that way.

So, the doga was sending *soldiers* in response?

What was going on in Tiverius?

There was a time it would have been easy for him to find out, because he'd grown up in Tiverius and his family lived there. But since both his parents had died in quick succession, his brother had relocated his transport business to Peria and he now lived in the City of Glass, because *The doga is not interested in encouraging business initiatives. They only want our taxes.*

Belo was doing very well now, judging by his correspondence.

While he waited for the telegraph office's response to his request, Javes visited Ysherra's bath house, because that was an excellent place to catch gossip.

And there was plenty of gossip.

Yes, it was true that there were military camps not only at Watya, but also at Lekata. It was also true, according to a man whose family came from Lekata, that the soldiers didn't go into town. They'd brought their own supplies.

The man described this as, *They don't even want to support our local businesses,* but another man said the military commanders probably didn't want to spook the locals.

At that point, an elderly gentleman in the corner of the bath house said, "But then explain this to me: if they told us what they're doing, they wouldn't need to fear spooking us."

That remark stuck in Javes' thoughts.

Yes, the doga was up to something, and no one knew what. Of course, the administrators of affected regions had asked. The reply from Tiverius was *exercises.* Very predictable.

Javes received a message from Saree in Whitesands Creek to keep an eye out for Trini, who had left without telling her mother where she was going. Saree worried about her daughter.

Ysherra was the next town down the road from Whitesands Creek, so logic dictated that she would come through town.

Saree worried that her daughter would return to *those people,* presumably those she thought were related to Mindo.

But if those people were in the area—and Javes asked, but everyone said that where strangers had visited, they were now gone—Mindo showed no sign of wanting to return to them.

In fact, as Javes watched him work from the office window, every time someone unfamiliar to Mindo came to the farm, Mindo hid in the shed or, in one case, behind some hay bales.

Time came to prepare for his trip to the northern council meeting.

Deep in his heart, Javes didn't want to go. He didn't like people. He would have to take Mindo, but was having difficulty justifying to himself why it was necessary. Mindo was a competent worker and could just as easily stay. Javes' distrust of him had waned again, because Mindo had done nothing to justify that distrust. He hadn't tried to go into town, he'd avoided people, and he was learning Chevakian, even if telling Javes how he had ended up on the desert coast was still beyond his ability to explain.

Since Renko had also attended the youth meetings in town, Javes asked him about it.

"They call themselves the people of the Gathering," Renko said.

"What—like they do in the ancient culture in Samira on the coast?"

"Yeah." Renko shrugged.

Javes went deep into his memory. This was stuff they'd learned in a subject called *Lands and peoples* at the Scriptorium. He recited from his memory. "Traditional Samiran customs are about community consensus. They hold a gathering every night."

"Yes, like that."

Huh. That was interesting. "When I was at the Scriptorium, there was a student who came from that region. The Samiran movement is very old and very small and very secretive."

"They're not small anymore. They're sending people into all the towns and asking the young people to join."

"You went to those meetings."

"A few." He looked aside. "It sounded like fun."

At the time, Javes had also suspected a girl was involved, but a relationship had never eventuated, so he'd never pressed Renko on the subject.

"But it wasn't?"

"Not so much that, but they wanted us to do stuff that I can't, like travel for months. Another young guy said he couldn't because he needed to help his mother with the shop, and they tried to make him tell his mother that this was more important, and I left when that happened, because that was stupid."

"Did he go?"

"No. But some of the girls did."

Javes hesitated before asking the next question. "Do you know if any of them were… violated by the men?"

"You mean, raped?"

"That and other things."

"You sound like you've heard something about this."

"Yes, I have." And then he explained what he heard from Trini, and also made it clear that he didn't know how Trini had decided Mindo was from the same group or had anything to do with them, but that something strange and inappropriate had definitely happened to her.

Renko shrugged, his face looking uncomfortable. "They only left not long ago, so I wouldn't know. I haven't seen any of my friends who went since they left." He met Javes' eyes. "Should I be worried? You know… with him here?" *Him* being Mindo.

"That's what I'm trying to find out. When poorly behaved men and young women get together, bad things happen. I don't want to assume that it's a fixture of the movement to provide the men of the movement with girls to rape."

Renko's expression continued to be uneasy.

Javes pressed ahead. "Is there anything you could tell me?"

Renko hesitated. "I don't want you to think this is a fact, but when you just said Trini was certain that Mindo was one of them... I can see that. When I talk about these meetings, the people there were locals, mostly. They came from the hamlets or were from town. One was from Watya. But there was one guy there... he wasn't from around here. He was like..." He shook his head. "I can't describe it. You know when you go into Watya and you go to the shops of the serious clothes sellers? You know how mama made me go in because she wanted me to have at least one set of clothes that made me not look like a farmer? You go into this shop and the shop person comes to you and offers you tea and takes your dusty overcoat and looks at it like it's the dirtiest thing he's ever seen, and then he shows you all this stuff that's like wow that has to be so expensive and when will I ever get to wear it? And you feel like you don't belong there because these are obviously not people like you and they're way above anything that you could possibly ever be? That's what this guy was like. The kids adored him. But he looked down on us and made it clear. I don't know why he was there, because he didn't seem to enjoy the meetings at all. Mindo reminds me of that guy. He's not the same, obviously, because Mindo is nothing like that. He's learning quite quickly and can be funny."

"Any word about where he came from?"

"Mindo? No. He seems to know things like how to do up a harness without much explanation, but then he tells us he can't remember."

"I mean the stranger who was at those meetings, the one that Mindo reminds you of. Do you know where he came from?"

"They called him Garu or something like that. I never heard him address the people in the meetings I attended, but they seemed to have to ask him about everything. He had these beautiful clean pale hands with long nails."

Javes thought uncomfortably about how he'd noticed Mindo's sophisticated hands.

"Where is he now?"

"He left. The young people still hold their gatherings in the back of the fruit shop, because Haro's dad owns the shop, but not many people come anymore, because most of us are just too busy for that kind of stuff."

The next day, Javes then went to the fruit shop where Kamat, Haro's father, told him of the "gatherings" the young kids held in his shed.

There was nothing sinister about them, he said, just a few kids getting together. They mostly played games.

Haro himself came in while Javes was in the shop and he confirmed this.

"It's just a bit of fun. Nothing special."

"Are you still in contact with the people who told you to start these gatherings? There was a man called Garu?"

"He was there. He is very important."

"Why?"

"That's what they all said. That he was from the Gathering."

"Like the group on the coast at Samira? Was he Samiran?"

"I don't know. He didn't tell."

"What did he say to you?"

"Oh, he wouldn't talk to me. Only the leaders got to talk to him."

"About what?"

He shrugged. "I don't know."

"Weren't you curious?"

The boy looked a bit uncomfortable. "I didn't see the harm. It's just fun. We're friends."

"But what about the people who left to travel with the group?"

"They wanted it. Nobody told them that's what they had to do. They're mostly girls. They don't..." He stopped as if he had been about to say something that he knew would not be all right to say.

"The girls don't..." Javes prompted.

Haro shrugged. He was a few years younger than Renko, still in that stage where teenage boys are lanky and don't seem to know how to hold themselves.

"Tell him, son," his father said.

Haro looked at the ground. "They say that the girls, you know, at my age, don't have anything useful to do and they should spend the time more wisely."

"And spending the time wisely includes going with those men to secret camps."

He shrugged. "I don't know. I didn't go."

"But for those who went, aren't you a bit worried?"

"They chose to go."

"That doesn't answer the question. Are you worried about those boys and girls? Where they are now? Whether they are all right? I'm guessing they are the brothers and sisters of your friends. Have any of them come back yet?"

Haro didn't say anything for a while, and then he burst out, "Look, it's nothing to do with me. I didn't make them go, all right?"

"I didn't say that. I'm just trying to find out what's happening. You can help me."

Haro said nothing.

"Hey, I'm not blaming you for anything."

Haro shook his head and continued to look at his feet. He said in a soft voice, "Some changed their minds after a few days. They're mostly very quiet. They say they missed their families and that's why they came back early. They never got to where the others were going."

"The kids say it's for a year," Kamat added. "They haven't been gone a year, most of them at least. When they come back, you can ask them."

Javes chatted a bit with the boy's father about the upcoming northern council meeting. He thought Haro had left, but when he was about to leave the shop, Haro blurted out, "I am worried about them, all right? I should have stopped them. I don't think these people care about us."

Javes stopped. Haro stood in the door to the living areas of the building, and he'd obviously waited for this time while weighing up the things Javes had told him.

Javes asked, "So, you do know any more?"

"No, I don't. I should have asked. Falina's mama is always asking me about her daughter when she comes to the shop. She thinks I know where she is. I don't, all right? I don't know what to say to her. It's not my fault. Falina chose to go. She asked her parents, and her parents never said that she couldn't. And now it's somehow my fault that they haven't heard from her? She's angry, right?"

"Why doesn't she ask the people in the movement instead of you?"

"She doesn't want to talk to them. And also—they wouldn't know. They're just local kids."

His face had a haunted expression. His father looked uncomfortable. These were practical people, not people who spent lots of time on philosophy about the big questions in life.

"I believe you," Javes said. "I should have looked into this, but I've been busy, and I didn't pay this the attention I should have. I'm still busy, but when I go to Watya, I will ask around to see if I can find out what's going on. You can do something for me. Anything you remember or find out from others, anything at all, come to me and tell me about it. Or if I'm not here, write it down."

The boy's cheeks coloured. "I'm not so good at writing. I make lots of spelling mistakes."

"I don't care. Write it down so you don't forget. If I have time, I'll help you fix the mistakes."

Javes walked home feeling more worried than he had when he'd come.

At his house he walked past Mindo hard at work in the olive grove with one of the farm hands, pruning back olive trees.

He did not disbelieve Trini or Kamat or his son. He also did not disbelieve Mindo, who genuinely showed no sign of ever having been in this area before. But he did fear that the two were connected, and he had no idea how.

Tali was in the office with a guest. A woman who sold wool, Lissa told him.

Javes made Lissa some lemonade in the kitchen and then went upstairs to pack a bag for his trip. He didn't want to go, but he had to.

He had felt safe in this area, where he didn't have to worry about what happened in Tiverius or in the rest of the world. But it looked like that time was over.

He was in the bedroom, trying to decide what travel clothes to take, when someone came into the kitchen.

Tali was still with the visitor, and he could see Renko outside.

Javes abandoned his packing and walked down the stairs.

He found an employee of the telegraph office in the hallway downstairs.

"Well, that's a surprise, seeing you here," Javes said.

"I agreed to let you know when I had some time to check the telegraph messages for the day you asked me to check."

"You could have asked me to come into town."

"I was on my way to my brother's farm, anyway." He handed Javes an envelope.

"Thank you."

"Wait until you've seen it."

Javes opened the flap and took out a single sheet of paper.

Scrawled on the paper, presumably written by the man who stood before him, were some very strange words and numbers.

Javes stared at it.

"What does this mean?"

"This is what was sent from Whitesands Creek that morning."

"What does it mean?"

He shook his head. "I'm just the telegraph operator."

"Where did he send it?"

"To Watya. According to the office there, the message was delivered to a house in town."

Well, that was interesting.

Javes again looked at the letter, but the characters on the page just made no sense.

Yet Mindo had shown no interest in going to Watya.

When the man had left, Javes changed his mind about whether he'd take Mindo to Watya. Let him ask about it. Let him admit that he did know people in the area.

CHAPTER 26

Ravi's Aranian lesson the next day didn't go well.

Apart from the fact that he hadn't done his homework, he found it hard to concentrate.

His tutor was an old Aranian refugee. Ravi understood from his father that many of those were people who had supported one of the old princes and that with the demise of those princes, and the abolishing of their trappings, like mothers' houses, many had packed up and gone elsewhere.

The ones who had a lot of money had gone to Peria, because once they'd paid the entry fees, the taxation laws were friendlier to people with money, so those who'd come to Chevakia either had family there or they didn't have enough money to pay the settlement fees to Peria.

Ravi judged his tutor to be one of the latter variety.

The man came with good recommendations, which mattered to Ravi's parents, but he was also petty and vindictive, and that mattered most to Ravi.

No, of course, he didn't already know a basic level of Aranian and also, he didn't consider learning Aranian to be the pinnacle of his studies. And he tolerated, but didn't like, the types of texts the man pulled out for him to study.

So instead of learning by rote all the tenses and conjugations—which he had no time for anyway, because he'd left it too late—he answered the questions the tutor had set about the text.

He tried to say *I'm glad that Chevakia has no royal family, because the Aranian tradition of princes fighting each other to the death for the throne seems pretty dumb to me*, and he got all the tenses and conjugations wrong, as his tutor told him in a voice that sounded like he was on the brink of shouting.

"Besides," the man said in his Aranian accent. "The han Chevonian family, to which you belong, might as well be royalty."

"But we're not. We're elected."

And the long-term Proctor Sadorius han Chevonian was dead. He had been Ravi's uncle once removed. The han Chevonian extended family was quite big. Uncle Sady's wife was Perian, and their only daughter Lana was now queen of Arania.

"Elected," the man said in a sneering tone, and lifted his chin. "You have to be very naïve to believe that these so-called elections are fair. But. Let's keep to the subject matter. You will rewrite all these answers in a correct manner with appropriate answers. I think I don't have to tell you what constitutes an appropriate reply. You will have trouble securing a place as a diplomat when your replies show this type of attitude."

Ravi was seething, but he kept his mouth shut, because to continue to speak up would only result in bad marks and complaints to his father.

As it was, the tutor already complained to his father, who asked him, at dinner in front of his mother and the house staff, whether he was dumb enough not to see that he embarrassed his family or whether that was the intention.

"I don't know what's going on with you, son, but I have to admit that your recent behaviour puzzles me and disappoints me."

"The tutor asked me a question, and I answered it."

"He didn't ask you to be smart about it."

"It was one sentence in a longer reply, and he didn't tell me I couldn't give my opinion."

His father pointed at him. "You, son, are too young to have an opinion."

"There it is. That's the reason!" Ravi half-rose from his seat.

His mother looked horrified. "Ravi, don't shout like that. It's unbecoming and invites gossip."

"I don't care. That is another reason. I'm twenty. What were you doing when you were twenty? Were you being told, for every step you took in the day, what you could do and couldn't do?"

"That was different. We were at war, so we grew up quickly."

"And I'm going to be treated as a child until I'm thirty?"

His father glared at him. "Just what do you want? I know I've asked this before, and I don't hold hope for a sensible answer—"

"It's not that hard! I want to be taken seriously. To be treated like an adult. To make my own decisions. When I want to see friends in the evening, I don't want to have to sneak around and make excuses or present my friends' life histories for approval. Like normal people my age."

"You should be studying."

"I can't study every waking hour of the day. I want to have friends I choose."

His father glared at him in a long moment of silence that dragged on for what felt like ages.

Ravi's heart was thudding in his throat.

Then his father snorted. "Well, I guess the damage has already been done."

Damage?

What did that mean?

"So? I can go?"

"As long as there is no more funny behaviour. And you keep your tutors happy. I don't understand what's wrong with you these days. I give you every opportunity I can think of, and are you grateful? No!"

Ravi glared at the table. He was tempted to say that he couldn't see why he should be grateful, but he knew that would be petty and wrong. It was not even that he didn't see that his parents acted with the best intentions. It was that he was old enough for them to… stop doing so much of that.

He was also tired of arguing over all this. Arguing was not a strong point of his. His father argued all the time in the doga. Ravi couldn't compete with that.

So he said he would make sure he got his work done, and was finally allowed to go. The meeting would have started already, and he hoped that Dana didn't think he wasn't coming.

He got changed into casual clothing and went off to the horse market, where it was very busy with men wanting to sell horses and buy horses and leading horses to pens and arguing over prices.

The place smelled—unsurprisingly—of horses and because it was almost dark, Ravi had trouble finding his newfound friends. He only remembered for certain what Dana looked like, but didn't remember any of the other faces.

He pushed his way through the crowds.

Horse traders came here from all over the city and the surrounding country. He'd been surprised to hear, a year or so back, that the horse trade was still very lively. People used horses for transport, if they couldn't afford a truck. People used horses to work fields where tractors couldn't get through. And they used horses for the mail. Those were stubby little ponies that would either pull a small cart or carry bags with mail to be delivered.

Ravi finally found the group gathered under a tree, sharing biscuits from a tin. One or two people held drinks, some kind of juice or cordial.

Ravi sat down next to Dana. She looked up at him and smiled.

"I'm sorry for being late," he said. "You don't know my father…"

"Actually, I do know him. He has a bit of a reputation."

"Not a good one, I assume?"

"No."

Ravi looked down. "I don't know if I should be here. If you don't want me…"

"Of course we do. You're not your father."

He shrugged. Suppose she was right about that, but living in a house like his with a family like his was going to make him very different from the others.

"I can't stop you from going back home, but I thought you were stronger than that."

"I'm not, really."

"Yes, you are. It was amazing that you dared talk to the proctor like that."

"Huh. My father gave me a real talking to. And then I did badly with my Aranian tutor and he refused to give me a decent enough mark to move to another class and be taught by someone else. I hate that man."

"I bet it's an old guy called Sarak."

'That's the very one. Do you study Aranian?"

"I did, for a while. He's such a bore, isn't he?"

They laughed.

Then an uncomfortable silence passed. A silence in which he might have asked who her family was, because their previous conversation about this subject had only made him more curious. If she belonged to the di Fabrioli family, he could use that fact to impress his father with his friends. But he also didn't want to ask, because Dana would know why he wanted to know and that this was the reason she didn't want to talk about it.

There was some activity in the group that indicated that the talk was about to begin.

The young man whose turn it was to speak had chosen business opportunities for young people as a subject.

To be honest, Ravi didn't find the talk half as interesting as the day before, but Dana listened intently. She stood next to him, and each time she looked aside, their eyes met and he felt hot, even more so when he thought of his embarrassing dream of her. By the same token... what did she look like under that boyish outfit?

No, that was a bad idea to think about right now.

Still, she would probably clear his parents' high requirements for someone he would be allowed to have an interest in. *Especially* if he could say her name was di Fabrioli.

The discussion went on about how young people in Chevakia didn't receive relevant training to be good business owners, only on how to be academics. And academics only cost money because they sold nothing and produced nothing. Ravi wanted to argue how this was untrue, but that urge dissipated quickly. These people didn't understand what the Scriptorium did, and that the academics had saved society much pain through being able to predict the weather and saved many lives through working out how to resurrect the old sonorics machines that protected the continent.

Then an older man spoke up. "Training people correctly is what we do in the camps."

This was a man who was a few years older than those in the group. Ravi hadn't given him much attention and wasn't even sure if he'd been there at the meeting in the ulli hall. But now he wondered why he was here. Obviously, he was a foreigner, because he spoke with a heavy accent.

"What camps?" he asked Dana. And what did he mean by *correctly*?

But the foreigner heard his question and answered. "The young people come together in groups away from the city and other bad influences. They can talk about what they want with their lives. There are exciting things happening and good discussions taking place. Then people learn to do the work. The young people come from all over the land."

Ravi wondered where he was from. The accent didn't sound Aranian, or at least he didn't sound like his tutor. Ravi wasn't sure what a Perian accent sounded like. But Perian people were supposed to have dark hair, pale skin and blue eyes. This man didn't. His skin was too dark to be Perian, his eyes brown and his hair was a strange reddish-brown. He wore local clothes.

"Where are these camps?" he asked.

The man replied, "In different places in the country. Usually old farms."

"And what happens there? Just talking and working? What sort of work? Farm work?"

A young woman said, "And other work. Making things. Skills our parents don't teach us."

"It's an honour to go," a young man added. "We're working for the country, so we can make everything ourselves and don't need to get stuff from Peria."

That seemed innocent and noble enough. "And people who go there don't tell their parents, right?" He thought about the petition letters in the mail office, about young people having gone missing. He guessed this was what happened to them. They went to work in the camps and didn't tell their parents because their parents wanted their kids to do learned things.

—Except some of those parents had seemed quite simple themselves, judging by their spelling skills. He couldn't imagine that *all* those parents wanted those kids to study at the Scriptorium.

The stranger said, "Parents are not allowed."

That wasn't really an answer to the question.

"I'm going," said one of the young local men.

Ravi looked at Dana. "Are you going?"

She nodded.

"Are you not going to tell your parents?"

"They know. They're fine with it."

Then Ravi said, before he could stop himself, "I can go as well."

He didn't know where it came from or what possessed him to say this. His parents would not need to think about this for more than a second. They would never allow him to go.

When everyone had affirmed that they were also going, the meeting broke up when a group of students said they had to go home.

Ravi walked with Dana in the direction of their homes.

"That was a brave thing to say, that you were coming," she said. "You didn't have to do that. During Gatherings, people are free to be honest."

"But I wasn't lying. I want to come."

"Really?" She narrowed her eyes. "Your parents are very strict."

"I'm also an adult. I can make my own decisions."

"I guess..." She hesitated.

"Are you saying I can't come?"

"No, not at all. I'd like you to come because you could bring a lot to our discussions, with the knowledge you have about the doga, but on the other hand, if you disappear from your home, your father is not going to let it rest so easily. He's not going to write petitions to the proctor like those poor people in the country. He's going to send the army."

"He wouldn't do that. My father is very strict, but he's also very strict for a reason: because he's ridiculously principled. As a politician of influence, you never use the army against your own people. That is called a civil war."

She met his eyes with a serious look. "Never underestimate what people in power will do to hang onto that power."

That remark chilled him deep into his bones. "Is that the sort of thing that goes on in the di Fabrioli family?"

"What makes you think I'm from the di Fabrioli family?"

"Because you said your family was old money and—"

"Do I look like a di Fabrioli?"

No, she didn't. Di Fabriolis were all kind of… chonky people.

"I'm sorry, I just sort of assumed and made you a di Fabrioli in my head. But I guess you're not."

"I'll tell you, but I'd like it to remain quiet. Mainly because I don't see eye to eye with my family about many things. And my family and its presence in Tiverius has been controversial ever since my great-grandmother fled there."

Oh. He knew. He suspected…

Not that family.

Seriously. He couldn't believe it.

But they ticked all the boxes: rich, exclusive, secretive, manipulating.

"What is the proper name again?" Many years ago, the cruel King Caldor of Peria and his family were killed in the City of Glass. His son's widow and unborn child fled to Chevakia. The woman married a Chevakian merchant, who also looked after her son. But she and the merchant never had children. Her son, direct heir to the throne, had a Chevakian family. He, in fact, had several children with different women. The family was known by their Chevakian name han Trevasa. But recently they had indicated they wanted to be known by their royal Perian name.

She said, "Thillei. My name is Danaithe."

"And you're…" He chuckled uneasily. "A princess?"

"Not really. The palace in the City of Glass has plenty of successors to the throne. It wasn't always like that, but that's the situation now. If I could make a claim, it would come at the bottom of quite a list. But yes, I'm a direct descendant of King Caldor. And I don't want that to be known to those who don't need to know."

"And you worked in the mail room?" It still felt surreal to him.

"I have to pay my bills."

"But you're living with your parents?"

"No, I'm not. I told my father I wanted to be independent, and that meant I had to find a job."

"At least you were paid for your work."

"Well, there's a lot wrong with the families that run the doga for sure. I could talk about that for days. But I suspect I'm not telling you anything new, after your outburst to the proctor."

He grinned, and she chuckled.

They stood for a moment in awkward silence.

"Well…" he said after a long silence. "I guess I'll see you in the mail room tomorrow?"

"Yes, sure." Tomorrow was good. Tomorrow was close enough that he didn't need to worry about how he was going to get out of the house to go with her to this study camp, or whatever it was that the young people from the Gathering did there. At this point, he didn't care. He just wanted the same level of freedom enjoyed by Dana.

He walked home with a spring in his step.

At home, he found his mother in the kitchen, checking on him, as usual, but it didn't make him angry this time. He'd expected it. She'd give up, eventually.

He told her he'd just met some friends, and she didn't ask much more.

Then she said, "Your father could have used your assistance."

Ravi gave her a strange look. Wasn't his father in bed, like usual?

"The guards interrupted a burglar trying to break into the proctor's residence."

And his father needed his help? "I might be doing some training, but I'm no good at catching burglars."

"The man was going through the proctor's documents when the

proctor and his wife were coming back from a night spent with friends."

Ravi still didn't see what he could contribute.

"The proctor needs to know if the man stole anything important."

"Should I… go over there to help?" Ravi still wasn't sure what he could do or why this was so important it couldn't wait until tomorrow.

"They're probably fine now."

"All right, then I'll go to bed. I'll be in the doga building tomorrow, anyway."

But as he was going up the stairs, it came to him why his mother mentioned this to him: because she wanted him to feel guilty for not being at home when something happened.

CHAPTER 27

For most of the days following Harek's visit to the tower, Kotori wondered if he had now really blown his chances.

The prince's words *You're here because you want to be surrounded by women who adore you. I'm here because I'm interested in the house* echoed through his mind.

He'd finally gone too far.

Harek was right: he had talked about having a mothers' house, but not once had the prince interacted with him on that topic. He'd assumed it was for a mothers' house, but the prince had never confirmed that.

But if he didn't want the house for mothers, then what was it for?

And, worse, Kotori had told Pertak to find some pretty girls from the regions that gave the capital the most grief. What was he going to say to Pertak? What was he going to say if those girls—and their parents—started turning up at the Citadel?

A few days later, Kotori led another stargazing session on the top of the astrology tower. Although the princess didn't come this time, some of the other students did and they brought their friends. They scoured the sky for the blinking object, but Kotori had chosen his time better, and the object was not going to be visible in the sky in the evening.

When one of the students asked about it, he said that it was probably a freak occurrence and a trick of the light. He spent the rest of the evening talking about much safer subjects. But the students were not as keen. They started talking to each other and making jokes.

When Kotori finally came back to his room, feeling frustrated, someone was waiting for him there.

One of the royal guards.

He turned around when Kotori came down the stairs onto the landing.

"Good evening, astrologer."

Kotori looked the man up and down. "Can I help you?"

"The queen wants to talk to you."

"Let me put down my books."

As he turned to the door, he noticed an envelope stuck behind the door handle. His name was written on the front in a neat hand.

Mother's breath, what was that? Was everyone after him now?

He pulled the letter loose and stuck it in the pocket of his cloak.

Then he opened the door with sweaty hands, under the guard's constant gaze.

The guard remained in the hallway.

Kotori scurried into his room and stopped inside, a wave of panic coming over him.

The queen.

Having grown up in Chevakia, the queen had never asked for a casting that wasn't also required by ceremony. Kotori had done a casting for her when the king officially married her, and also at the princess' birth. But he knew she had deep contempt for the art of casting fortunes.

She would never call on him for that reason.

In fact, she didn't like him and would avoid him if she could.

Which meant she called on him because she couldn't avoid him.

So this had to be an occasion where she would admonish him for something he had done or hadn't done.

And out of the many things this could be about, she was sure to raise the mysterious blinking object, because the queen was very knowledgeable—if far too skeptical—about astrology. She even refused to use that word.

After the previous astrology session, the princess would have mentioned the object to her mother. The queen had a keen interest in astrology and she was devilishly good at it.

Kotori knew she'd been too busy and preoccupied to do much stargazing lately, but after her daughter's report, she would have studied the sky and had seen the object for herself.

And she would roast him for not saying anything about it earlier.

He checked his book of notes about it—it still lay in the drawer. He pulled the key from under his robe and locked the drawer.

Calm, calm, he had to stay calm.

He had to consider carefully what to do, like he had done all his life.

Go through the motions. Tell people what they wanted to hear.

He took off his cloak because he didn't need it inside, and straightened his robe. He took the letter out of the pocket. The handwriting looked familiar. Yes, he was pretty sure it was from Pertak. Whatever he wanted would have to wait.

First, the queen.

She hadn't asked for a casting, so he left his map and stones on the desk.

He breathed deeply in and out a few times.

Let's face the queen's anger.

Then he went outside again, where the guard waited patiently.

They set off down the winding staircase of the tower, into the courtyard, where a chilly breeze made Kotori regret that he hadn't kept his cloak on. He would have had somewhere to hide his hands, because they always gave away when he was nervous.

The royal family occupied an entire wing of the main and oldest building of the Citadel. Kotori and the guard went in through the grand entrance and up the staircase. Not so long ago, the court's carpenters had built a smooth ramp that allowed the queen to take the king outside in his wheelchair. They would wander around in the garden that surrounded the old mothers' house. The garden that she had planted. These days, the garden beds were overgrown with that detestable orange-flowered weed whose seeds stopped conception in women. It was a travesty. A woman's function was to be a mother. Why would any woman forego that glorious feeling?

They walked past the guards in the royal livery, who nodded at their colleague and Kotori and let them through.

Into the king's private quarters.

King Orik himself would probably already be in bed.

The guard led him into the royal sitting room. This was usually where the queen received guests. Was it a good thing that she didn't call him to the office?

Probably not. The office was next to the bedroom, and from the bedroom, one could probably hear what was being said nextdoor, especially at night when the rest of the building was quiet, and if the windows were open. Orik might be feeble, but there was nothing wrong with his ears.

The queen stood as a silhouette in front of the window, looking out over the city, when Kotori entered.

"Good evening, your highness." He bowed as much as his stiff back and his time standing on the viewing platform on the tower allowed.

She turned around.

The light from the oil lamps hit her face. It softened her expression compared with the daylight. Her hair was very bushy and curly, a legacy of her Perian heritage. These days, it was flecked through with grey. Her pale eyes had not lost any of their sharpness and because her skin was so pale, she never spent much time in the sun. Unlike Aranians of similar age, she didn't have skin that resembled that on a turtle.

She didn't tell him to sit down, so Kotori remained standing.

"I'm sure you're wondering why I called you here at this time."

"You can call me whenever you want, your highness. It's not my position to wonder about it."

She snorted.

Kotori looked down, in his mind going over all the different ways he had rehearsed talking about the blinking light, knowing that she'd dismiss all of them before he'd even finished the sentence.

"It's about my son."

Wait—total change of subject.

"Your son, your highness?" He looked up.

"I believe you heard me."

"Is anything wrong with him?"

She was going to roast him over the things Harek would have told her. But then his rational mind took over and he reminded himself that if Harek was thinking about having a mothers' house, his mother and sister would be the last people he'd tell about it.

"I believe you took him to the old armourer's house outside the gate." Kotori opened his mouth, and then didn't know what to say, so he closed it again. "I have an eyewitness account from someone who saw you walking down the street with him. In fact, they also saw you two walking in the harbour before that. Why are you meeting him and what are you telling him?"

"That house is empty. He wanted to explore what he could use it for."

"And? Did he find something?"

"He didn't tell me."

"Nice try, astrologer. Why were you involved with this venture, anyway? If it had been his own idea to look at this house, he would never have come to you to ask about it, right? You're the astrologer, not the Citadel's property manager. So clearly you went to him to tell him that the house was free. Now why would you do that? What is your agenda?"

Every single one of her words vibrated with implied threats. Kotori strongly suspected that she already knew everything about the trip and about what he had been doing. She just wanted to hear it, as a confession, from his mouth.

And he was not going to give her that satisfaction, because as uncomfortable as this subject was, while she questioned him about this, she wasn't talking about blinking lights in the sky.

"My task is to keep the members of the royal family safe." He stuck his chin in the air.

"That doesn't answer my question."

"I'm very sorry, but that's the only answer I have. If the prince wants to look at the house, I show him the house, because he's the prince and I am only the court astrologer."

"Huh." She snorted. "Well, you might want to stick to astrology, because not to put too fine a point on it, but I have a thing or two to say about that, too."

No! Kotori's heart jumped.

He scrambled for a reply that would please her. "I'm happy to leave looking at houses to the people who deal in the Citadel's property. I was doing him a favour, but I'm happy to hand the task off to someone else in the future."

"Good." She met his eyes with an intense look. "It's late now and we should go to bed, but one of these days you can expect a visit from me to talk about some important questions about the study of the stars. You may go."

Kotori didn't know how fast he had to scurry from the room. She knew about the mysterious object. She knew he'd known about it for a long time.

His life was unravelling before his eyes.

He refused the company of a guard with a torch, so he stumbled through the Citadel's halls and courtyards in the darkness.

In his room, he sank down on the chair in front of the window. The courtyard below was lit by the glow from the lamps under the archway that led to the next courtyard. A guard often stood there, but Kotori couldn't see him.

Then he remembered the letter that had been stuck behind the door handle.

He went into the wardrobe and took it from the pocket of his cloak.

He folded out the paper inside. On it, Pertak had written a simple message.

I have some news you might find interesting.

That was all?

Couldn't he have simply—no, Kotori had been on the astrology tower and Pertak wouldn't have known that. He'd knocked on Kotori's door, found he wasn't there, so he had written this note.

Which, Kotori assumed, was about a pressing bit of news he'd found out.

Normally, Kotori would have waited to do something about a message like this until the next day, because it was late, but he'd asked Pertak for unusual things that people from the regions had reported to him. This was sure to be about that.

And it wasn't that late, was it?

He checked the time.

Well, it was kind of late, well after his stargazing session had ended and after he had spoken to the queen.

But he knew he'd be unable to sleep with the knowledge that Pertak wanted to see him, and, knowing Pertak, he might be off on a trip the next morning.

So Kotori donned his cloak and went to see Pertak, anyway.

The courtyards and passages of the Citadel lay deserted.

The guards stood in their guard stations, looking exceedingly bored. They nodded politely when he passed, and one or two might have raised their eyebrows. Kotori was normally in bed long before this time.

Pertak lived in the block of houses on the mountain side of the Citadel. While the Citadel occupied a hilltop and was the highest point in the city, the range behind the city was taller. The area behind the Citadel, facing away from the river, was a kind of low saddle pass. A lot of the homes of well-of citizens were in this area that caught the sea breeze, but was not close enough to the ocean to suffer from the salty humidity.

Pertak was, like himself, not tied to a woman or family, and he lived alone in a small apartment on the top floor of a building that consisted of ten or twelve such housing units.

A few sparse lights burned in the stairwell, trailing coils of smoke into the air as Kotori trudged up.

He could hear very little of what went on behind the doors on each landing. The inhabitants would be asleep.

He listened at Pertak's door, but couldn't hear anything. What to do now? Pertak hadn't said anything about a meeting time.

Then he knocked anyway.

It took a long time before some scuffling noises came from the other side. Then the door opened a crack.

"Who is there?" That was Pertak's voice, muffled and confused.

"You left me a note."

"Kotori? What are you doing here?"

"You left a note that you wanted to see me."

"Whenever you had time. Tomorrow. I wasn't in this much of a hurry. But come in, before the neighbours complain about talking in the stairwell."

He opened the door further. He was wearing a long white nightgown. Well, that was embarrassing.

"I'm sorry if I woke you up."

"It's all right, I'm awake now."

Kotori entered the apartment's hall and followed Pertak into the living room.

The apartment was just the right size for one person, and Pertak kept it exceptionally tidy. He asked if Kotori wanted a drink, but Kotori said he wouldn't stay long, just long enough to hear about the news.

So Pertak started. "It's about your question asking if anyone in the regions had noticed anything unusual with rocks falling from the sky."

It was as Kotori had thought. "So somebody did report about it."

"I received a written report out of the border region of a strange streak of light falling from the sky. They're close to the Chevakian border, and the Chevakians are known to experiment with weapons. It wouldn't be the first time that they're careless, and projectiles or patrols stray across the border. The village sent out a few people to look for Chevakian weapons, but the boys found a huge hole in the ground that was bigger than any Chevakian weapon can make. But what made them specifically contact me is that a few days after finding the hole, the boys came down with a horrible illness. Fortunately, both are recovering, but a couple of the farmer's cows have died."

"What sort of illness?"

"Their skin went red and then came out in blisters, and then they developed fever and illness of the bowels."

"But they recovered?"

"That's what the report says."

He met Kotori's eyes. They both knew that if this was a weapon of a type that used icefire, any improvement would only be temporary.

"Did anyone find fragments of the weapon?" Kotori asked.

"The report isn't that detailed. It just says people noticed sounds like thunder and some farmers saw a flash in the sky and then the next day, they found the hole. If there had been an object, then I assume that would have made it into the report."

That was true.

But also, the report didn't specifically say that they'd checked for an object and hadn't found one.

They would have checked, he was sure of that.

So this meant… that they had found something, but they didn't want to use this report to notify the Citadel? After what he'd witnessed, on top of the astrology tower with his students, he didn't believe the report. If he'd seen the object fall, and there was a hole in the ground, there would be fragments.

Pertak didn't have more information, so Kotori left him to go back to bed and walked through the darkness back to the astrology tower. In the streets in the city, many of the oil lamps had burned out and the last stragglers had come home from the bars.

The visit hadn't filled him with a lot of hope that he'd have an easy answer that would satisfy the queen. Not that, after twenty years of wondering and looking for answers, he'd expected something simple.

Well, after twenty years, he was finally forced to do something about it. So that he could show the king and queen that he was working on unravelling the mystery, while also covering up that he'd known about it for years. By taking himself out of the Citadel. It had finally come to this.

He took out his bag and packed most of his travel clothes in it. He took a clean notebook because he needed space to write. He hung his astrologer's robe in the wardrobe, and packed his star map and his stones.

He put these next to the door. He went to sleep until the calls of the Citadel's peacocks woke him up. Then he got dressed in his travel clothes, picked up his bag and slipped out of the Citadel before anyone could see him. He walked through the deserted streets where the only other people were the city's drunks and vagrants and the merchants turning up early for the markets.

He would not be there to buy dried prunes.

He turned to the station.

Once he had left the city, he would send a message to the queen that he'd gone on a brief study trip. Because he "recognised the severity of the discovery". Hopefully, most people in the Citadel would buy that explanation. If they could be made to believe that somehow, the astrologer didn't look at the stars at night and had never seen this thing before.

If they were dumb enough to believe that.

The guards would. The king… probably, but the queen… no, she'd see him for the liar and coward he was. Not that she'd ever seen him differently, but now she would have proof.

CHAPTER 28

Lana stopped a few paces into the living room. The table looked magnificent, with fresh bread and jams and fruit and all the king's favourite dishes, but the king himself was sorely lacking.

"Where is my husband?" she asked of the servant woman who stood at the door.

"I'm not sure, your highness," she said.

"Then wouldn't you go to find out?"

The woman's face went red. "We were very busy. I assumed that he would come. He's always keen to come by himself."

It was true, at least within this apartment. He insisted on moving himself around. When Orik could no longer walk, courtesy of an old battle wound, they'd made the floor smooth and installed ramps so that he could move his wheelchair.

"Go and find out where my husband is. Please bring him here."

Lana sat down at the table, but admitted to not feeling terribly hungry herself.

The tableware cupboard against the wall held two more plates for the children.

But Loriane was very busy practicing for a trip. Now that her music studies were finished—and she should be concentrating on other subjects—she wanted to spend more time with the orchestra she had formed with a group of people from the course. They'd given a few performances in the market hall in central Kadrish, while lamenting that Kadrish didn't have formal performance venues, only crude stages for street fights, and the musicians baulked at using those blood-stained stages.

The group was now to have their first formal tour. Loriane had always wanted to perform in the City of Glass. Lana had taken her there on trips, to come to grips with a family heritage that not even she understood well.

But now King Selinor had officially invited the group, and yes, Lana understood how big a deal that was, but also, Loriane should be studying statecraft, because time was running out. To her argument that her father was not getting any younger, Loriane had said, as recently as this morning, that Lana had been wielding that argument for at least ten years.

That was also true, but Lana knew from her own experience, that holding power didn't come naturally. It resulted from long years of experience doing many different things that increased your understanding of who the players were and how to outfox them if necessary.

She poured herself some tea and walked to the window.

The many domes and turrets of Kadrish basked in glorious sunlight. A riot of colour marked the fruit market that was on today.

"Your highness!"

Lana turned around. "Yes, what's wrong?" It was the serving girl who had gone to get Orik, *without* Orik.

"The king… There is something funny going on with his face."

Lana set down her tea with such force that it sloshed over the side. "Where is he?"

"In his bedroom."

Lana strode out the door, left into the hallway and two doors down to Orik's bedroom. The first thing she noticed was how stuffy the air in the room was.

Also, that Orik had moved quite a lot of furniture in here. He didn't like it when people invaded his domain and questioned his independence.

It had been a very long time since she had last spent a night here. Her unwritten agreement with him had been for one child. She had given him two.

Orik sat in an arm chair by the window. Or maybe *sat* was not the right description for the way he half-hung sideways against the armrest.

She crossed the floor in a few steps and knelt before him.

"Orik!"

His hands were cold, the skin scabbed and paper-thin.

His eyes were droopy and desperately intense. Half his lip hung down. A drop of saliva was about to fall off. He tried to speak and his lips moved, but no sound came out.

"I'll call the medic immediately." She jumped to her feet and made for the door, her heart thudding.

"W—w—-wait."

His voice sounded so feeble.

"I need to find the medic to look after you."

"N—no p—point."

He was struggling to get the words out.

"M—my mmm—mm—mouth d—doesn't w—www—work."

"That's why you need the medic."

"N—nnn—no."

"What no? There is something wrong with you."

"O—old aaa—age. L—lll—lori—lori—ane. Get hhh—her."

With a deep sense of dread, Lana realised what he wanted. Loriane to come to his room, with the book of primary laws, with the crown, to transfer power. And to the best of her knowledge, Loriane was in the harbour packing for her trip to Peria.

"I'll do it." Heaven help the poor guard who'd have to tell her that her trip to Peria was off.

She opened the door.

"A—nd K—kkkk—kkkkk"

"Kotori?"

He nodded.

Lana ran to the guard station. She told them to get a medic as well, even if she also knew that Orik was right: no medic would fix the effects of old age. They had all known for years that this was coming.

Then she ran to the king's office, the place where she did most of her work, opened the cabinet in the corner with the key on the chain around her neck. She took out the book and the crown and put them on the desk.

The book contained the primary laws of Arania, of which there were many, but not by far enough. The laws did cover the simple, practical aspects of succession.

She turned to that section. She had read it before, but had always thought they'd have more time to study the details.

The king shall only transfer his rule to his chosen son—why had they never changed that?—*when in the presence of the court astrologer and only if the omens of succession are favourable.* Yes, she knew this. Kotori could sink the entire deal.

She'd hoped that Kotori would have dropped off the perch before Orik, being the older of the two. Then she could have appointed a younger, more reasonable astrologer.

But no.

After moving into the King's quarters twenty years ago, she had disposed of many of the old guard. But Kotori was untouchable through the sheer number of people whose fortunes he had spoken at important points in their lives.

Now she would have to go and find that despicable man and the fate of her family would be in his hands.

She left the office again, ran down the hallway, down the king's private stairs to the courtyard, across the garden and up into the astrology tower.

It was not a place where she came a lot. Kotori disliked her, and she disliked him, and they kept out of each other's way. If ever the law called for an astrologer, she would send someone up here to get him.

But now she climbed the winding staircase into the tower. It was not just Kotori's room at the top. There was a viewing platform where you could set up spyglasses and study the skies, but since they had extended the library, there was also a tower on top, and the view from up there was just as good, if not better.

Lana reached the door to the astrologer's room.

She breathed in deeply and knocked.

There was no response, so she knocked again.

When there was still no response, she asked, "Kotori. I would like to speak to you. The king needs you."

There was still no response, so she pushed the door.

To her surprise, it was open.

The room beyond was shrouded in semi darkness. Light came in through a small window, but because it was about to go dark and the window faced east, the light was already dim.

There was no one in the room. The bed was untouched, the cupboard was shut, a cloth lay on the table with a couple of dice on it. Wherever he was, it looked like he had only just walked out.

The library.

He'd be teaching.

So she went down the stairs again and crossed the short distance to the library.

It was quite busy in the main study area. She held a fleeting hope that she might find Loriane here, as she should be, but the students in the library were all much younger.

She didn't see Kotori either. She asked a few students, but they hadn't seen him.

"He sometimes meets people at the back of the library," a student said. "There is another study nook there. He doesn't like us sitting there because you're meant to be quiet and he says he prefers to keep the noise to this part of the library."

Lana walked in between the shelves made of heavy wood, groaning under the weight of thousands and thousands of books. Years and years of history. It was not for nothing that the library of Kadrish was one of the wonders of the world. It contained more books than anyone could ever read, big leather-bound tomes with golden letters on the spine, some books so old that they almost fell apart, and were written in languages few people could understand.

The shelves stood close together and were so tall that you needed to use a ladder on wheels to get to the top ones.

She knew the study nook the student referred to. It was a very old setting, with velvet-covered benches and a tabletop inlaid with mother-of-pearl that reflected the light from a flapping oil lamp that burned on a stand in the corner. The table was empty.

Lana walked past all the aisles, looking into the darkness of each, but there was no one.

Well, that was annoying. The one time she had a genuine need for the astrologer, he was nowhere to be found.

Lana went back to the student. "What sort of people does he meet in the back of the library?"

"I don't know. Old people."

"Do you recognise any of them?"

"No, I'm sorry."

Lana left the library and stood at the entrance, wondering what to do now.

She spotted a guard go into the entrance of the king's quarters in the presence of the court medic.

And a moment later, Loraine ran into the courtyard.

"Mother! What's going on?"

"Your father has taken a bad turn."

Her mouth fell open. A moment of unspoken horror passed between them.

"I tried to find the astrologer, but he seems to be out."

"He's probably gone to the markets."

"The markets?"

"Kotori has a liking for dried prunes," Loriane said. "Apparently last week he ate so many that he went to the latrines three times during a lesson. Wherever he walked, he left behind a waft of smelly air."

"That's disgusting. Where do you even hear stuff like that?"

"Students talk."

They'd reached the top of the stairs and turned into the private apartment.

The door to Orik's room stood open, and the voice of the medic drifted into the hallway. "No, get that pillow for me."

Inside the room, a couple of servants stood around the bed, where they had moved Orik. The sheets and blankets had been pulled back. Orik lay on his side, his head on a pillow, while the medic used a cone to listen to his heart and his breathing.

Orik met Lana's eyes.

His mouth moved.

Lana knelt next to him.

He whispered, "M—mmmy b—b—brother?"

"I can't find the astrologer. He might have gone into town. But I have all the things ready."

"N—nnn—no p—point with—without m—my b—brother."

Sadly, he was right.

Lana went to the lone palace guard in the room. "Have you seen the astrologer today?"

He frowned. "I don't think so."

The medic came up from behind. "I don't think the king is going to leave us just yet," he said. "But his health is definitely not getting better. He's taken a turn, and usually that leads along a downward path. For the time being, I've asked for a personal nurse to help him, because he won't be able to do a lot for himself."

"He's been unable to walk for a long time."

"This will be worse. He'll need someone to be with him all the time. He'll need a nurse to feed him and roll him over and change his soiled clothing."

"He won't be happy." He had been very adamant that no one should have to feed him.

"If no one helps him, he won't last long."

A clear female voice said, "I will do it."

Lana turned around.

Loriane?

"But what about your studies?" What, indeed, about the trip to Peria that she had been so looking forward to?

"I can sit with him and study."

Before Lana could ask if she truly understood the level of care required, the medic said, "Good. I always believe this type of work is best done by people whom the patient trusts. Talk to the nurse, and she will tell you where you can help and will give you some tips on how to lift frail people."

Loriane went with the nurse before Lana could speak to her daughter.

Orik still lay on his side in bed, but his eyes were now closed. A track of drool ran from his lips onto the pillow.

"He's asleep," the medic said when they were in the hallway.

"Will he get better?" Lana asked.

"Sadly, this sort of thing rarely gets better, only worse."

"How long?"

"Could be less than a day. Or more than a year."

"Can you provide Loriane with plenty of help? I don't know that she understands what's involved."

She didn't want to say that she thought Loriane might tire of the tedious work of looking after someone. Lana knew a bit because she had seen her own mother go down this path. It was very tedious and often thankless work.

The medic said that he would, and he left with the message to call him straight away if Orik's situation got worse. Lana thought she heard in his comments that he didn't think that would be too far off.

She went to her office, where the circlet and the book still lay on the table. She realised that—and she wondered why she had never considered this before—the circlet might be too big for Loriane.

And she still didn't know where the astrologer was.

CHAPTER 29

Ravi's parents were still talking about the break-in at the proctor's house the next morning.

His father had come home late, after having sifted through all the documents in the proctor's office. Normally, his father went to bed really early, so now he was tired and cranky, and complained about the amount of work that needed to be done.

But because there was no official record of which document had been where—Ravi wondered why not?—nobody knew for sure whether everything was accounted for.

The thief had clearly been after the doga's documents, Ravi's father said, because he had ignored money sitting openly on the desk, which he would have had plenty of opportunity to grab before fleeing out the door when the proctor and his wife came back home.

Had the guards caught him yet, his mother wanted to know, but they hadn't found a trace of him, which also added to the evidence—according to his father—that the burglar knew what he was looking for and was a professional.

Ravi wondered why the proctor was allowed to take these documents home anyway, but he didn't ask that question since he was pretty sure his father wouldn't appreciate it.

Because it was probably true that these documents shouldn't leave the doga building. That was why the senators had offices, he'd always been told.

And he wondered, because proctor Calidius han Pasaki was not considered to be good or effective at his job, if this break-in was staged by his rivals in the doga to demonstrate the level of inappropriate movement of documents and the availability to people who shouldn't have access.

But he didn't say anything, because his father would tell him off for commenting about *things he wasn't familiar with*. Besides, he was glad that this commotion meant that no one asked him any further questions about where he had been and with whom last night.

So he let his parents talk about the break-in and, after breakfast, got ready to walk with his father to the doga building.

The prospect of working again felt so different from his earlier days there. Now he could look forward to seeing Dana and thinking about how he was going to ask his parents if he could go on a study camp. Surely they'd allow people to only stay a month or so? They'd be somewhere in the central highlands, as far as he knew, and he could easily travel back to Tiverius on the train. He knew how to do this.

But when Ravi and his father arrived at the doga building, it was oddly busy in the forecourt.

That was strange, because it was not normally busy at this time.

When they came closer, Ravi saw that the guards had put up barriers at the bottom of the steps into the building.

The group of people gathered in front was familiar: these were all the usual petitioners who, when Ravi and his father came closer still, were all talking about where in the line their place was so that they could take up their proper positions once they were allowed into the building again.

Many of them turned around when they noticed Ravi's father.

"Senator Gerinius, do you know if the proctor is seeing people today?" a man asked.

"Step aside for the senator," a guard at the front yelled.

The people shuffled aside to let Ravi and his father through.

The guard moved the barrier aside for them.

"Anything going on?" Ravi's father asked.

"See for yourself upstairs, senator," the guard said, his voice serious.

Ravi followed his father up the stairs and into the building. The sound of the voices outside faded.

They went up the broad staircase to the first floor, that marble, cavernous space that was normally busy and noisy but was eerily quiet today.

The secretary's desk in the foyer at the top of the stairs lay deserted, but the door to the proctor's office stood open.

No—wait, the door was damaged. The doorknob hung loose. Splinters of wood lay on the ground and a section of the door where it was attached to the wall was clean ripped off the hinges.

That was a pretty solid wooden door. Who was strong enough to do that?

"Oh, senator, there you are."

The secretary came out of the room, wriggling sideways through the door opening. The man's normally immaculate uniform had ink smudges over the front.

"It seems someone came in here overnight and smashed the proctor's office."

"As well as his home office? What time did they come here?"

"None of us saw them. We're not even sure how they got in."

"You know the way to the mail office, Ravi," his father said.

That was a pretty clear order: go to work. While his father shimmied into the proctor's office through the broken door, Ravi turned into the hallway and walked to the mail office.

The sound of his father's and the proctor's voices drifted through the corridor.

In the mail room, only Marlo was in. He sat in his usual spot, leafing through a big book where he would enter all correspondence that passed through the office.

"You're early," he said.

"My father had to come in early because of the break-in to the proctor's house and office."

"That's where we will be spending most of our time today," Marlo said, while turning a page.

"Doing what?"

"He wants to know what documents were taken."

"Why is he so sure they took documents?"

"They took nothing else. No money, no valuables. They knew exactly where the documents were and didn't touch anything else. If we know what's missing, we know where to look."

Siman came in. He had no connections to the doga and had no idea what was happening, so Ravi had to explain, and then Dana came in and he had to explain again. But explaining to Dana was not so bad. At least she understood the importance and the implications if sensitive documents were taken.

Meanwhile, Marlo collected a stack of drawers on a trolley. He set each of the drawers on a table. They contained stacks of folders. Each folder was numbered, and they spent the morning going through them and checking the numbers against a list of all the documents in it registered as belonging in the proctor's office.

Ravi asked if the proctor was allowed to take doga documents out of the building.

"Officially, the senators are not allowed to do that," Marlo said. "But the proctor works a lot at night and he has his private transport, so the risk is very small."

The sheet and drawer Ravi had to check was a perfect match. He felt a little disappointed about this. It would have been exciting to discover something missing. Not that the others had more luck.

They finished the task just before midday.

Marlo announced that he was going to get more boxes. He left the mail room and then didn't come back.

Ravi, Siman and Dana remained in the room.

He asked Dana if she thought the break-in could have been staged by a political opponent of the proctor's.

She shrugged. "Could be. Could be not. I don't know about that kind of thing. My father is not a senator."

She sounded so different here than she did at the nightly gatherings. She feigned disinterest, but with her family history, she was sure to be interested.

Ravi was hungry and wanted to go out. In fact, he wanted to ask Dana if they could go for a walk, but he didn't want Siman to come, because Siman seemed rather… simple and Ravi didn't know what to say to him.

But they waited and waited, and nothing happened.

Eventually Dana said she was hungry, and she was going to get something to eat and she walked out.

Ravi unpacked the lunch he had brought from home, even if Marlo said they shouldn't eat in the room, because crumbs would attract vermin. Siman hesitated for a bit, but then he did the same, wolfing down the sweet bun he had brought.

Marlo came back in the company of Dana, who had been to the markets and brought a packet of biscuits.

She offered it to Ravi and Siman, but Marlo reminded them of the "no eating" rule.

Ravi and Siman met each other's eyes.

Marlo had brought more material to check, but again, they didn't find anything missing.

"Well," he said, while stacking the boxes back onto the trolley. "At least we can be glad they didn't steal any of the sensitive documents we checked."

Ravi walked back home with Dana.

The day hadn't quite gone as he had hoped. In fact, it had been a long and frustrating day in which he'd learned nothing useful. And tomorrow he'd be at the Scriptorium.

"Well, I'll see you in two days' time," he said, when the time came for each of them to go a different way.

"You won't."

"Why not?"

"I was going away, remember?"

"Already? I thought this wouldn't happen until later."

"There is never a set date. They just let us know when we can come. I got the notice this morning."

A deep hole opened inside him. She was the only reason he liked working, and now she was leaving already?

"What are you actually doing in this place… wherever you're going?"

"Talking about the future. Making plans, studying. There is a bit of farm work involved as well, I think. Or stuff like that. We'll go to fix things that the doga has neglected."

Ravi snorted. "I guess opening petitions all day has given you a good view of what needs to be done."

The words had already left his mouth before he realised this remark could be taken entirely the wrong way.

But she smiled. "Exactly."

His heart was thudding. He'd almost suggested that she spied on the doga.

"Do you know you look cute when you blush?"

"I do?"

"Yes. Biscuit?"

She held up the bag she'd bought and hadn't been allowed to share.

As he took one, his hand brushed against hers.

Her eyes met his, intense.

She said, "But you can see for yourself what we do. You said you'd come as well."

"Uhhh, yes, but I didn't expect to have to leave so soon."

"Does that mean you can't?" She looked disappointed.

"I'll…. I'll have to think about that."

"Does this mean you don't want to come?"

"No, it doesn't. Of course I do, but… you know my parents."

"You don't have to be afraid of them. You're brave."

"No, I'm not. I don't know why you keep saying that."

He looked down. He'd expected so much, but like everything else in his life, this was turning out to be a disappointment.

She put her hand over the top, so that his hand was enclosed by hers.

His heart was thudding. She was very close.

"Have you ever kissed someone?" she asked.

Had he—what? "Aren't you supposed to only do that when you get married?"

Dana laughed out loud. "Rules! Stop caring so much about rules! Kissing does no one any harm. Everyone does it."

"Do they?"

She gave him a sideways look. "Not you, obviously."

She left a silence where, obviously, a reaction by him was meant to go. But he didn't know what to say, because he wanted to kiss her very much except he had no idea how, and also, his mother constantly reminded him how inappropriate those kinds of actions were. He still remembered her outrage when she went to an arts class only to find that the models weren't wearing clothing and the point of the class was that they put themselves in highly suggestive poses for the artists to practice drawing titillating portraits.

Scandalous.

Back then, Ravi had wondered how to gain admission to this class, but that was as far as his forays into this subject went. Yet there were young men out there—labourers mostly—who had families by the age of eighteen. Yet he was twenty and had never even seen his mother naked. This was yet another way in which his parents sheltered him from living a real life.

Dana said, "I need to go."

He looked at her, his mind pleading for her to stay so that he'd muster the courage to tell her that he wouldn't mind if she taught him how to go about kissing.

And he also couldn't also suggest they'd meet again at the mail room, because she was leaving. Which made the situation all the more desperate.

And so next time, he'd be in the mail room with Marlo and Siman, having to do Dana's work on top of his own, and having to put up with awkward conversations with Siman and admonishings from Marlo.

Then, in a split second, he made a decision.

"Yes," he said. "Yes, I'll come."

She smiled, and in that smile, he could see the promise of kisses in a farm barn somewhere, wherever they were going. And where there were kisses, there might be much more of these forbidden fruits.

"Come tomorrow morning. Sunrise. At the main station. Bring a small bag with practical clothes."

"I will be there."

"Great." She bent forward and gave him a little peck on his cheek. "Now I really have to go."

She turned around and strode off in the direction of her house.

Ravi walked home with a mixture of dread and excitement in his heart. He'd have to sneak out of the house and he'd disappoint his parents. His mother would wonder where he was. Maybe she would even send a petition to the proctor. On the other hand, he was going to go on an adventure with Dana. They didn't have to tiptoe around parents and their rules and opinions. He could say and do whatever he wanted.

Go to gatherings. Work in the field, sleep next to Dana. Work out all the things that adults did. He'd save Dana from having to marry a much older man. And his father could no longer stop him.

CHAPTER 30

*L*ana entered the bedroom into the stuffy heat and the sickly sweet smell of soap that she had become accustomed to in the last few days.

Loriane sat next to the bed, feeding her father a from bowl of porridge with a small spoon.

Lana stopped to watch, with a sense of dread-inspired wonder, how incredibly patient her daughter was when the porridge dribbled out of his mouth. She would carefully scoop it up and try again.

Occasionally, she would touch and hold her father's hand, when it looked like he tired of the procedure.

"How is it going?" she asked.

"Slowly," Loriane said.

Each time she got some into his mouth, half of it dribbled out the corner, onto the bib he wore. Loriane then took a damp cloth and wiped it off his face with those dainty hands that normally played music.

"I can't wipe it with a dry cloth, because the skin goes raw from wiping too much," she said, while bringing the spoon to his mouth again.

"Thank you so much for doing this," Lana said. She honestly didn't think she would have had the patience to do this. Oh, she would have done it, but her mind would have been racing with other things that she should be doing instead.

Loriane shrugged. "He's my father."

"I mean it. I saw my father do most of this kind of stuff for my mother. It's hard work."

"You have things to do I can't help with."

It was true, but it was just that Lana hadn't *expected* Loriane to offer to help so freely. It made her reassess her daughter's commitment and determination.

"We must talk about some of those things I'm doing," Lana said, with her mind on the upcoming transfer of power.

Orik mumbled some inaudible words. He pushed away Loriane's hand with an uncoordinated gesture.

"What is he saying?" Lana asked.

Her heart was thudding. Definitely, when he'd first fallen ill two days ago, he had been able to speak better than this. And was it only two days? It seemed like a lifetime ago.

Orik mumbled. His lip drooped in one corner and a glob of porridge slid out. Well, he wasn't eating very much at all.

"Speak slowly," Lana said.

"Mmmm—mmy bbbbb—"

"Your brother? Kotori?"

He nodded.

"I've tried to ask him to see you several times, but he's avoiding me. That's not unusual, of course—"

"Nnnnnnnn—"

"No? Has he been here?"

"Nnnnnnn—"

"Do you know what he's doing?"

"Gggggggone!"

"What do you mean, gone?"

Orik's lips trembled, but he couldn't get a sound out.

She frowned at Loriane. "Have you seen the astrologer recently?"

"I attended his stargazing class a few days ago. He was there."

"I went to his room when Father first fell ill. He wasn't there. I went to the library, but he wasn't there either. But I let the guards know that I was looking for him and assumed he'd turn up."

Orik protested. "Nnnnnn."

"What do you mean?"

"Gggggone."

"Do you know where he went? Did he tell you?"

Orik couldn't answer that. One side of his lip hung down and just wouldn't come up. Lana could feel the sense of urgency pressing on her. Orik would not last much longer, that much was clear. And they needed Kotori to transfer powers to Loriane.

She said, "I'll make a bit more effort to see if anyone has seen him or knows where he went. I'll talk to the guards and ask them to look for the astrologer."

Loriane raised her hand to her mouth. "I hope he hasn't jumped off the tower."

A few years ago, a guard had done that. Underneath one section of the Citadel's wall was a rocky outcrop and a patch of bushland. No one had known the man's body had lain there until a stray dog dragged a disgusting bone into the courtyard of an apartment complex.

Lana said, "If he was going to do that, he would have done it many years ago, especially when I came and he was no longer the master of the mothers' house."

Loriane undid the knot in the strings of the bib around Orik's neck.

He had barely eaten half the bowl of porridge, and half of that had dribbled down his chin.

The nurse had given her a pot of salve to rub on his raw skin, and as she was doing that, a vicious gurgling noise came from under the blankets.

"Uh oh," Loriane said.

"Is that what I think it is?" Lana asked.

It certainly smelled like it.

Loriane pulled the covers back.

"Wait, let me help you. You don't have to do this."

"Better that we do it than anyone else," Loriane said. "Because the servants will talk and the next thing—that the king shat himself—will be all over town—urgh."

She had pulled back the loincloth and pad over Orik's bony buttocks.

It was bad alright. Watery, yellowish and foamy. In one part of the pad was a stain of blood.

Loriane saw it, too, and they looked at each other.

"We need Harek to come," Loriane said.

Yes, and why wasn't he here, anyway? He'd been at breakfast in the morning. Lana had told him his father wasn't well, but he had come up with some sort of vague excuse about training.

She didn't understand what he was doing and liked it even less.

The kingdom was stable only for as long as Orik lived. Many Aranians still considered her a foreign usurper.

Many also, especially the men, didn't think a woman should be in charge, much less on the throne.

And despite years of trying, she had not been able to establish clear protocols for Orik's succession. Her panicked thoughts went to her room in the apartment, where she should have kept a small bag with everything she needed to flee to safety, but she had not done this. Besides, after twenty years, there was no longer a safe place to flee to, at least not in Chevakia, where she had grown up. And she had to protect her children.

Cleaning the bed was a big job. Because Orik lay on his side, the shit had run out along his leg. They dragged Orik into the chair and changed the entire bed. The smell was disgusting. There was more blood.

By the time the bed was clean, Orik almost fell off the chair because he'd fallen asleep. They dragged him back into bed and quietly left the room.

Only in the corridor did Lana realise how haggard Loriane looked.

"Go to bed," she said.

"It's daytime. I have to do some study and practice."

"You won't be able to do much useful study when you're tired."

"Probably not, but I have to…" Loriane looked down.

"I'm very sorry about your trip to Peria," Lana said.

Loriane shrugged, but Lana could see the glittering in her eyes. "There will be another time."

Lana nodded. Yes. There might be another time. Or there might not. For now, it didn't matter. Matters were out of everyone's control.

Lana sent Loriane to sleep and went to the guard station at the entrance of the king's private quarters.

The two guards in there hadn't seen Kotori, but informed her that a colleague had already gone to warn Harek.

"I don't understand where Kotori could be," she said.

"He retreats into his room sometimes," one of the men said.

That was true. There had been weeks when Kotori had refused to come down from his tower, when his students brought his food, and he allowed no one in the room.

So Lana went back to have a closer look in Kotori's room, even though she had already looked there and didn't expect to find anything.

The books still lay in exactly the same position as before. The bed was neatly made. The pens on the desk lay in the same position.

But the air in the room was also stale and cold. Dust had accumulated in the hearth. Kotori disliked the cold, and it had been cold enough even for her to use the fire in her room these past few days.

It was very obvious that he hadn't been here.

Then she opened one of the cupboards, and found it completely empty save for his astrologer's robe.

Her heart skipped a beat. Kotori had gone, indeed. He had made it to look like he had only walked out, but he had taken all his spare clothes and his travel pack and everything else in the cupboard.

She pulled open a drawer and found a big book that looked fairly new. Its cover was made from board rather than leather, so it was likely to be a note book.

When she lifted it out, it fell open at a page dated a few weeks back with star observations.

A sheet of paper was inserted in the back—wait, that was Loriane's handwriting.

What was that doing here?

Kotori had scribbled in pencil in the margins, checking the calculations. Lana chuckled, because she knew how much he hated calculating anything related to the stars.

According to him, astrology—although she despised that term—was about deeper feeling and intuition about the meaning of star signs. About divination and casting.

But when Lana had formally become Orik's only consort, Kotori had been forced not only to acknowledge that she was right about the position of the world in the sky and that the stars were suns very, very far away, and that stars that made up star signs were not even close to each other, but he'd also been forced to learn to calculate their positions. And found that he was not that great at understanding the concepts.

The notes by Kotori in the front of the book made some mention of a strange phenomenon he had observed in the sky, *Like a blinking falling star that never falls.*

The second page held a drawing of the sky with stars with a line through it. He had made this same observation over several nights. He called it a streaking star, but it was not not one of the type that fell to the earth. It winked, growing briefly brighter and then fading, repeating this over and over and over, not just for that one night, but for all the nights that followed.

He had made a note that he wanted to discover what this thing was before *the southern woman* did, meaning her. And this phenomenon had completely bypassed her, because she hadn't been up to the astrology tower to look.

She went through the book looking for other notes about it. She found records from years back, even before Loriane was born.

He had made a long string of very similar observations, pointing out that each night when he went back to look, the thing seem to be a bit further to the north, until it disappeared for a period of time but then it came back, always moving at the same speed, in the same direction and blinking consistently at the same speed.

On one page, he had listed all the possible options for what this thing could be.

That it was a small rock or a moon. But he noted that they didn't blink.

That it was a wanderer, but it moved too fast, and also wanderers didn't blink.

That it was a falling star, but it didn't fall.

Small rocks sometimes came close enough to be clearly visible when tracking through the sky. They often returned day after day for a short period, until they were gone again for a stretch of time, sometimes years. They also didn't blink.

And then, in the most recent notes, it said that he had clearly observed something splitting off the thing and veering down. He didn't see the usual flash made by the tail stars that came too close, but the bright dot vanished over the horizon and definitely would have fallen down on the surface somewhere. Loriane had made calculations of where the thing would come down—somewhere in the highlands. Kotori had—with great difficulty, judging from the messy calculations—determined she was right.

But that didn't solve the question: what was this thing?

He'd written the question in big letters in the middle of a page.

He'd written, and crossed out, the options he had already investigated: a moon, a falling star, a tail star.

In a corner on the same page, Kotori had written another option: *visitors from the skies.*

That made Lana take a sharp breath. There had once, many, many years ago, been a vast civilisation that spanned the continent. The people that built the machines that protected the land from sonorics. The ones that built the City of Glass. The ones that built the strange constructions in the northern desert, and it was likely that they'd built similar structures in Chevakia, but they had long since been erased by the passage of time.

And yet she could not fault Kotori's conclusion:

Something that moved in such an unexpected but regular way, something that blinked so regularly, something that had definitely not been there in the past, *had* to be artificial.

And the question was, *who* or *what* put that thing up there, what was it doing, and where did it come from?

Did that mean there were *people* up there? Creatures or monsters? Was this where those mysterious old people had gone? If they could build machines that no one understood way back before anyone else, then what could they do now?

The blood roared in her ears so loudly that she almost didn't hear the guard knocking at the door.

"Your highness?"

"Yes?"

But she could tell by the look on his face what he'd come to tell her. And he confirmed this.

"I'm very sorry to inform your highness that the king has passed away."

THANK YOU FOR READING MIST & Dawn. The story continues with book 2 of the series, Iron & Rock. In that volume, our characters make important discoveries: Tylve in the City of Glass, Ravi at the farm, Javes follows Mindo on a wild goose chase, while everything goes wrong for Kotori and Lana.

ABOUT THE AUTHOR

Patty Jansen lives in Sydney, Australia, where she spends most of her time writing Science Fiction and Fantasy.

Her career started in earnest when her story *This Peaceful State of War* placed first in the second quarter of the Writers of the Future contest and was published in their 27th anthology. She has also sold fiction to genre magazines such as Analog Science Fiction and Fact, Redstone SF and Aurealis, before making the move to independent publishing.

Patty has written over fifty novels in both Science Fiction and Fantasy, including the *Icefire Trilogy* and the *Ambassador* series.

pattyjansen.com

BOOKS BY PATTY JANSEN

For a complete list of books, scan the image below with your phone.

9 781925 841305